MONARCH OF MENACE

Old Bark.

The great silver bear.

Mother otters used his name to frighten their young into obedience. Aged badgers told stories of catching a glimpse of this monstrous creature from afar. Somewhere in the depths of the forest he dwelled in eerie isolation. None was so foolish as to cross his path or seek his company.

But now he alone could stand up to the ravaging, ruthless invader who had cast his savage shadow over all the woodlands.

And now the animals would have to conquer their fear and offer Old Bark their crown—before they themselves were conquered and enslaved. . . .

Dragon Winter

by Niel Hancock

POPULAR LIBRARY • NEW YORK

Published by Popular Library, a unit of CBS Publications,
the Consumer Publishing Division of CBS Inc.

March, 1978

For Beth,
who's been there and back

STORM WARNINGS

AN END OF SUMMER

The summer was ending, and a faint note filled the air with the promise of cold to come, although it was still sunshiny and warm, and the wind wasn't anything more than a cooling breeze.

Throughout the forest all the citizens, large and small, were preparing for the long months ahead, when the snow would become their constant companion and the north wind would chase them across the frozen lakes.

From all signs, and there had been many, it promised to be an especially harsh winter, and there were even rumors that there could be dragon blizzards, which those in the Wood had never seen themselves, but only heard of through folk tales or hand-me-down stories. But a dragon winter was, they all agreed, the very worst thing that could happen to the Wood, and no one much wanted to talk about what that dreaded winter might bring.

The one animal who was not affected by all the scary stories was Bramble Otter, who lived in a snug holt right at the very edge of Rambling Pond. He simply wiggled his ears at all those who came to his door trying to frighten him into going to work laying in extra wood for his stove,

7

or gathering more turnips against the famine that was sure to follow such a horrible winter.

"It's nonsense," snorted Bramble. "All tales that Mrs. Hedgehog and Mrs. Muskrat have been making up to liven their tea gossip. There's been no such thing as a dragon winter in so long I doubt there is anyone around now who could tell you exactly what a dragon winter was."

"It's awful," moaned Basil Beaver. "Worse than oak blight, or sapsuckers at the spruce trees. We've been lucky, all these winters, and it's always been mild, up to now. But my own gibber, who lived past twenty turnings, told me stories he had heard his sire tell him of a dragon winter. Why, animals were frozen solid where they stood, just by poking their noses out of their holes to see what the weather was."

Bramble shook his head.

"Not a word of truth to it," he said, walking about his kitchen, and finally finding the honey spoon he had been searching for. "And I wouldn't hesitate to say that your graymuzzle had a good ear for a story, and if there was anything that would get a young pup's attention, it would be something to do with a dragon's business, whether it was his appetite or his winter."

Basil paced uncomfortably about.

"Well, I know it's so, all the same. Everyone says it's true."

Bramble had taken down the teapot boiling cheerily over the fire, and poured two mugs, and placed them on the green table.

"Here. And there's the honey."

"Why don't you believe it, Bramble?"

"Who said I didn't?" asked the otter. "All I said was it's merely folk tale and gossip."

"Isn't that saying you don't believe it?"

"Not at all. And I want to check out these stories with someone who knows the workings of them, and who might know what they're about."

Basil's eyes widened.

"Who would know that? Granny Badger?"

Bramble shook his head slowly.

"She knows all there is to know of the Wood, and all of the folk in it. But even she isn't old enough to really know any more than gossip about a dragon winter."

"Well, who, then?" shot Basil shortly.

"I think I'm going to take a little journey downriver, and see if I can't find Old Bark. He would be one that would know, if anyone would."

"Old Bark?" cried Basil, almost spilling the dripping honey he had been putting into his tea.

"Old Bark!" breathed Branch Otter, who had heard the commotion in her kitchen and come to make sure no one was sampling her blueberry scones she had baked for lunch.

"Old Bark," repeated Bramble. "He's lived beyond all count, and I have seen him once or twice on my outings downriver. Almost silver all over, and twice as high as an oak seedling."

"But he's dangerous," groaned Basil, and placed his cup loudly down before him.

"I wouldn't be so sure of that," laughed Bramble, "although I'm sure he would like everyone to think so."

"Mrs. Muskrat said her Sam said that Old Bark was the one that murdered that elk cow last fall, and that he had done the same to more than one of the deer that cross into our wood in the spring."

"It may have been a bear, but it was not Old Bark," said Bramble. "He hasn't hunted or tasted flesh in many turnings. I know he's too old for the hunt, and I also know that he's more than fond of berries and grubs, and sweet gum roots." Bramble shook his head firmly. "No, I don't think it was Old Bark. We'll have to lay the blame for the murders on the proper culprit, when we find him."

Branch Otter, who had stood quietly near her mate, wrung her paws nervously.

"When are you planning on making your journey?" she at last asked, her voice hesitant.

"Not I, my dear, but you and Bumble and I."

Basil grasped the edge of the table.

"You can't take your family into danger like that, Bramble. Why, it's certain darkness."

Bramble paced slowly to stand in front of the hearth, and studied the merry blaze a moment before he answered.

"That may be as it may be, but it won't be danger from Old Bark. No, there is more afoot here than mere danger from something with as fine a name as a dragon winter. I think there is more to it than that, and if I'm right, we shall need to know all we can, before it's too late."

Try as they might, neither Branch nor Basil could get anything further from him, and he excused himself at last and went into his small, snug study alone, and there finished another cup of tea, and watched the sky through the open window, and wondered at the dark white patterns the clouds made across the late afternoon sun.

At last he pulled himself upright, and crossed to the tiny desk that stood by the bay window that looked out over the landing to the river, and drew open a top drawer. From it he took an old, worn volume, bound and stitched in a most ancient fashion, with tiny gilt letters on the front that sparkled and shone in the mellow light that filled the room.

He sighed once, and picked up a rather battered-looking reading glass, and wiping it twice with a paw to clean the dust off it, he sat down and opened the old tome carefully, and spread it before him on the desk.

THE ANCIENT LOREMASTERS

In very small, delicate letters was printed the title:
Upon the Matters of Seriousness
or
An Otter Primer

Below this were listed the names of each otter scholar who had penned notes in this ancient lorebook, which had been passed down to Bramble from his own sire before him.

The list of names ran something like this: Orion Lakewalker, Colder Shallows, Shore Meadows, Runner Pondlily, Greystone Treemender, and Stolter Millweed.

Those were of the first generation of lorewriters, and many, many other names filled the book, although Bramble had never been able to make out the tiny paw scrawls, and he had given up ever daring to hope that he would be called upon to write in the worn lorebook the exploits of his own adventures. He knew that merely entering an entry that told of swimming in the great Shelter Weir would not be important enough to add to the tales in the book, which described horrible dragon wars and narrow escapes from mountain wolves, or the settling of the distant waters that were more than all rivers together, and of which there was no ending ever spoken.

Branch, who had often read to him aloud from this vaguely disturbing book, although he loved it, too, always assured him that the blank pages in the end of the volume would one day be filled up by him, and that it would be the best story of all.

He wrinkled his whiskers, and smiled to himself, and looked about him sadly. There was nothing at all interesting or exciting about the one wall lined with books, or the small fireplace, or the desk, which had never been involved in anything more adventurous than penning a few lines to mark the Summer Solstice or writing himself a note to remember to caulk the boat before spring launching. He had written an occasional poem or two, but distrusted his talent in that area, and kept them hidden carefully away.

It seemed he would face the certain task of handing on the lorebook to Bumble, with those blank pages still as empty as they were now, looking up at him accusingly, as if to say that his life had lost its flavor, and that all the old mystery to it, of waking on deep winter mornings, and anticipating a nose ride down a long, snowy slope, or looking forward to the coming of summer, had gone.

Bramble sighed again, and closed the empty pages, and turned to the front part of the book, where Orion Lakewalker had put down his journal from the earliest years of otterdom.

Soon his eyes filled with the wonder of the yarn, and he was so engrossed in the telling of it, he quite forgot himself, and began whistling and chirping to himself so loudly that Branch came quickly into the low study to see if he were all right.

The gray mist of the tale receded, and he blinked, wiggled his ears, and looked slowly around him.

"I was really there, for a moment," he managed at last, holding a paw to where he had been reading. "They were preparing to do battle with a dragon."

Branch crossed to the desk, and took up the book.

"I haven't read that for ever so long. Shall I read it aloud for you?"

Bramble nodded, delighted to remove himself to a position nearer the fire, where he pulled his chair close to the hearth, and called out for Bumble to come to a reading. Before the echoes of his voice died, the stout little pup was on his knee, chittering in a high voice, and rolling a small spoon about the smooth gray fur of his stomach.

"Hush now, your mother's going to read us of your great-great-great-great-great-uncle Orion Lakewalker. They are fixing to battle with a dragon."

Bumble's eyes opened wide.

"We're going to have a dragon winter. Is that anything at all like that?"

"We are hearing wild enough stories without having to repeat that one," replied Bramble. "These stories your mother is going to read are all history. What you're hearing from all these silly geese is nothing but foolishness. It is merely the onset of a more severe winter than we are used to."

"Do you think we should be seeing to our tender and sweet turnips, rather than sitting here reading?" asked Branch, laying the book back on the desk.

"No. I've been thinking that perhaps we might winter farther down the Rambling. I've had it in my mind for some days now, and it might be easier to travel there now, rather than try to lay in enough wood and food to last us through the winter. And I have mind to talk to Old Bark."

"Old Bark!" shouted Bumble, jumping up and down on his father's lap. "Why, he's eaten a forest, and stolen all Mrs. Hedgehog's recipes, she said, and I know he's the one that murdered all the poor animals that live beyond our river."

"Nonsense," snorted Bramble. "He is a very wise and learned being, and he certainly must have more news on this dragon winter business than all the tea tales we've been hearing here."

"Oh, when do we go?" cried Bumble, dashing down, and beginning a hard scamper around the study floor.

"Yes, when *do* we go?" asked Branch, her surprise showing in her voice, and all interest in reading gone.

"I would have told you sooner, dear, except that I hadn't really thought it through until just now. And reading all about Orion Lakewalker has convinced me that something is very wrong this year. I don't go so far as to say anything about a dragon winter, or any of that, but it does seem odd that none of the summer swallows stayed late this year, or that we've seen no sign at all of the lake salmon. That's never happened here as long as I can remember. There have always been lake salmon, and then too, there have always been the migrating animals that come and stay a bit, then move on. We've seen no being, outside our own little community here, for the whole last part of the summer. And that is the oddest of all, for we have bountiful food here, and sweet water. That is what has been at the bottom of my thoughts all along. Not so much what we *have* seen, as what we haven't."

"You know those traveling kind," said Branch gently, but her words carried no conviction, and her worried frown gave away her uneasiness.

"When do we leave?" asked Bumble again, very loudly.

"Hush!" cautioned his mother. "We'll leave when it is time to go."

"And I think that should be soon," said Bramble. "We have much water to cover to reach Bending Willow by first snow. And I would rather be stormbound there than here. And that leaves only a short journey to reach the home of Old Bark."

"Then you are determined to do this, in spite of Basil's warning?"

"I do not fear Old Bark," said Bramble. "What I fear is something else. And I think he may know of these dangers, or have heard some news of something."

"What is it?" asked Branch. "What has upset you so?"

"I can't put my paw to it," said Bramble doubtfully. "I guess it started with the murder of the two deer at Frond Dell last spring. Then that business with the muskrat family disappearing, and not so much as a trace of where they've gone."

"You know Chappie Muskrat. He's the wandering sort. There wasn't anything unusual in that."

"But Bernice was a good swimmer," chimed in Bumble. "And she could balance gooseberries on her nose."

Bramble ignored this interruption.

"I know Chappie well enough, and I know it would be the sort of thing he would do. I wouldn't have thought twice about it, except that he was to be the head oarsman at the rowing meet. He didn't even show up for that, and I know how much he had been looking forward to it."

"And don't forget the tea things," shouted Bumble. "All out on the table, and none of it touched."

"Do hush up, Bumble!" admonished Branch. "I'm sure there is nothing any more dangerous at work here than a little natural boredom. I'm sure the muskrats simply had had all they wanted of Pine Hollow, and were anxious to be off."

"Whatever you want to believe is fine, dear, but you can't overlook what the two song sparrows told us."

"They knew nothing. I don't think they had ever even seen the whole family of them at full gallop, going away toward the east, on the morning that the deer were found below the lower weir."

Bramble shook his head before going on.

"No, my dear, I think something more than a dragon winter is already upon us, and I think we badly need the advice of Old Bark, to see us through."

"Do you think any of the others will go with us to find him?" asked Branch.

"Perhaps Basil. He's not too tied down at the moment. And we might get Oakstaff to go along."

"He'll never leave. Nor will Oakstaff. Their whole life is spent on this river."

"We'll call a council meeting tomorrow, and find out who will accompany us."

"I hope Cabbage will go," put in Bumble.

Cabbage was the youngest pup of Basil Beaver.

"And then we'll have enough trouble on our hands that we won't need to go seeking after more," concluded Bramble.

He tried to smile, although it felt as if a dark cloud had settled over his heart.

GRANNY BADGER

In the snug, low-ceilinged room, the animals gathered there talked quietly, and helped themselves to Mrs. Badger's tea biscuits. Everyone was ill at ease and very shy, and they all talked in their most polite, quiet tones.

It had been a long time since they had been in the sitting room of Mrs. Badger. Their last visit was when old Gruff Badger was laid to his final rest in the very deepest corner of the large maze of tunnels that made the Badger home. That had been a sad and solemn affair, and one which called for one's utmost in good manners and seriousness.

Of course, all the animals understood what had happened, and knew the perfect change in all things. Still, it was Gruff Badger, and he had been a friend of them all, and it had come very suddenly one day, as the old gray muzzled animal had been working in the patch of turnips that he always prided himself in.

Granny Badger had found him, and quickly fetched the others, and just at sundown, they had covered him with sweet clover and honey blossoms, and gently carried him to the hole he had asked to be placed in.

19

"I've been weaned in these woods and lived here all my turnings, and I have no doubt that when the day comes, I'll call on the decency in you all to carry what's left of this old sack to the place I've prepared, far down in the heart of the earth, where I may rest safe and warm on cold nights, and where one day I'll rise up again, to go on once more."

Gruff Badger was always frightening, and speaking of things no one understood, and as often as not, he was locked in his library, reading pages of strange books on mysterious subjects.

And Granny Badger was just as frightening, in her own kindly way. Some of the animals even said that she read to the spirit of Gruff every night, and baked him apple pie for every birthday.

Bramble Otter believed none of the stories, and only knew that Granny Badger was as wise as she was old, and he wished with all his heart that Gruff had not gone so suddenly, for he could use his advice now.

Granny Badger brought around another tea tray, and everyone dutifully took more, and had more of the delicious tea cakes even before they were asked.

Seated in a circle around the fire was Morley Muskrat, a distant kin of the family of muskrats who had disappeared, Branch and Bramble Otter, Basil Beaver, Beryl Beaver, his wife, Acorn and Ash Squirrel, and a very cranky mole by the name of Stump.

Granny Badger at last seated herself in a high-backed chair next to the hearth, and placed a comforter over her lap. She put her spectacles on, and looked hard at each of the faces that gazed hopefully up at her.

"Now," she said, her deep voice almost a bray, "we have here tonight a decision to be made, and an important one at that."

She paused, and looked at Bramble.

"I think we all know Bramble well enough that no introduction is needed, and I am going to ask him to put forth the dilemma we are faced with, and the choices we have."

Bramble blushed gray, then rose uncertainly.

"Thank you, ma'am," he mumbled. "I have brought with me tonight something I would like you all to see, and perhaps it will help make a little clearer what I am trying to explain."

He crossed the floor, and laid the well-worn volume of otter lore in Granny Badger's lap.

"In this book, I have found evidence that every so often, I don't know how many years between exactly, we experience an outbreak of violence and trouble. I've done study in my lore, as well as in others', and find this to be true of everyone. Something happens, and the next thing you know, you've got stories of wars, and slaying, and robbing, and burning, and destruction, and all the rest."

Bramble paused, and an uncomfortable murmur swept over the gathered animals.

"Here, here, we don't need any of that talk, old fellow. There's ladies present," said Acorn, frowning disapprovingly.

"I assure you," explained Bramble, "I am not trying to upset the ladies. What I am trying to do is explain the fact that a lot of odd things have been occurring in our quiet little end of the Wood, and with too much regularity."

"I think what he means is that we've all been off our toot working, instead of playing," interrupted Basil. "Bramble does get frightfully bored when he's forced to tend to his own games."

"I think we have neglected him," pouted Ash.

Bramble raised a paw.

"This has nothing to do with our summer fun. What this has to do with is a business which frightens me, and I've only my lorebook to go upon, but it all has happened before, and has been happening all along. And every time it happens again, because no one is looking for it to, and everyone is caught with their paws down all over again."

"We all know that," grumbled Stump. "There's no good in any of it, if you ask me."

"Hush, you old prune," said Granny Badger to the mole, who smiled, surprisingly, and settled back once more in his chair, taking loud slurps of his tea.

"The good of it is this, Stump. I have read and reread all the passages in the book about dragon winters, or anything to do with that sort of thing."

"What about them? Freezing cold? How much wood should we lay up? Do we need more than a normal winter's food supply?"

Morley shot his questions rapidly at Bramble, who let him finish before he went on.

"There is a lot more to this business than meets the eye. It is more than just cold weather, or a shortage of food, or a need to have a good store of firewood. This is also a thing that means attacks and slayings, and mankind, and savage animals down from the north. And I think we have already gotten a taste of all that with the murder of some of our friends last spring, and the disappearance of our muskrat family last summer."

Basil Beaver leapt from his chair, and paced furiously until Bramble fell silent.

"Nonsense, all of it. We know who killed the unfortunate deer, and where the muskrats have gone. This is all poppyrot you've dreamed up out of that silly antique rag of a book you've got. I dare say half the things those fellows wrote about were tales to put their cubs to sleep with."

He halted, panting, looking about the circle of friends for support. All nodded in agreement with him, their eyes wide with fear and amazement.

Only Granny Badger stared ahead, as if in a trance, and she spoke aloud at last.

"Bramble is speaking the truth. Gruff knew it, and so do I. These tales are not such fancy bedtime stories, and I don't think they're fireside stories for the young ones. Both Gruff and I knew Greystone Millweed, and I know for certain that he wasn't an animal who was tended toward exaggeration when it came to storytelling. He liked his fun as much as the next fellow, but he was a serious sort, and I know he spent much of his time in various parts of the Wood, and Gruff told me once that he and Greystone had been all the way to the Falls, and beyond."

All the animals gasped aloud at the mention of the Falls, for that was the absolute border of the Wood, and no one had ever dared to see them, or travel in that direction, for there were dark things that lived in those regions of the Wood, things they knew would harm them if they could.

Granny Badger went on.

"Gruff and Greystone never spoke much of what they found beyond, or why they had gone on such a perilous journey. All that Gruff ever said of it to me was that there would come a time when we would all need all the courage we could muster, and all the stout hearts we could find. And that was that.

"Afterward, he and Greystone would disappear every so often, and be gone for over half the winter. Scouting parties, they called them. Little outings to work up their old bones, or some such. But every time they came back, they seemed older, and sadder, until at the last, they couldn't go any more, and gave it up, but not easily."

Granny Badger looked down at the timeworn volume in her paws.

"Greystone was always Gruff's dearest friend. They were brothers, those two, as alike as peas in a pod. And I know that whatever Greystone might have to say in this lorebook is only the truth."

"Thank you, Mrs. Badger," said Bramble, bowing. "My grandfather was certainly a most remarkable animal. It would take such, to be a comrade to Gruff Badger."

The silver-tipped old she-badger smiled gently, and nodded her gray muzzle in agreement.

"But what's all that to do with us?" asked Acorn. "We all know they were the best of animals. What's the rest of this story you were talking about? Or does it all have to do with all those horrible things you were speaking of?"

"Those horrible things have already begun to happen," continued Bramble, serious once more. "We are all talking about a dragon winter as if it were only a case of snowstorms, and ice flows, and no more than a matter of mending our roofs, or making sure our fires won't go out."

"And isn't that exactly what we're faced with?" asked Beryl.

"That, to be sure. But the most important thing of all is to be ready for the worst."

"That being?" chorused Acorn and Ash together.

"That being that the Wood is already full of danger, and has been for some time, now. We need to look to our own defense, or we shall soon enough find ourselves in the belly of some adversary we don't even know the first thing about."

All the ladies but Granny Badger gasped aloud.

"That's not called for, Bramble," cried Basil angrily. "We've lived her long and peacefully, ever since that marauding creature left our wood. And there was nothing we could have done against a bobcat, at any rate."

"But there is," persisted the small gray otter. "We can enlist ourselves in our own defense, and we can seek out instructions from Old Bark. There are not many creatures of prey who don't fear him and his sires."

At the mention of the great bear, the she-animals squealed, and more than one teacup was upset. It took Granny Badger rising grandly in the middle of it all to calm the gathering, and when at last order was restored, Bramble went on.

"And the other purpose of this council here tonight is to find out who will go with me to find Old Bark, and seek his guidance and aid?"

A dead silence crept over the animals there, and hardly a breath was heard after the echo of Bramble's voice died away.

UNWELCOME NEWS

"There's none of us that could match Gruff Badger or Greystone Millweed, no matter what we might do," said Stump at last.

The mole had shifted his position, and now stood before the fire, looking disgusted. He hitched up the old threadbare frock coat and paced a step or two.

"But that all may be as it may; Bramble has hit on the unwelcome news that I think we've all known about all along, but just wouldn't take notice of."

There were murmurs of disagreement, and Ash Squirrel began to fidget in her seat as if she were rising to leave the room. A look from Granny Badger soon quietened the animals, however, and Stump went on after clearing his throat loudly.

"I don't need the yarns out of a book to tell me that I've been losing good spinach to some scofflaw, or tomatoes, either, for that matter. This doesn't amount to anything much, and I'm not one to deny a morsel to any living soul, if I know he's needy. But this has been just plain ornery mischief, digging up, or ripping out, and trampling down, for no reason."

"My vegetables have been disappearing, too," offered Beryl. "I thought Sandrat was taking them."

There were titters from Branch and Ash, and Stump glowered fiercely at them, until they fell quiet.

"Sandrat is not the sort of animal that any of us need fear," he snorted. "And the poor creature has cause enough to fill his scrawny hide. No. The creatures I am talking about have crept here in the dark part of night, while we're all asleep, dreaming of cupcakes and jugs of berry tea, and been at our food supplies, so that we are going to be short if this winter turns out unusually long and harsh."

A dim gleam of understanding flickered in Acorn's eyes.

"You mean you think someone, or something, is trying to destroy our food supplies?" he asked cautiously, raising an eyebrow.

"I don't know how much plainer I could paint it, you fluff-tailed tree merchant," snorted Stump. "And I also have a rumor or two of mankind moving in this very end of the Wood where we sit talking now."

At this, Ash and Beryl squealed loudly, and covered their eyes with their paws.

"There's no need to deny it by carrying on like a pack of stoats," grumped Stump. "It isn't so unusual anymore to run across mankind, nowadays."

"It is here," snapped Morley. "And that might explain the ruined crops, and the disappearance of my kindred."

"Maybe," agreed Stump. "Yet I think otherwise. My vegetables were destroyed long before I heard of the coming of man."

"Then who could it have been, Stump?" asked Basil. "We've seen no strangers in our community, nor known of any passing."

"We wouldn't be likely to meet these sorts in our travels," said Stump, his voice low.

He looked from face to face, then went on.

"These were the killer wolves, from the far Northerlands."

A teacup and saucer shattered loudly on the stone floor, followed by silence.

At last Bramble Otter spoke out.

"Thank you, Stump. I am as surprised as the rest to hear of the killer wolves, although I have known for some time about the destruction of the crops."

"I only found out about the wolves," said Stump.

"But how could they come to be here without any of us knowing?" asked Basil. "Surely, some of us would have spotted them, or at least seen their trail."

Granny Badger answered his question, although he had directed it to Stump.

"Gruff once came across one of those beasts when he and Greystone were on one of their journeys. A most nasty sort of fellow, he said, and they were hard put to escape with their lives. Of course, Gruff made it all into an amusing tale, and it served to liven up many an evening around the fire in winter, but Greystone told me later that it had been a near thing, and that the only thing that saved them was the river. Gruff never was much of a one for water, other than to drink, but Greystone said Gruff outswam even him that day. And it seems that those other nasty chaps like a good fast stream even less."

"Oh my," breathed Ash. "I've left the two babies at home all alone. I'd best go look to them."

She rose, wringing her paws, her voice quavering.

"I'll go with you," offered Branch, and she followed the trembling squirrel out of the low, comfortable room.

She smiled over her shoulder to Bramble.

"I'll be along back after we find the children," she said, and was gone.

Morley Muskrat was drumming his paws loudly on the arms of his chair.

"Do you think that might be an answer to the disappearance of my kindred?"

"Most likely answer of all," shot Stump. "Perhaps one of those beasts showed himself at teatime, or perhaps someone warned them that one of them was in the neighborhood, and they decided to take to their heels. Those savages are certainly nothing for the likes of a family of muskrats to take on."

"Or any of us, either," went on Basil. "I've heard tales that they are as tall as trees."

"Hardly," said Granny Badger. "But they are quite dangerous, and especially if they are in a pack. What we may be dealing with here is perhaps one or two of the killer wolves, if killer wolves they are."

"I agree with Stump," put in Bramble. "All my investigations of the matter seem to bear out what the lorebook says. And these wolves begin creeping into everywhere at the outset of one of these dragon winters. Their food is normally found in the far northern reaches, where they find many old or sick animals. But in a dragon winter, almost all the northern wastes become frozen, and everything is forced south, to warmer climates. And along with the weather come the wolves. In my grandfather's day, he spoke of a pack of wolves so great that it took him the better part of an hour to count them. They were traveling at night, and he saw them as he came back from upriver. Fortunately for him, he found a reed bank close by the water's edge, and they never sensed he was there, or I wouldn't have been reading his story. He said the moon was full, and the pack looked like silver death flowing across the hills. They marched through these very woods, and although there were many animals living here then, too, they all kept to their dens, and hunger drove the wolves farther on, where they hoped they might find better foraging."

"I remember my dame telling me of that," said Granny Badger. "I was only just weaned then, myself, but I remember her story, almost imagining myself hiding in our deepest hole, and hearing the horrible howling that went on at night. And Gruff was there, and almost caught, trying to reach the safety of his hole. He carried a nasty scar on his hind leg, where one of the beasts had bitten him just as he was jumping for his front door."

Stump cleared his voice loudly again.

"Well, that's a nice kettle to boil, all these little tales we're spinning, but it's not leading us anywhere closer to an answer to our problem. Or to any reply to Bramble, as to who might go with him to find Old Bark."

"I'd go myself," said Granny Badger, "if I had enough energy left not to be a burden. I'm sure Gruff would have jumped at a chance for an adventure like this."

"I don't know about any adventure involved with it," replied Basil, curtly. "It sounds more to me like an animal would be lucky if he were caught by the wolves, rather than do all that walking to end up supper for that renegade bear."

"That's all you know, Basil Beaver," said Granny Badger. "All of us have had our ears poured full of gory stories about poor Old Bark, and we've just got enough of a gossip in us to believe anything we hear, especially if it agrees with us."

She paused, and pounded her silver-handled tea mug loudly on the arm of her chair.

"Gruff only had good things and praise to say of that

poor, slandered animal, and I think he and Greystone dearly loved the fellow."

"And even if he were of a mind not to eat us, what good would he be?" asked Morley. "He must be almost dead by now, on any account."

"Hardly," said Bramble. "True, he's got gray in his muzzle whiskers, and I don't doubt that he's seen many turnings, but that is why we're going to seek him. He may know of ways to help us get through a dragon winter, wolves and all."

"Wouldn't it be just as simple to lay in a good stock of winter forage and wood, and all just stay close to our own hearths? If Greystone said that all those wolves he saw disappeared after they got hungry, then all we have to do is not go out, and we could outwait any attack."

"That would be wonderful, Acorn, but you see, a dragon winter is so harsh that all the food and wood is used up quickly, and then you would have to go out searching for something to eat, and wood to keep you warm, and then the waiting wolves would be most happy to oblige you with a special dinner party."

"What if we all moved the settlement farther south?" asked Morley.

"I have thought of that," replied Bramble. "It seems like a fair plan, if all else fails. But the snows go on for many leagues, even going south, and I think we would have to journey even beyond the Falls to really find any sort of haven from the dragon winter. And to get that far, we would have had to have left at the first of the summer."

"There's nothing beyond the Falls," said Acorn, his jaws shut tight.

"Nothing that would interest you, Acorn," chided Granny Badger.

The squirrel turned a darker shade of gray, and fell silent.

"I think the point our hostess is trying to make is that we can't solve anything by running away from it. I must admit that I had given some thought to the idea of wintering elsewhere, and taking the missus and the pup beyond harm's way."

Bramble paused a moment, studying the teacup in his paw, then went on.

"However, after today, I'm sure it would be more dangerous to take them on a journey like that, without knowing where, or how far I was bound for, or what dangers might already lie ahead."

"Do you really think there are things already here?" asked Basil.

"Stump says so," said Bramble simply.

"Stump is always full of gloom and doom. What I would like is some solid proof that it's something more than Sandrat or a band of swamp stoats out for a quick meal that they won't have to work for."

"It's no stoats," snapped Stump. "Not with paw prints as big as pie plates. At least it isn't any stoats I ever heard tell of."

"But then if we aren't going to go, what can we do?" pleaded Acorn, who was growing more concerned by the moment.

"We can, as I have suggested, find help," said Bramble.

"And I think that is the wisest choice by far," agreed Granny Badger. "You can't fight an enemy you don't know, and you can't escape from something if you don't know where it is to begin with."

"I'm still waiting for an answer," went on Bramble. "Is there any of you here who would accompany me to find our friend, so that we may at least have some counsel on the subject, if not outright help in facing whatever we need to face."

Stump looked shrewdly at Bramble, then at the others.

"It seems as if it's going to be up to us," he said at last, after a long silence.

Bramble shook his head sadly.

"I understand. I can't ask any of you to give up your safe homes here to go with me, or force you to do anything at all. Yet I hope you all do understand what a grave peril we've fallen into. And I know you all know that without each other's support, none of us will be able to last long alone."

Bramble had stopped to gather his breath, when Branch hurried in, breathless.

"They've been here," she gasped, her eyes white-rimmed and terrified.

"Who?" chorused all the animals, jumping up from their chairs and rushing to the shivering form of Branch.

"The wolves! They've trampled down our new potatoes, and torn out all the winter carrots. And they've taken what was left of our emergency honey and scattered all the hives."

"How do you know it's the wolves?" shot Bramble.

"I saw them!" cried Branch, and burst into tears.

BEYOND THE KITCHEN WINDOW

There was such a clamor and commotion that it took Stump finally climbing on the mantelpiece and shouting at the top of his lungs to quieten the screams and squeals and shouting of the animals.

Bramble had helped Granny Badger into the kitchen, and found her a warm cup of elderberry tea to calm her jangled nerves. She was not in the habit of company, and certainly not able to handle the noisy guests that filled her sitting room now.

Branch came into the kitchen, followed by a hysterical Beryl Beaver and a rapidly talking Basil.

"Look here, Bramble, you can't still be thinking of going off, not with these beasts in our very midst? We've got to come up with a plan, somehow. We've got to drive them off."

Stump, who had come in last, handed Basil a fire poker, and smiled his lopsided smile.

"There you go, old fellow. Dash along now, and ask those chaps if they would mind awfully much running along, and leaving our wood as it is."

"That's not amusing," glowered Basil, handing the poker back viciously.

"All we need do is ask them," went on Stump. "I'm sure they're very understanding about it all. And you noticed that they don't get hungry enough to eat those vegetables, or the honey. What they're waiting for is a hungry beaver to come galumphing along, and then they'll have a proper roast, I dare say."

"Shut up, Stump," put in Acorn angrily. "You make jokes out of it now, but I wonder what your tune will be when those things are at your hole door?"

Stump grinned wider still.

"I imagine I shall inquire if they've already had tea. And if they haven't, I'll show them my newest development in tea servers."

He went through the motion of throwing scalding water on an imaginary killer wolf.

"Oh, so you say now. I don't doubt it would be a different story if one of those things was breathing his hot breath down your back, with his horrible red eyes glaring through you."

Stump turned to Bramble.

"The lad has a good imagination. He'll be writing his own lorebooks soon enough."

Granny Badger had collected her wits, and raised a frail old paw for silence. It took a moment, but soon the gathered animals grew still.

"As you may know, I haven't been well these past few months, and I hope you'll forgive me acting like some senseless pup. Fact is, I'm feeling all right now, and I think we had better lay a plan of some sort to see what must be done, and to see what we can do to defend ourselves here."

"We must gather all the animals first," declared Bramble. "It won't do to have some of us separated, and cut off from the others. And we had best start laying in all the winter stores in one common cellar."

"How will we get it there, if the wolves are already here?" asked Acorn.

"That shouldn't be hard," replied Stump. "These beasts aren't too active until after the sun has gone. And I know for a fact that Mrs. Badger's hole has many tunnels that open out not too far distant from almost all our own homes."

Granny Badger nodded slowly.

"They were dug in the old days," she explained. "Our hole has been passed down to us from almost the beginning of this wood. There were holes in all directions, and I think if you look, you'll find a map of the tunnels. It should be somewhere in Gruff's library."

"Did you get a good look at them?" Morley asked Branch.

"Good enough to almost frighten the wits out of me. Ash and her babies are safe in their tree, and I don't think they saw me. I came back down the shore of the river, just in case."

"How many?" asked Bramble.

"I couldn't really tell," apologized his wife. "But I saw at least three, or maybe four, coming out of Beryl's turnip patch. And there were two or three others where the hives were kept."

"Seven, then," mumbled Bramble. "Not a pack, but certainly enough to cause the likes of us more than enough trouble."

"What can we do?" moaned Acorn, thrashing his tail about wildly, and chirping in short, screechy explosions of breath.

"We can start by calming down," said Granny Badger. "The fact is, we are all safe for the moment, and none of us are in any danger. There's never any good trying to make plans when you've lost your head. Always end up doing the most foolish things, then."

"Well said, Granny. That is the first order of the day," said Stump in agreement.

"Where is Bumble?" Bramble asked his wife.

"He and Cabbage have gone to the Willow Pond to look for water bugs," she answered, then threw a paw to her muzzle. "They were supposed to be back by supper."

Bramble's eyes darkened.

"That is right on the path past where you saw the wolves."

Basil had leapt up, and darted for the door.

"Where do you think you're off to?" asked Bramble, turning quickly to his friend.

"To warn them," he said, opening the door.

Bramble motioned for him to halt a moment.

"Wait. Let's see if we can't find a back door. They may be watching all our homes by now, and it seems as if they are familiar with all our gardens, and where we get our honey."

"But the boys!" pleaded Basil.

"I know. Bumble is along, too. But we won't help them if we find them and frighten the wits out of them. And I don't like the idea of being in the open and aboveground when there's something like these wolves about."

"Bumble and Cabbage are out there," said Branch, her eyes filling quickly.

"You must take them for complete fools," said Granny Badger, and everyone turned to her.

"Those two lads are more than a match for a mere few

killer wolves. They've been here often with their tales and schemes, and I wouldn't be too surprised if they don't have those wolves trapped somewhere, even now."

"We've taught them well," reassured Bramble.

"Perhaps you're right," agreed Basil, closing the door, but pulling aside the freshly starched curtain to take a peek beyond Granny Badger's kitchen doorstep.

Outside, the afternoon was fine, although growing chilled by a slight breeze that had sprung up from the north. There was nothing at all to be seen, except the lovely fall trees, their leaves already changing, dancing softly in the wind.

Looking further, Basil saw movement in a low berry thicket, but breathed easier when he realized that it was only the breeze, and nothing more. His heart had stopped, for that was the favorite berry spot of Cabbage, and for a horrible moment, he half expected to see his chubby young pup come waddling along up the path, happy and unsuspecting, to be pounced on by seven starving, vicious killer wolves from the terrible north, where they had dragon winters every year.

He shuddered, then turned quickly to face Bramble.

"Quickly, then. Let's find our trail, and be off, before it's too late."

"I've never known Bumble or Cabbage to be anywhere on time," soothed Bramble, more to himself, he realized, than to try to comfort Basil.

However, he realized that it was true, and that if the two young friends had instructions to be home by supper, then they could be counted on to drag in somewhere between dusk and midnight, depending upon where they had gone or what their errands had been.

Granny Badger showed Bramble where to look in the

large, well-stocked bookshelves, and after a short search, he and Basil had found a tunnel that was indicated on the diagrams as running to almost the very banks of Willow Pond.

As Bramble prepared to show the sketch to Granny Badger, to find out where the start of that particular tunnel lay, he heard a renewed outbreak of raised voices and cries coming from the kitchen.

"What now," groaned Basil, hurrying through the study door before his friend.

"More news, it sounds as if," replied Bramble.

"That's all we need," muttered Basil grumpily. "It seems as if the only news we're doomed to get is all black."

"Perhaps not," said Bramble, for he had picked up a familiar voice among the rest, and now hurried forward eagerly.

"Bumble!" he cried, entering the crowded, low-roofed room. "Cabbage!"

"Yes, sir," said the chubby otter pup, and lowered his head, embarrassed by all the attention he was receiving.

Cabbage sat happily on a small three-legged stool, and was gratefully attacking his second helping of Granny Badger's tea cakes.

Basil bolted into the room as he caught sight of the young beaver.

"Where have you two come from?" he blustered, his eyes wide in fear and relief.

"Through Auntie Branch's back yard," answered the young animal.

"You mean you were both just out there walking around, as free as you please?" roared Basil.

Cabbage stopped eating long enough to nod.

"We found some swell pond lilies," he added, picking up another tea cake.

Branch was having a difficult time keeping herself from hugging her small, gray son, but Bramble shook his head, and took her trembling paw.

Bumble looked up.

"There was sure some funny things happening," he said at last, in a low voice.

"Funny things?" asked Granny Badger, before any of the others could speak.

"Well, we kept hearing all this funny breathing. Like what it sounds like when you've had a long swim, and you're sort of low on breath. But there wasn't anybody else swimming at Willow Pond, or anybody anywhere around."

"And don't forget those growls," added Cabbage, wiping his paws on his muzzle, to get the last of the cake.

"What sort of growls?" asked Morley.

"Loud," replied Bumble.

"Do they know yet?" asked Stump.

"Know what?"

"Well, you see, Bumble, it seems we have all been a bit worried about you and Cabbage, since we have found out that there are some marauders in our community."

"You mean the bobcat is back?" cried Cabbage.

"Worse. It seems like for some reason we have attracted the attention of a pack of killer wolves."

"Oboy!" shouted Bumble. "You mean like the kind Graymuzzle Greystone always wrote about in his books?"

"It's not anything to be glad about," scolded Branch. "And we certainly don't feel any excitement about being invaded by those things from the north."

"Well, it sure beats looking for water bugs on Willow Pond," said Cabbage.

"You two," chided Basil, but not too harshly, for he was still feeling the relief of finding his son safe, instead of wandering about loose in the Wood, with seven hungry killer wolves that had somehow descended upon their quiet community and in one single afternoon wrecked the peace and tranquillity, and changed all their plans for the oncoming cold season, and suddenly reminded them that the horrible weather that a dragon winter always brought was not the most dangerous thing that it threatened. Here, in their very midst, was a pack of the killer wolves, which were said to be as tall as trees.

"Can we see them?" asked Bumble.

"Certainly not," snapped Branch.

"Aw, I knew it wouldn't be any fun. They're just old wolves."

"And just hungry enough that they might take a fancy to anything," said Morley.

"Especially young whelps with rude manners," Granny Badger added. "Now you two march right to the sink and wash your paws good. I don't want blueberry track marks all over that clean tablecloth."

The two youngsters sheepishly followed the old she-badger's commands, and busied themselves at the pump.

After pumping the worn handle a few times, Bumble put the pail under it and began to fill it. Cabbage was already dipping his paws in the cool, clear water, when Bumble happened to glance out toward the walk that led to Granny Badger's front door.

His eyes met the cold, frozen glare of a great gray wolf, whose lips had curled back to reveal deadly white fangs and the yellow froth that drooled past his chin.

Bumble had hardly time to call out before Stump and

Bramble had darted to the window and slammed the inner shutters closed.

A great, bloodcurdling howl went up from beyond the kitchen window, and it was answered by two more, fainter, and farther away.

ATTACK OF THE KILLER WOLVES

A shattering roar split the air, and the animals stared at the window in horror. The inner shutters rattled and shook on their hinges, and the faint tinkle of broken glass reached their ears.

Bramble had leapt to the door, to throw the bolt and shut the winter door beyond it. Not a second later, terrible blows fell on the dark green painted wood, and icy howls of rage filled the afternoon outside.

"I thought you said they didn't go about until after dark, Morley," said Basil, his voice trembling.

"They're not supposed to," the muskrat replied.

"I think these chaps are ready for a meal," put in Stump. "They don't ordinarily act this way, from any account of them I have ever read."

"Then why are they out there?" asked Beryl, her tears coming freely, and holding on tightly to her son, who fidgeted uneasily.

"Hungry," replied Stump. "They know where their next meal is coming from." Stump smiled lopsidedly, and indicated the spot he was standing on.

"What are we going to do?" wailed Acorn. "And what

45

about Ash and the little ones? They're all alone in the nest, and they don't know but what the wolves have gotten all of us."

"Stoke up that fire," ordered Granny Badger, wrapping her shawl tighter around her frail old shoulders.

"What?" chorused Morley and Acorn.

"Stoke up the fire. You'll find plenty of wood in the pantry. And start that big kettle, will you?"

"How can you think of tea at a moment like this?" shot Beryl, wringing her paws and dancing about the room nervously.

"Just remembered what Stump said," answered Granny Badger. "Something to do with teatime, all right, although I don't fancy those things outside will enjoy it so much."

Stump's eyes widened.

"You mean you're going to open the door?" he managed at last.

"Oh, quite so. And we're going to invite those poor fellows to warm themselves up a bit, to get rid of that chill they must still be feeling, being up there in those cold climates of the north so long."

"We can't open the door, Mrs. Badger," cried Morley. "They'd have us all in a second."

"Not if they can't get through the boiling water, they won't."

Slowly the old she-badger's plan had dawned on Bramble. He smiled and nodded.

"It might work, Granny. It just might be the thing that would do it."

"But there's six or seven of them. Maybe more," snapped Basil.

"Whether or not there's a hundred is no matter. We are trapped here until we drive off the intruders and can come up with some plan that will rid us of them for good."

"Or enable us to escape, and go on farther south," went on Stump.

"You, Stump? You would think of giving up that precious hole of yours, and just desert all your old digs?"

"When confronted with the choice I have now, yes," answered the mole. "At the moment, I'm homeless just as much as if I were ever so far from the Wood."

"Are we going to get to make a journey?" cried Bumble, tugging on his father's arm.

"Hush," warned Branch. "Your father is trying to think."

"We may be taking a trip, son. I'm not sure. If I thought there was a chance of reaching safety before the first of the snows, then I'd be all for it. Of course, there is still our problem outside to be dealt with."

Bumble threw up his paws, and scampered hard around the room.

"Me, too," shouted Cabbage. "I want to go, too."

Both the youngsters quietened when they saw the look coming from over Granny Badger's eyeglasses.

"You're not going anywhere," hissed Beryl Beaver, "except straight to bed without your supper."

"I don't even have a bed anymore," said Cabbage. "We're going to have to live with Granny Badger now."

"Hush!" snapped Bramble.

The door jarred horribly again, and dust flew from the frame and the wall.

"They must be using something to try to batter it down," said Morley, his voice coming out a terrified squeak.

Bramble's brows knitted into a worried frown.

"I have never read of the northern wolves knowing how to use tools."

"It does sound like a ram," confirmed Stump.

"Get on with the kettle," commanded Granny, more urgently. "Get all the hot water heated you can, and make sure it's boiling. And come along with me, you two, to fetch some torches from the tunnels," she said, motioning for Bumble and Cabbage to follow her.

The two young friends muttered, "Yes, ma'am," under their breath, and followed the old badger from the kitchen.

With a persistence that was terrifying, the dull roar of wood being battered against wood went on. The air in the snug kitchen was filled with dust from the jarring of the door, and all the animals shuddered each time the crashing jolt came, as if they could feel the blows within themselves.

"Stack up anything you can in front of the door," shouted Bramble, and he and Morley brought the stout oaken table, and turned it sideways, and braced it behind the splintering shape of the inner shutters.

They piled up the two benches that went with the table next, and after that, Morley, Bramble, and Basil, with a little help from Stump, who complained of a bad hind leg, pushed the tall sideboard into position next to the benches. Over the noise of the battering ram, they could hear the snarling voices of the wolves.

"I think they're talking," said Basil, pausing a moment to listen, putting his ear as close to the pounding door as he dared.

"Impossible," said Bramble. "There was never mentioned a single clan of animals that lived in the north as having anything more than basic speech. And certainly nothing at all like what we have in the south."

"They *are* talking," insisted Basil, beckoning Bramble to come and stand beside him.

The otter crossed the room and stood next to his

friend, straining his ears to hear anything above the dreadful rhythm of the battering rams and the creaking noise of the door and shutters as the wood was ruthlessly smashed from its hinges on the wall.

Bramble's eyes widened.

"I think they *are* speaking," he finally agreed. "It sounds like some sort of a chant, or a snatch of a song."

"They're calling out so they can swing the log all at once," said Morley. "It's just like rowing."

Just at that moment, Granny Badger returned, followed by her two small assistants, who were weighed down and almost hidden by tall stacks of torches, oiled, wrapped, and ready to light.

Beryl and Branch had been responsible for the fire, and now kept exchanging steaming kettles for fresh, and passing the scalding buckets to Acorn, who was lining them all up on the floor.

"Now," said Granny, "you, Bumble, and Cabbage, you take one of these torches, and light them in the fire."

They moved forward, and soon had their torches flaming.

"We're going to have to move all that furniture away from the door," said Granny Badger calmly. "Or else we won't be able to welcome our guests."

"Oh no," hissed Basil. "They've almost gotten both the doors and the shutters down. They'd be in already if we hadn't stacked this up."

Granny Badger eyed the beaver sternly.

"And just how, you young whelp, do you think I'm going to have my supper, with my table stacked against the door like that?"

The withering look and the calm way she spoke moved Basil to start removing the pile of kitchen furnishings they had heaved in front of the endangered door.

"Now, children, everyone light themselves a torch off the two youngsters' here, and let's get ready to do a bit of reckoning."

She straightened her old, wrinkled form, and for a moment, she looked as she must have looked as a young she-badger, all those turnings ago, when Gruff had first courted her and won her heart.

"There's nothing else for it, Basil," shouted Bramble. "This beats anything I've ever heard of. First, those wolves are actually talking, and next they've learned how to use tools. It's beyond anything I can imagine."

"Can't we use one of the tunnels?" cried Acorn. "I really should find Ash and the young ones. There's no telling what danger they're in."

"No more than what you're facing," replied Bramble grimly, lighting a torch off the fire his son held out to him. "We shall have to stand them off. They aren't going to wait about for us. If we left here now, they would simply track us down and slay us all in the tunnels. No, Granny Badger is right. It's here and now, or we won't need to be making any more plans, ever."

Branch came to stand beside her mate.

"Do we stand a chance?" she whispered to him, trying to keep her voice low, so that the others wouldn't hear.

Bramble turned a quick smile on her.

"An even one," he said. "Even if those beasts are able to use tools now, and even if they've begun to be able to use high speech, I don't think they've mastered heat and fire yet."

"You were wrong about the speech and tools," Basil reminded him.

"Yes, I was. I've never known of any of the animals of the north knowing anything beyond killing and destroying. That was their purpose, and they have served that well. But something must have changed them, or changed something to do with them. They have begun to learn all the ways of the southern beings."

"Look sharp!" warned Stump, who stood beside the door with a large pail of steaming water clutched over his head.

As he spoke, the splintered remnants of the outer door and the inner fitting, bolt and all, came crashing in with a deafening roar. Dust was everywhere, and so thick that the friends had barely a moment more before the awful gray shapes of the killer wolves of the north were loping into the room, braying harsh, guttural victory howls, and preparing themselves for the sweet taste of a massacre.

Stump struck first, with a bloodcurdling screech. The scalding water he threw caught the leading wolf full in its broad, ugly muzzle, and blinded, it stumbled and fell onto its front paws, directly at the feet of Beryl Beaver. She touched her blazing torch to the stunned brute, and a moment later, it was shrieking and writhing in pain, its fur ablaze.

Before the others realized what had happened, Bramble swung the heavy club of a torch he held, and with all his might, struck the snarling, savage thing that had leaped directly at him over the broken door. The wolf caught the flames of the sizzling and sputtering torch in its mouth, and a great scream tore its throat, and the horrible red eyes rolled back in pain.

Bramble dodged quickly aside as Branch struck the beast a stunning blow with a fire poker. Howling wildly, the wolf turned and bolted toward the door.

The smell of burnt flesh and fur hung heavily in the wrecked kitchen of Granny Badger, and it was a few moments more before the terrified animals realized that they were alone in the ruins of the hole, and that the only sound at all was coming from a faint, agonized, faraway braying, and their own short, gasping breathing.

They stared dumbly at one another, hardly daring to move, until Bumble and Cabbage raced past and went tumbling over each other, on past the wrecked door.

Following them, Bramble looked out beyond the splintered wood of the entryway, and on to where the path turned. Bumble and Cabbage were standing beside the still smoldering form of a gray northern killer wolf. Bramble shook his head, and realized how badly shaken he was. Branch put her paw in his, and the two walked out, followed by the rest.

"My mom did it," Cabbage was insisting loudly.

"Well, she didn't do it alone," argued Bumble.

"Here now, hush up," cautioned Bramble sternly, looking with mixed remorse and relief at the still form of the great wolf.

He shuddered, and turned away.

"Let's bury it, quickly," he said.

"And then you can all help me put my kitchen back in order," said Granny Badger. "There's a terrible draft coming in the door."

As the friends dragged away the heavy wolf and covered it with rocks and branches, Basil asked Bramble the question that had been bothering him since the fight had ended.

"Do you think they've had enough?"

Bramble looked gently at his friend, and shook his head sadly.

"I don't think they mind losing a few of their number, if they get to eat eventually. And unless we get Granny Badger's door fixed, and soon, the loss of one wolf will have accomplished just what they wanted, and that was a way into the larder."

"I was afraid you'd say that."

And as the animals hurried back along the path to Granny Badger's to repair her broken door, a great wailing howl went up from the Wood, away behind their small community.

"You can bet they are making more plans," said Bramble. "And if we've any sense left about us, we'd best be making our own."

Working frantically, they managed to get the outer door replaced on its frame, and hung a new, heavier set of shutters inside, and behind that, they placed three stout oak timbers to brace everything into place. After making sure of their handiwork, and making sure Ash and her babies were gotten safely to their new shelter in Granny Badger's house, the animals sat down to take stock of their situation, and to make what plans they could before the killer wolves struck again.

BATTLE PLANS ARE LAID

A wild, high moon shone weakly through the skittering dark clouds. In Granny Badger's kitchen, all the animals huddled close together near the fire. Bramble returned from the shuttered window, where he had been peering cautiously outside.

"I can't see anything unusual out there," he said. "The dead wolf is gone, though."

"Did they come to get him?" asked Bumble.

"I don't know."

"You don't think they attack at night, do you?"

Basil Beaver frowned as he spoke, and paced nervously back and forth.

"I don't know. But we have to make what plans we can."

"Is there enough food in the house to feed us all?" asked Branch.

"I should think there is," replied Granny. "We have enough turnips, I know. I hadn't gotten all my garden in before all this excitement."

"How long do you think we'll have to stay here?"

55

asked Beryl Beaver, knotting her hands together anxiously.

Cabbage was fast asleep at her side.

"I'm not sure it's a question of how long we'll have to stay," put in Stump gravely. "It's more like how are we going to get out?"

"Well, if we stay out of harm's way, won't the wolves get hungry, and go on? They won't eat roots or grubs, and I think they've already destroyed most of our gardens."

"They seem to be a strange lot," muttered Bramble. "I'm not sure at all what has occurred here. They have a language, crude as it is, and they are able to use simple tools. That doesn't bode well."

"And they seem to be organized," went on Morley.

"I would say our best bet is to wait for daylight, and send out a scout or two to see what there is to see. It may be that the wolves will get hungry and pass on through our wood."

"All to the lament of someone else, Ash," said Granny Badger. "Our good luck would be the next animal's downfall."

"We can't do anything to stop that," complained Acorn.

"We might, if there's any decency left in us. Who says we have to lie about like a pack of stoats while these beasts run roughshod over us? They're part of the order of things, but they are only to take the weak and over-numbered. There is nothing that says they are to be all-powerful, or have whatever they want. And as long as there's a breath left in this old body, I'm not standing for that gang of cutthroats to keep me terrified in my own house."

Granny Badger paced back and forth before the fire angrily.

"And if Gruff were here, he'd know what to do," she added defiantly.

"Perhaps we might take down his old notebooks and see if there's anything there that might help," suggested Bramble.

"Why, bless me, that's an idea. He kept notes always on his travels, and was forever writing down things he'd heard about, or seen. There might just be something there that could help us."

"Let's hurry, then," said Bramble. "I don't like this at all. It's too quiet. They're up to something."

"I know. I feel that, too," said Branch softly.

"Here. Here they are," said Granny Badger, pulling down a thick bundle of notebooks from a shelf beside a crude desk near the hearth.

She spread them on the table, and began separating them.

"Here's a description of the year of the turnip blight," offered Basil.

"That won't help out here," scolded Ash.

"Here's one of Gruff's trips. And look, here's a drawing of a killer wolf," cried Branch.

"Why, so it is," agreed Granny.

"Brrrr. Just looking at it gives me the jitters," said Acorn. "It was one thing to read about these brutes to make a good story to pass a long winter evening. It's all different when you know they're outside somewhere, in our own wood."

Basil opened another page of the book.

"And look. Here's something."

The animals all crowded around, and studied what the excited beaver was pointing out. In Gruff Badger's bold

paw, there was a rough description of the language of
the killer wolves of the terrible north. Flowing across the
page were the symbols and sounds they had heard in the
afternoon, when the wolves had attacked Granny Badger's
home.

"Can you make any of that out?" asked Basil, looking
at Bramble.

"It's all funny. But look. This might be something like
we speak."

Bramble wrinkled his whiskers and tried to form the
sound that was described in Gruff's ledger.

"That sounds awful!" cried Morley.

"But it sounds like what they were saying," went on
Bramble, trying the guttural sound again.

This time, it woke up the two pups, and they cried
aloud, and called for their mothers.

"Shhhh, you've scared the babies," scolded Beryl.

"They're all right. They won't be, though, unless we
can figure something to do. We can't stay holed up here
at Granny's for long. And I think our friends outside are
up to something that may make staying here any longer
out of the question."

As Bramble finished speaking, a faint noise reached the
animals.

"Hush!" said Granny. "Hush. That's from the lower
tunnels."

Another dim noise drifted into hearing, followed by a
slight whiff of burning wood.

A blank look crossed Basil's face, then the dark cloud
of fear covered his eyes.

"They've set fire to something," he muttered, half
aloud.

"But they don't know how to use fire," snapped Stump.
"Or do they?"

"They have a language, and we know they can use tools," said Bramble. "So they may well know about fire."

"Which direction is that tunnel, Granny?" asked Stump.

"I think that's coming from the upper level of the basement. There's an opening they might have found. It hasn't been concealed since the last time we were in danger in these woods."

"Can we shut it off?" asked Bramble.

"There's a door to the lower tunnels in that direction. And there's another kitchen and sleeping rooms down below the upper levels. Gruff used that sometimes to work, when he didn't want to be disturbed."

Bramble wiped a paw across his muzzle, and fell silent. After a moment his eyes cleared, and he spoke more surely.

"Well, we must go there. This is too open here, and there's no better defense than to be somewhere your enemies don't know about."

"Is there food there?" asked Beryl.

"If there isn't, we'll take all of what we have left here."

"And take the ledgers. And the maps of the tunnels," cautioned Granny. "Gruff had a map of every tunnel here, and where it went, and where it came aboveground. We may have need of knowing that."

A loud popping sound, followed by a dense cloud of black smoke, silenced the animals for a moment, then Granny Badger's voice rose above the rest.

"Quickly, quickly, children, pick up all you can carry, and follow me. We have to reach the lower tunnel before the smoke is too bad to get through."

In the stinging cloud that was rapidly filling the room, the animals began grabbing what they could, and followed the old she-badger as she quickly slipped away into the swirling black darkness.

In another moment, the upper hole of Gruff and Granny Badger was deserted. And in another instant, a great sheet of flame engulfed the heavily barred front door.

FLIGHT

The animals had barely left the warm kitchen of Granny Badger when the killer wolves had set fire to the heavy wooden door and shutters. As the smoke grew thicker, and the floor and walls caught fire, horrible howls went up in the darkness outside, and the gaunt shapes of the wolves danced about madly in the dirty light of the raging fire.

Far down the tunnel where Granny Badger had led them, Bramble halted, and counted heads as his terror-stricken friends rushed headlong away from the fire that threatened to engulf them all. Branch remained at his side, and held the wide-eyed Bumble close to her. The pup whimpered sleepily, but was too curious about all the excitement to complain much.

Cabbage went by with Basil and Beryl, followed by Morley Muskrat.

Stump, marching solidly along, and giving encouragement under his breath, stopped momentarily as he drew even with Bramble.

"It looks like we're dealing with a lot more than we were bargaining for," he said under a low grumble.

"These wolves not only can speak some rough language, but they know about tools." He paused, a worried frown crossing his muzzle. "And they know about fire."

He fell silent, gazing for a long second at his friend.

"That means that something has happened, somewhere. No one from the north has ever known about fire, or tools, or had any more of a language than a few snorts or grunts."

"I don't know what's happening, Stump. But it all has to do with this business of the dragon winter. It's all tied together some way. When we reach a safer spot, we'll try to go through Gruff's ledgers to see if he and Greystone had any thoughts on this matter. And then we'll try to see what we are up against, and what we must do."

"Are you still in favor of trying to make our way to Old Bark's camp?"

"I think that is the only thing that we have left to us. If we are dealing with these things that are outside now, we won't stand a chance at trying to hold them off. They've found out how to smoke out their victims now, so they won't be put off by a few doors between them and their supper."

Granny Badger passed, hobbling rapidly for all her years.

"We're almost to an inner level. Another few turnings, and we'll be there. And out of reach of those rude fellows." She snorted, and clucked her tongue. "If only Gruff were here." She snorted again. "He would have had a thing or two to give these rude fellows."

"I hope it would be a lot more than we have to offer," said Stump gloomily.

"We'll find some way out of this fix, you young whelp," snapped Granny. "I'm sure we'll find something helpful in Gruff's writings."

A loud, long wail echoed through the musty tunnel, and everyone was rooted motionless for a moment. It was followed by another, and then another, and then there came the loud roar of the fire burning furiously out of control.

"It sounds as if they've ruined your house, Granny," said Branch gently to the old she-badger.

"I wouldn't be sorry for a bit of it," she replied, "except that Gruff's favorite chair was in that study, and all my fresh cranberry preserves."

A faint tremor was in the old gray-muzzled animal's voice, and her eyes had gone misty and distant.

"We'll replace that chair as soon as we're settled," reassured Bramble.

"And I have that recipe for cranberry jam you gave me last fall," offered Beryl. "We'll have a new crop in no time at all."

"Oh, you pups. You're all so quick to humor an old baggage like me. Well, I'm tougher than you think. And if anybody is showing me my work where jam is concerned, I'm sure I'm farther down the path than I would like to think. I may be getting on, but I'm by no means helpless yet." She threw her head back resolutely. "Now, let us find our shelter. I'm tired of all this smoke up my nose."

Without any further halts, the small band of friends hurried on down the darkening tunnel, chattering aloud to keep each other's spirits up, and peering ahead into the gloom, hoping against hope that they would arrive soon, wherever they were bound, and not daring to look back, for fear they would see the grisly forms of the killer wolves loping after them down the narrow shafts.

After another few minutes of hard trotting, Granny Badger drew up before a seemingly solid wall of earth and stone. There was a smell of fresh earth and grass, although there was nothing around them but what appeared to be an unpassable barrier of heavy stone and solid earth.

"This is the entrance to the first level," said Granny Badger, taking a flickering torch from Ash.

"Where?" asked Bramble, struggling to make out an entrance in the uncertain reddish orange light.

"Here. It's just as we left it. I haven't had reason to be here in ever so long. I just hope everything is in order."

Before their eyes, a small hole appeared low down on the wall, and the fresh earth smell grew stronger. It seemed to come from beyond the dark circle in the wall. There was also a definite freshness to the air, after the stuffiness of the tunnel.

"Let me check it out," cautioned Bramble. "Here, give me a torch."

He very carefully held out his light before him, and poked a wary muzzle into the small opening in the shaft wall. Soon he was gone, and the other animals waited anxiously, hardly daring to breathe.

"Does this lead outside, Granny?" asked Basil, his eyes narrowed, straining to see into the dark opening.

"It did once. There is an air hole. That's what you're smelling. Gruff dug it to keep his herbs fresh in the winter. But the air hole is so small a good-sized grub worm would get stuck in it if he weren't careful."

"Do you think those things out there might smell us through it?" asked Morley.

"It's possible. But even if they did, they wouldn't be able to get to us," replied the old she-badger.

"What if they just kept on following us, and kept on trying to smoke us out?" asked Acorn Squirrel.

Granny Badger turned slowly.

"I hadn't thought of that. They could, if they knew

where to find the aboveground opening. That would take some doing, but it might happen."

"How far away from your hole are we?" asked Stump gravely.

"Perhaps not far enough," went on Granny.

"Then perhaps we should press on, until we reach somewhere a bit safer, and a little more out of range of our visitors."

"Quickly, then," said Granny. "Let's be off. On you go, there, Bumble. You next, Cabbage. Hurry along now. You'll be able to see Bramble's light. Just make your way toward it."

Just as the otter pup was preparing to enter the hole, Bramble's head popped through the opening, and his whiskers were quivering.

"I heard something in the tunnels up ahead," he blurted out. "I couldn't make out exactly what, but it was just beyond the torchlight."

Cabbage started to cry.

"There, hush now," snapped his mother. "It's going to be all right."

"I want to go home," he mumbled jerkily. "I'm sleepy."

"We'll be there in a little while," said Basil, who turned to his friend grimly.

"Are we going to have to make a stand of it here?"

"I don't know. Can you shut this back up, Granny?"

"I can. But if we can't get on this way, the only other way is back the way we came. The entrance to the lower tunnels is beyond this wall."

"What did it sound like, Bramble?" asked Stump. "Was it a lot of noise, or what?"

"It was just noise. Sort of like someone trying to be quiet."

"What is our course, Granny?" asked Morley.

"We go on, I say," she replied, her voice hard. "There seems to be nothing for it."

"Then what say you, Stump?" asked Basil.

"I'm as well for Granny's plan. It's that, or turn back and end up supper for those things behind us."

"Shhhh," whispered Bramble, turning his head to the opening in the wall, and listening intently.

"What is it?" hissed Beryl.

"I can't tell. It sounds as if it's coming this way, though."

"Get rocks, everyone. We'll attack as they come through the opening."

"What'll we do with the torch?" asked Morley.

"You hold it, Branch. Move back there, so you'll be out of the way, and whoever it is won't be able to see anything but the flames."

"All right, let's get to it," said Bramble, and positioned himself beside the opening in the dark wall.

Morley faced him on the opposite side, and next to him was Stump. Beryl and Basil, with Cabbage behind them, stood armed with large stones, and beside them was Acorn and Ash.

A tense silence grew louder as the friends waited, their hearts thumping wildly inside them.

And then they heard the first of the strange noises.

SHADOWS

Nothing could be heard in the tunnel but the hissing of the flickering torches. From the other side of the wall, strange sniffling noises were heard, and the friends raised their crude weapons, and prepared to defend themselves as best they could.

A terrifying silence began, and the snorting, shuffling noise stopped, and an absolute stillness reached the horrified friends.

After a few moments, the strain began to tell, and Bramble cautiously poked his nose in the direction of the opening. Stump growled, and tried to warn him back, but the waiting was too much for the otter, and he eased himself forward.

Just as he bent to peer into the opening, a black snout, covered with flecks of gray, poked through, and Bramble met the inquisitive stare of a large pair of deep brown eyes, which blinked once in surprise.

"Hullo," said a deep voice warmly.

Bramble bolted out of the shaft opening, and sat back on his hind paws breathlessly.

Everyone had jumped at the voice, and there were

more than a few squeals and squeaks. Bumble recovered
first, and raced to stand in front of the stranger.

"Hullo, my name is Bumble, and you really gave us a
start."

Two powerful paws appeared and began widening the
hole, and a moment later, the black and white face of a
stout badger showed through.

Granny Badger caught herself before she cried aloud,
and went forward.

"Greetings, brother. Our hole is yours."

The newcomer shuffled through the opening, and shook
the dust off his sleek coat. He raised a paw and bowed
low to the old she-badger.

"My service, mother. I am called Blackpaw."

The stunned animals broke into a relieved clamor of
paw-shaking and back-slapping.

"One at a time, one at a time," snapped Granny
Badger, as the animals chattered questions out of control,
until all were speaking at once. She raised her voice
again, and the frightened friends quietened.

Blackpaw raised his voice over the new chorus of questions everyone was trying to ask him at once.

"Settle down, friends. Mother here has it right, one at a
time. First of all, let's lower our voices, for there are ears
everywhere, and I have reason to suspect we may be in
danger here."

"That's exactly what we were trying to tell you," said
Bramble, positioning himself beside the stout figure of the
badger. "We've been set upon by killer wolves, and
they've fired Granny's house, trying to drive us out."

"And they knew how to use a log to batter down the
shutters with," offered Basil.

"And they can even speak a rough tongue," explained

Beryl. "We heard them outside when they came to try to get us out of Granny's house."

"And we killed one of them," chittered Bumble, almost beside himself.

Blackpaw listened carefully to everyone's story, nodding his head grimly, and narrowing his eyes in deep thought. After a short silence, the badger cleared his voice and spoke.

"I fear my news is going to be ill tidings, as well. It is a sad affair to meet on such a note."

"What news?" demanded Bramble.

"I had hoped to find a safe haven to bring our settlement to," said Blackpaw softly. "But I see it is already too late."

"Where is your settlement, and how many are you?" asked Granny Badger.

"My settlement was beyond the Bent Oak, and we were a family of twelve. There were others, three muskrats, and a large crowd of rabbits, and two squirrels, as well as a number of hedgehogs. We have lost half that number since the plague that is on you struck us three days ago. I have been traveling since to find safe haven for those that remain."

"I think I know your family," said Granny Badger gently. "Gruff had cousins and uncles who lived near Bent Oak. If I think carefully, I can probably recall who your own sire and dame were."

"Our ties have always been strong with the Wood. I'm sure our families have many names in common. That's also how I came to know of these tunnels. Badger holes are always common knowledge to kinsmen. I remembered these digs from stories I was told as a pup, although I never thought I would have need of them."

"I'm glad you learned well," said Granny. "It doesn't seem that it's helped, though."

"Can you get word to those you left?" asked Beryl.

"I don't know. I can try."

"We're no safer here than we were at Granny's," mumbled Stump. "And I imagine there are plenty of those things out there right now counting on us for their supper pot."

"We're not through yet, Stump. Come on, get out your ledgers. I want to see those maps Granny said Gruff had," said Bramble.

"They're all there," said the old she-badger. "And we're on the right level now to find most of them."

Bramble spread out one of the tattered ledgers, and carefully folded out a finely detailed map. It appeared as a maze at first glance under the flickering torchlight, but Bramble soon made some sense of it, and could roughly guess almost where they were.

He proved himself not far wrong when Granny pointed a gray-tipped paw to a spot on the carefully inked map.

"This is where we are. And not far from one of our storerooms."

"Then let's make for that, so that we can stop long enough to plan what we're to do."

"Is that tunnel still open?" asked Basil.

"That's the tunnel I just came down," said Blackpaw. "There was no sign of anyone, until I met you."

"Why weren't you afraid?" asked Cabbage. "I mean, we were. We thought you might be one of the killer wolves."

"I've never met anything disagreeable in a badger's hole," replied Blackpaw simply.

"Nor have I, ordinarily," shot Stump. "Until recently."

"Well, let's move on. We're wasting time here."

Granny Badger took the lead, and the companions trailed after her single file, with Bramble bringing up the rear.

Far behind him, he thought he could hear the savage, guttural cries of the killer wolves, as they called back and forth to themselves in the upper tunnels of the badger hole. He felt if they could reach somewhere that had food and water for a day or so, they might possibly elude the killer wolves, and make good their escape toward the Falls, and into Old Bark's territory.

It seemed like years since he had sat in his study before the hearth, pondering what was to be done about the impending danger of the dragon winter, and it had been such a seemingly long time since he had sat down to his dinner at his own table that he had difficulty for a moment remembering what his own holt had looked like. And it seemed certain that it would be a long time before he would sit down to another peaceful late evening supper with Branch and Bumble, to read from the ancient lorebooks of his grandsires, or to stare into the wonderful adventures that you could find in the fire.

A faint tremor passed over his heart as he looked at his waddling pup trotting along beside Branch. He hoped with all the earnestness that was in his steadfast nature that they would find a way free to get beyond the grasp of these terrible wolves, so that their settlement could grow and flourish once more.

ECHOES OF THE HIGH CLAN

Granny Badger led the friends deeper into the maze of tunnels and false shafts that ran beneath her home, until at the end, all of them were confused and turned around.

"Are you sure we're going right, Granny?" complained Basil, who was beginning to believe that the old she-badger was beyond her prime, and had gotten them all helplessly lost in the darkness, and that none of them would ever see the sun again, or breathe fresh air.

"We're almost there," assured Granny.

Blackpaw, who had gone along beside Granny, turned to her in admiration.

"This is a lovely dig," he said. "There's a real symmetry to it. And all so well proportioned."

"Symmetry!" cried Basil. "Why, it's nothing but a mess of cobwebs and stale dirt. Why animals can't live in a sensible hole is beyond me."

"Hush, Basil. Granny knows what she's doing."

Beryl's voice was tight, and although she wanted to believe the old she-badger, she was also frightened by the endless tunnels, and the darkness, which seemed to grow heavier as they went on.

"Well, it's beyond me to know what anyone would be doing spending so much time underground, when they could be out and about outdoors."

Badgers are badgers, and beavers are beavers," said Blackpaw, in the way of explanation.

Before Basil could ask about that, Bumble had darted ahead of Granny Badger, calling excitedly.

"There's a door there. I can see it."

And before anyone could stop them, Bumble and Cabbage had broken away at a fast gallop, toward the shadows ahead.

"I'll bet it's the place Gruff always wrote about in those stories," shouted Bumble.

"It might even be where he kept all the treasure he found," added Cabbage.

The two pups drew up before a heavy oaken door that was joined to the earth and stone wall by great brass hinges.

"It must be the treasure house," chittered Bumble.

"It's neither," said Blackpaw. "Unless I miss my guess, this is one of the places of the ancients. All good digs may have one or more of these."

"This was here when we moved into these woods," said Granny. "Gruff always thought it had been here since before the First Turning. I've only been here twice, but I remember that I agreed with him, at the time."

Bumble and Cabbage were beside themselves, and jumped up and down shouting.

"It's a treasure house, a treasure house."

Bramble grabbed his chubby son and held him still.

"There's no treasure house, Bumble. This is a place your Great-Uncle Gruff used for work."

Bramble secretly believed just as his young pup, however, and thought there might be some treasure indeed behind the impressive door.

"There has certainly been no work like this in a while," said Blackpaw, feeling of the smooth metal where it joined the stone, and the fine finish of the heavy wooden door. "I have read in our old stories about the ones who knew how to do these things. But that's been so long ago now that no one is left that remembers, except to write of it in the legends."

"Gruff said he thought this was done by the High Clan. If the light were better, you could see the Cross and Crown that was their sign."

"The High Clan!" breathed Blackpaw. "That goes back even further than I suspected."

"There were other things in the writings that they left behind that made Gruff think so. No one ever knew where their clan disappeared to. They had the greatest knowledge, and the fairest settlements, and it is said they held commerce with even mankind."

The animals gasped.

"You mean they dealt with the furless ones?"

"But it was different then. All kinds lived in peace, and there was no discord," said Granny.

"I've never read that," said Blackpaw.

"You have missed your lessons, then, you sassy pup. But come. Let's see if I can still remember the way in."

Granny Badger shut her eyes tightly, and began to make a noise like a running stream low in her throat. She swayed back and forth in front of the heavy door, and her voice grew more sure of itself. The animals were silent with the dignity that the old she-badger displayed, and as she continued on, she seemed to grow younger.

A fine, high note, so soft and faint as to be almost unheard at first, began to echo Granny's song.

When Bramble looked from Granny to the door, he was amazed to find that where the door had been before, it no longer stood.

"It's gone," he said, his voice trembling.

"Oh my," breathed Branch.

Granny Badger opened her eyes and sighed.

"Well, at least I can remember something," she said, relief showing across her grizzled muzzle.

"What happened to the door?" asked Bumble, looking around blankly.

Granny Badger laughed.

"The High Clan of badger lords that built that door knew many secrets, Bumble, and they knew that any door was only as strong as its key. They fashioned a lock that only opened to the certain notes of a song, and that is just what has happened. As the notes are sung, the door swings open. If you don't know the song, then you can't gain entry."

Cabbage was staring into the gloom.

"But where did it go, Granny?"

"Here, step back, and I'll show you."

She motioned for the young beaver to move aside.

Once more she began the odd-sounding song. Silently, and almost before anyone could move, the stout wooden door with the brass hinges was tightly locked into place again.

Blackpaw shook his head in undisguised admiration.

"I have often heard of the High Clan's works, and their wonderful powers, but I always suspected it was just a batch of stories without any truth to them." He turned to Granny, and spoke in a lower voice. "But you have shown me how great our grandsires really were, mother. They were indeed wonderful."

"This was only one of their accomplishments. It's

merely a trinket, compared to the other things they knew."

Bramble had stepped forward, and ran his paw over the smooth wooden door.

"It's almost like touching water," he said.

"Gruff used to tell all us little ones about the old days, and the High Masters of animaldom. And he even knew the names of the others who were there. It must have been truly grand."

"It was grand," agreed Granny. "And it lasted for ages and ages, and no one ever grew old, or suffered, and all the houses and holts and holes and digs all over the land were filled with bread and honey. It was a grand time indeed, Bramble. Mankind was yet reasonable and peaceful, and there were many alliances of all kinds across Creation."

"What happened, Granny?" asked Cabbage. "All mankind does now is hunt and kill. They're nasty. My dad says so."

"They have their place, Cabbage," said Basil, "but I would just prefer wherever that place is to be somewhere away from me."

"Granny was going to tell us what happened," put in Branch. "Or why the animal kingdoms faded."

"It wasn't overnight that they came, and they didn't disappear all at once, either," explained Granny. "There are some who think so, but it took a long time for the end to come to those golden years. At the last, it is said, the beings were given a choice to stay, or go Home, and for the most part, those who knew the real truth went. Those that stayed began to forget where they had come from, and after another long time, they had even begun to lose their ability to speak, or use tools, or fire. We are dealing with the direct descendants of some of those now. They have a purpose in the plan, and under the Law, they are given the right of death to those that are old and weak."

"Are they after you, Granny?" asked Bumble.

"Bumble!" shot Branch.

"No, no, it's all right. Yes, they may be after me, but it is only the old and weak they catch. That is the Law. And I'm not about to give myself up without a good account of it. I shall make Gruff proud of me."

"Your mate would already be proud of you, mother," said Blackpaw.

"If Gruff were here, he couldn't have done more than you've already done," agreed Stump.

"Well, now that's saying something," objected Granny. "And coming from you, Stump, that makes it really something."

The mole looked away quickly.

"Well, badgers always have been sensible," he muttered.

"Come along, you wanton sharpster. No buttering up from you. If I didn't know better, I'd say you were trying to get on my good side, just like you always do when it's apple tart time."

"Oh, good," shouted Bumble and Cabbage together. "Are we going to get apple tarts?"

"We'll soon see what we're going to get," replied Granny, humming the song again, and leading the confused animals into the inner shelter beyond the magical door.

A strange light flickered and flared about the walls, and a thousand glistening mirrors seemed to blaze into life, reflecting back the torchlight so brightly that the friends had to cover their eyes.

And as the last of the animals stepped through the

opening of the strange gate, it slammed shut with a resounding noise.

"There's no going back that way," said Granny. "There were only a certain number of times the locks would answer to the same song. And it looks as if this door is used beyond its time. We shall have to come around the other way, if we ever can, and I'll have to give it new notes."

"That was clever. In case any enemy ever overheard the song, it was still safe, for the door was only able to be opened for a certain number of times by the same song."

"You mean you can't open this door again from this side, Granny?" asked Basil.

"I'm afraid not. We shall have no direction to go from now on but forward."

"Well, I at least hope that if we can't get back, the killer wolves can't get through this way."

And as if in answer, a bone-chilling howl rang out, seemingly just on the other side of the sealed shaft.

THE PATH TO THE FALLS

THE MASTER ERINOULT

In the high chambers the animals now found themselves in, the air smelled fresh, and the light from the walls seemed to grow in brilliance as they stared about in amazement. Blackpaw and Granny Badger had moved from the small cluster of friends, and stood with heads bowed before a carved stone statue of some sort that was brighter and more grand than even the light that sparkled from the dazzling walls.

Bramble was afraid to raise his voice, for fear that the spell would be broken.

"Was he a member of the High Clan you spoke of, Granny?" he finally managed, indicating the statue of the tall, muscular badger.

"He is Erinoult, the King," breathed Granny, barely able to speak, so moved was she. The tears glistened wetly in her eyes, and she clasped Blackpaw tightly.

And the younger badger was weeping openly.

"They are the Masters," he said at last, finally able to speak. "They have come and gone a hundred times, and always there is the promise that in times of need, Erinoult, and the High Clan, will ride from the Secret Hill to help all those who are threatened or in danger. They left this last time in the days that the Golden Age had settled upon, and they were no longer needed. There was peace across these woods and fields and prairies and seas, and there was no call for the High Clan to tarry longer away from their Upper Home, where they rest when they are not here."

"Where is the Upper Home?" asked Bumble, coming to stand by his father, his eyes wide and shining from the reflected light of the stone image of the badger Erinoult.

"Hush, Bumble," put in Branch.

"Upper Home is where you think you would like to go when you think of the nicest place of all," said Granny dreamily. "Or if you could think of someplace like Gruff used to describe when he would talk about the lands above the Falls."

"You mean like Briar Hollow?" persisted Bumble.

Granny Badger laughed, and looked down at the small pup beside her.

"Very much like Briar Hollow, only bigger, and nicer. And it would make you feel like you felt there, only much, much better."

"Is this the Upper Home we have in our own lorebooks?" asked Basil.

"It's the same, no matter what animal you have as Masters," said Blackpaw, turning to answer the beaver's question. "For us, it's Erinoult. For you, it must be someone else, although I think it is the same, except to me, he looks like this. To you, I suspect he will very much remind you of a beaver."

"You mean there's a beaver hole somewhere with a statue like this in it?" asked Beryl.

"I wouldn't be a bit surprised if it weren't in your old home, somewhere," replied Granny. "If we found Erinoult here, there must be a reason, and the rest of the Masters must have been somewhere nearby."

"I want to see the beaver lord," complained Cabbage bitterly.

"You will probably get to do just that," said Blackpaw. "Sooner or later, if we've bumped into this statue of Erinoult, we will find one of your kindred, Cabbage, or I'll miss my guess. And I suspect that there will be the same thing for all the rest."

"I'd like that," said Bumble. "And I remember my dad read me stories once about the High King Olthin, and how he tricked the hunters who had come to kill the otter tribe in the Old Wood."

"Olthin is one of the names of the High Clan," said Granny, "although I think my young cub here has hit the matter squarely when he said that they are all the same, except they might look exactly like whoever you are yourself."

"I'm hungry," said Cabbage, suddenly remembering that it had been a good while since he'd eaten.

"Good gracious sakes alive," muttered Granny. "I've lost track of what we were doing in all the commotion, and now all this. Come, let's explore here a bit, and see if we can't find the makings of a meal. We won't be able to think straight until we do."

"We've brought some of the things from your kitchen, Granny," said Morley.

"And there seems to be a fireplace here, with wood already laid on," mused Stump, bending to examine a neatly laid pile of kindling on a spotless hearth.

"Then see if it'll burn," said Ash, coming to stand by the mole.

"There's tinder there, Stump. See if you can brew us

some hot tea water," said Granny. "That might just hit the spot."

"And I've still got the makings of some journey meal," went on Branch. "I thought I had dropped it back there when we didn't know who Blackpaw was, but I knotted it up in my apron, so I've hung on to it after all."

"And I've got the bread," chimed in Beryl.

"We'll have a regular feast, then," said Bramble. "Now all we need is a fountain to drink from."

"There will be one here somewhere," said Blackpaw. "These tunnels always led onto an underground stream or river. There were times it was necessary to spend the entire months of winter belowground."

"Only decent," agreed Morley. "No one but some light-headed nit would be out and about during the worst of the cold months."

"Oh, there's fun to some of it," argued Bramble. "If you fellows would only get a good winter coat, and an appreciation for nose sliding, I'm sure you'd find winter most becoming."

"You can talk, you mud-brained water dog. You never stay in one spot long enough to feel it, and if the fancy suits you, you're off up some other river with no more thought for tomorrow than a jackrabbit. Just think it's simply a matter of finding a few new holes to swim in, or a watercress patch to fill you up, or a nice sunny spot to sleep in."

Branch had been nodding agreement during the mole's long dialogue.

"That's Bramble to a hair," she said. "And don't forget to add on that as like as not, he'll have his own pup out far past moonrise, showing him the way water looks when it's full of silver lightning bugs, or off downriver, visiting with all sorts of odd animals who are always here one day, and gone the next."

"They're good sorts, dear," began Bramble, but his mate cut him short.

"Oh, they're animals, right enough, and I'm sure they're serving their purpose, but they're not exactly the type I feel most comfortable around."

"Children!" hissed Granny. "No more of this nonsense. We have much to plan, and little time in which to do it."

"I thought we'd already decided, Granny," said Morley. "You said there wouldn't be any going back the way we came, because the tunnel gate can't be opened from this side any longer."

"That seems to limit our choices to merely going on, no matter what's in store," said Basil.

"Our choices are to go forward and find a way out of the Wood, and beyond the grasp of the killer wolves, or to hole up where we can outwait them. At least that's it to my way of thinking," grumbled Stump.

"Those seem to be about the limit of our choices at the moment," confirmed Blackpaw.

"There might be one further, if you are ready to receive it," came a strong voice, filling the chamber with an even more dazzling light, and frightening the animals badly.

A rainbow-colored music began to play, and as the terrified friends watched in awe, the statue of the Master Erinoult began to throb and shower sparks, and the voice seemed to come from the very heart of the stone. Blackpaw and Granny had fallen flat on their muzzles before the sacred altar of their High Master, and the rest of

the animals whimpered softly and covered their eyes. The
rainbow music spun the room full of more dazzling colors,
and the voice came stronger still, filling their hearts with a
strange combination of strength and fear.

A VOICE IN THE STONE

"This can't be," stuttered Bramble, looking into the fiery light that was given off by the bright golden halo that surrounded the statue of Erinoult.

"It can, and is, my good waterfolk. You have perhaps seen me many times in your travels, although I was always in disguise."

Bramble felt a little less frightened as he listened to the warm voice.

"But now you must listen, and listen well. The High Clan is coming forth once more from Upper Home, and we have been stirred upon these worlds again. You are fleeing from the first of the packs of killer wolves that have been set free by the dragon winter. Times are hard upon us that shall try all our mettle to the utmost. But we will rise to meet this challenge, I trust, and overcome, as we have always managed to do."

Blackpaw touched a forepaw to his muzzle.

"How are we to do this, Master? We are only a lost band of animals. We stand no chance against killer wolves."

"You are not to fight them alone, my brother. You are

not to fight them at all, if you can help. This dragon winter is merely the omen that it is time for those on the lower planes who have believed in us, and kept true to the Spirit, to begin their journey to join the High Clan in Upper Home."

"How shall we ever do that?" asked Bramble. "We're trapped here by the killer wolves, and we only have enough food to last a day or so at most. We can't hope to stay here forever. And these wolves have speech, and know about fire, and tools."

"They are the offspring of the new evil that is rampant in the dragon winter. It has affected the tribes of all. And mankind has become even more cruel and harsh."

"Then what are we to do?" asked Granny, thinking to herself that Erinoult reminded her very much of Gruff in his younger days. And in a quickening part of her, she felt sure that Gruff was with the High Clan, wherever they were.

"You must seek the star that glows beyond the Falls," replied the voice from the humming stone.

The animals gasped.

"The Falls!" they cried together.

"And beyond. You must follow the Trine of Erinoult. It is the brightest star you'll see in the lower heavens."

The mole recovered himself first.

"If you don't mind my saying so, we're a fine lot, sir, to be traipsing about topside, with a wood full of killer wolves, and good heavens who knows what else, and here we are with mates and pups, no food to speak of, and not much in the way of common sense between us, and we're supposed to make a journey to the Falls, and beyond?" Stump snorted a short ripple of grim laughter. "It sounds to me as if we might just as well stay here until we starve, for all the chances we'd have of doing that. At least I

wouldn't have to walk my paws off to end up in some
killer wolf's supper pot, or end up bird bait under some
thorn brake somewhere."

"Stump!" scolded Granny. "Your tongue is as rude as
even good mole manners might allow."

"He only speaks what little truth he knows, mother,"
said the deep booming voice softly. "It sounds like an impossible task, on the surface of it. And there are dangers
to be faced, to be sure."

"I wouldn't exactly say dangers," went on the mole.
"I'd call it a little nearer to disaster."

Bramble stepped near his friend.

"You've got a stout heart, Stump, although your opinions aren't always the cheeriest. Let's hear what else Erinoult has to say."

Bramble had lost all fear of the strange, gentle voice
that came through the stone. If anything, since it had begun to speak, he felt for the first time that they might just
be able to elude the killer wolves, and find food, and
make their way toward where Old Bark dwelled, which
was in itself beyond the Falls. And he knew that his
great-great-great-grandfather's father had been that far,
and beyond, and returned. Even Gruff Badger and Greystone had ventured there in his youth, and come back to
tell of it, although they would never really say what it was
like, other than it was a "far journey," and that it took
something more than time to reach.

"Thank you, my good otter. I'm sure you are correct in
your feelings, yet the sturdy mole has a grain of truth to
what he says. However, I'm prepared to assist you in
some small manner, so the trip won't be so pressing upon
you, and to give you what directions and other aid I
may."

"Will you be coming with us?" asked Blackpaw hopefully.

"It's very difficult for a stone leg to walk many miles," came the voice lightly. "But the answer to your question is no, I fear I cannot guide you myself. I shall, however, provide you with a chart which will show you the main trails and highways, and warn you against the dangers there. And I shall provide you foodstuffs along the way."

"How can you do that if you aren't coming along?" asked Basil.

"Very simple. It's like I said before, sometimes I go about disguised. But there are ways that are open to me to do these things for you. And there is reason that the High Clan wishes to speak to you."

"To us?" chirruped Bumble.

"Yes. And it will be necessary to meet them in that place below the Falls."

"Will we be able to make all these lights like you, sir?" asked Cabbage, staring intently at the glowing stone.

"Someday. But first you must make the trip to reach the spot the High Clan has given you. That is the first order they have given, and the first thing to be considered."

"What preparations shall we have to make?" asked Granny.

She was thinking of the lack of food, or other provisions they carried with them, and of the passages in the journals where Gruff talked about the wild lands that were near the Falls. Her thoughts went out to her baking stove, and the snug kitchen that she had almost forgotten about, although she had not been gone long from its smoldering ruins.

"Your baking will wait, mother," said the voice, startling the old she-badger. "There will be enough time at the end of this journey to do all the blueberry pies you want, and enough to satisfy all the hungry mouths that have been thinking of your tea scones."

"How are we going to get out of these tunnels without the killer wolves knowing?" asked Basil.

"The walking isn't what's worrying me. We can always most likely find something to eat, if we leave right away and go as quickly as possible, so that we may reach the southern limits of the Wood before the snow sets in."

"That part of the trip will be the hardest of all," agreed Bramble. "We'll have to travel day and night, and even then I'm not sure we can beat the snow. I've never been as far as the Falls, but it's a good two weeks' march just to reach Thorn Canyon, and I don't know how many more days after that to get anywhere near the Falls."

"Gruff always said Thorn Canyon was thirteen days' march from Hidden Wells, and another thirteen beyond was the Valley of Thunder. That's where the Falls begin."

Bramble counted silently, and shook his head gravely.

"It's already so late, we'd never make it, even traveling all day and night."

"We can carry the pups," said Branch. "They won't slow us down."

"I know," replied Bramble "We'll have to carry them. And even still, it's going to take us until beyond snow time to even reach the beginning of the trail that leads to the Falls."

"The first snows won't be as bad as your usual winter," said the humming, powerful voice from the stone. "And you'll find you'll travel easier in the coolness."

"When will the bad snows come, then? From this dragon winter?"

"The first of the bad blizzards will be upon the day past the last leaf fall. From that time on, you must be in a place where you can shelter."

Bramble had started to ask another question, but the golden light in the stone flared and dimmed, and then disappeared completely. Astonished and disappointed, Bramble stepped forward.

"What happened?"

"I don't know," said Granny, nodding her old head still to the rainbow music. "But there's a shaft opening that I never knew of, and I know Gruff never mentioned it in any of his journals."

The animals all stared at the spot in the wall where the old she-badger was pointing. Where the statue had been but a moment before, there was now a low, well-carved archway, filled with a faint, glowing mist that no one but Bumble recognized as sunshine reflecting back on the smooth rocks of the tunnel's floor.

AN ANCIENT GLADE

"It's sunshine," chittered Bumble eagerly, and started to scamper through the hole that had appeared in the wall when the mysterious voice stopped speaking.

"Wait!" cried Bramble, holding out a paw to restrain his pup, but it was too late, for the young otter had wriggled away, and was gone down the short shaft that led out into the dazzling sunlight.

It hurt the animals' eyes at first, for they were used to the dark gloom of the badger set, but Cabbage recovered next, and before anyone could move to stop him, he was close behind his friend, and they were on their way out into the open air.

"Come on, then," urged Bramble, "let's find out what Erinoult meant, and see if we have come far enough to elude our good friends from the north."

"Oh!" squeaked Branch, having forgotten their terrible danger, and realizing that her pup was running out ahead into an unknown place, where the dreadful jaws of a killer wolf might be waiting to devour him. She darted forward, her hackles raised, and tiny fangs flashing.

Stump, startled by this grim vision, jumped backward to save himself from being bowled over.

"What is it, Branch?" cried Beryl, drawing closer to Basil.

"We all want to go on and see what's there," put in Stump, regaining his composure. "Our delightful friends may have a pleasant surprise waiting for us, and we wouldn't want to disappoint them."

At these words, Beryl also shot through the tunnel wall, and disappeared into the golden halo of light.

One by one, the animals followed suit, crouching low, and hackles bristling, until they all stood blinking in the center of a grassy glade, which had a cheery fountain bubbling in its center and a green fence of low hedges and berry bushes, flanked by thick fir trees that went upward so high they almost blocked out the sky. It was fresh in the glade, and smelled of old forest floors, long undisturbed, and the green scent of trees, and the wonderful, silver clear tartness of the fountain.

Granny Badger broke the silence first, and bowed her old gray-tipped head.

"I think Gruff spoke of this glade once. He and Greystone had read of it in their old lorebooks, and it was always a thing between them who should find it first."

"Who did, Granny?" asked Bumble.

"They neither one ever found it," went on the old shebadger, lifting her gaze to meet the eyes of the young pup. "There was never a need for them to find it. But we have been in dreadful peril, and the great Erinoult has shown us his own personal home of old. This, according to our lore, was the golden glade the Great Power gave to the first of his children when the world was new, and all things came forth to begin their lessons."

"You mean this is where your forebears sprang from?" asked Bramble.

"It is the legend," answered Granny. "I think it is as well that it has someplace to start, although I have never fully believed that the Great Power could only begin in one place at a time. More likely, there were many of these glades, and many children, and it all went on that way."

"Hear, hear," grumped the mole. "I've not been overly industrious with my reading, but I think that's the way of it."

Blackpaw, who had been standing gazing about in silence, turned to the group, and in a voice that was hardly his own, he launched out into an almost memorized speech.

"In the Great Year of Erinoult, when he was born of the heavens and the sky, he came to dwell in the sacred glade known only as First Wood, and from there all the children of this lord came, even down until the present."

Granny Badger looked hard at the newcomer.

"You seem to have learned your lessons well," she said.

"Mine was an excellent teacher," he replied bowing.

"Do you think we are far enough from our old settlement that we have given the killer wolves the slip?" asked Basil.

"Or how much farther do we have to go, if we haven't?" shot Morley.

"When do we eat?" asked Bumble and Cabbage in unison.

"We'll come to that, you two," said Granny softly. "As to the other questions, I don't know. After the tunnels, I'm confused, and I'm not exactly familiar with where we are now. I can only hope we have given our pursuers the slip. We need time to scout out where we are, and how our situation lies, and to make plans as to what we are to do now."

"I hope those fellows are considerate enough to oblige us," said Stump, puffing out his cheeks and peering near-sightedly into the eaves of the forest that surrounded them.

"Here's what we'd best do, Granny, and correct me if I'm amiss," said Bramble. "Basil and Morley, and I, and Stump, and Blackpaw, if he likes, will spread out and see how we stand in these woods, and what, if any, will be our plans of defense here. You and the rest can gather any supplies you can from the shaft we've just left, and place them so we can take them along when we decide to move."

"That sounds all right," agreed Basil "We'll find out if there's a direction for us to go, and how matters stand in these woods, and the others can collect anything they can find for our journey, if there has to be a journey."

"Couldn't we stay here?" asked Ash Squirrel. "I mean if this was one of the Old Places, where someone like Erinoult lived, wouldn't it be safe from killer wolves, or beasts like that?"

"I think your friend is correct," argued Blackpaw. "This glade was sacred to Erinoult, and there are mystical powers at work here. I, for one, would be willing to stay here. I think it is protection enough against any killer wolves, or any other danger that might come our way."

"He could be right, Granny," said Morley Muskrat. "After all, why would Erinoult open the wall and show us this glade? Especially if he didn't mean for us to stay."

"And if we do stay on here, and set up a new settlement in this glade, I can go back and bring the rest of my clan," concluded Blackpaw.

"Is that your only reason for risking staying on here?" asked Stump.

Blackpaw glared hard at the mole before answering.

"I do not see that any others of your clan are with you, so I can only assume that you are either a loner or one dedicated to neither hearth nor clan."

"Hush, Blackpaw. You don't know what you're talking about. Stump's mate and pups were taken by a bobcat six turnings ago. He's lived with us since."

The badger bowed, and murmured an apology, although his voice was unconvincing.

"It's no matter about me," went on Stump, "but what I would like to know is how you stand. Are the reasons you give for staying, and possibly placing us all in grave danger, simply because you want us to wait while you go gather the rest of your clan? Or do you truly believe that this glade is safe from intruders?"

"I naturally want my clan safe," snapped Blackpaw, "but it does not color my decision here. Erinoult, the Master, dwelled in this very spot, and I believe in him, and in the magic he held as coming from the Great Power. I don't think there would be anything able to hurt us here, or I would not say as much."

"Then we know where you stand," said Granny Badger.

"I understand, and I think we all do. It is a bit mystifying when simple animals like ourselves run up against all the goings-on we've run into these past few hours, so we are going to need a bit of a breather to take everything in that's happened, and to look at things in their proper light," said Bramble.

"What do you think, Granny?" asked Acorn Squirrel.

"I think I'm tired and hungry, and need a nap," replied the old she-badger. "Furthermore, I would like very much to put those killer wolves out of my mind, and go back to my own kitchen, and finish my baking. That's what I think. What I shall have to do now, though, is not to my liking at all. I think that we shall have to find a place where we can set up shelter, and eat, and rest, and keep a sharp eye out to our surroundings. I have a strange feeling that our friends from the north are not ones to give up their supper so easily, even if their supper is hiding out in a glade known to a Master of old."

She paused and turned to the young badger.

"I have gone many turnings, young friend, and seen many strange things, and read the lore of our forefathers, and today I've witnessed what few animals ever have seen in their times, but I still feel as if this place is no more than a resting place, where we shall gather our senses, and whatever supplies we have, for a longer journey."

Blackpaw looked away from Granny, and although the animals could see he disagreed with her, his training was such that he did not raise his voice against her, at least not in the presence of the others.

"Then let's have a vote," said Bramble. "That is the only way to settle it. We shall follow the law of the many."

"I'll go along with that," agreed Stump.

"And us," said the squirrels.

"Us, too," replied the beavers.

Morley Muskrat nodded his agreement, and kept looking over his shoulder toward the shadows that lay below the tall trees.

"Granny, you're the oldest, you call for the show of paws," Bramble said, turning to the old silver-tipped she-badger.

"Then we shall have it. First, all who wish to stay in

this glade, and to attempt a new settlement, give a show of paws."

One alone went up, and that was Blackpaw's. He glared defiantly at the others.

"And all those who wish to gather what supplies we can, and go on in search of safer haven?"

The remainder of the animals showed their choice, and the decision was made.

"Let's get to it, then," said Bramble, assigning tasks. "We shall take a look to the woods to see our best route, and the rest of you see what-all we may be able to take with us. Bumble, you and Cabbage stay here and help your mothers."

The two pups whined and complained, but in the end they did as they were told.

Blackpaw, sitting alone by the fountain, looked glum and dejected, and occasionally looked grimly about, muttering to himself.

All the other animals soon forgot their new friend, however, and busied themselves with their tasks, and late that afternoon, toward sunset, Bramble and the other scouts set out to see what they could see of their new surroundings.

DISAPPEARANCE OF A FRIEND

Bramble had not gone far before he discovered what it was that he was most afraid to find. There before him was the distinct print of a large paw, three times the size of his own, and with four sharp marks where the claws of the wolf cut through the soft earth.

There were others, and the otter barely had time to try to check the direction before he heard heavy snorts and growls in the underbrush not far away. It sounded as if some unfortunate animal had met its end in the hunger of the killer wolves, and that they were settling down for a short nap after their meal.

It was, he thought, probably only the misluck of another that had saved his life, and he shuddered a deep shudder that left him weak for a moment. It was gone as quickly as it came, however, and he hurried back to the glade to warn the others, and to tell Granny that they had been right in not wanting to make their new settlement so close to the widening horror of the killer wolves.

He kept to the shadows of the trees, and ran as silently as he knew how, his hackles raised, and his nose testing every direction for any possible dangers. It had been a

good many turnings since Bramble had had to use his
senses to protect himself, and it felt clumsy to him at first,
although it soon came easier, and after a bit, it was as if
he had never been out of the habit.

He purposely went beyond the glade where his friends
waited, and doubled back twice more, to throw off anyone
who might be following him. After one more long circle
about, and one last cautious trip to within smelling distance of the glade, he became almost invisible in his
stillness, and watched carefully everything about him.

There was no sign of any enemy, but had there been,
the whereabouts of the friends would have been given
away by the pouting voice of Blackpaw, raised to a low
whine.

"I tell you, nothing could reach the glade of Erinoult.
It's as safe here as a set could be. It is a sacred glade."

Bramble's ears lay flat back, and his small, strong
teeth were bared. If he had been a killer wolf, he knew
which victim he would have gone for first.

He scampered hard into the camp, momentarily
throwing all caution to the wind, so that he could warn
the others, and shut up the loud brayings of the strange
badger. No one had seen him come, or heard his approach, and there were a good many squeaks of surprise
from the ladies, and a startled bark from Blackpaw.

Bramble held his paw to his lips, and pointed away in
the direction where he had seen, or heard, rather, the
killer wolves. He whispered very quietly, so that the animals had to come very close to him to hear.

"They are here. Not far away, either. They've just
killed, or at least I think they have, so I think we'll have a
chance to slip by. They sleep heavily after they've eaten."

Granny Badger wrinkled her brow.

"Was there any sign of what settlement was here?"

"No. I couldn't tell."

"Are the others still out?" asked Beryl, a worried frown tugging at her mouth.

Bramble had forgotten the others in his haste to hurry back to warn Granny Badger and those who waited. Seeing Beryl's fear, and trying to reassure her, and himself, he shrugged his shoulders calmly.

"They had farther to go to do their scouting. I'm sure they've seen the wolves, and are just taking a few precautions, just as I did "

"I'm sure that must be it," agreed Branch, patting Beryl's paw with her own.

"Shhhh!" hushed Bramble, for he had heard, or rather sensed, a movement at the shadowed edge of the glade. "Back into the hole, quickly, everyone. I think we can block it off from inside, if need be," ordered Bramble. "We'd stand no chance at all, here in the open."

"Quickly, children!" urged Granny, and they all hurried into the dark opening of the hole they had come out of after the strange voice in the statue broke down the wall.

Blackpaw and Bramble went last, and began searching for some means to close off the entry, if their visitors were the enemy, as they feared. There were large boulders and smaller stones lying about, but none the animals could shove into the opening to block it off.

Bramble raced back into the chamber where the statue had stood, and glanced around quickly, hoping to find something that might give him some clue as to what they were to do.

"All this soft living," he muttered under his breath. "When that renegade bobcat left our wood, we all assumed that there would never be any more danger, ever again, and I think we all must have lost our wits entirely."

He moved dusty old stacks of strange-shaped objects this way and that, sneezing now and then, until Granny Badger laid her paw on his shoulder.

"Here is what we want," she said softly, her voice barely above a whisper, but there was a thrill of excitement in it that quickened his heart.

"What is it, Granny?" breathed Bramble.

"It is the bane of the Dragon Hordes, and curse of Erinoult's enemies," she answered, in a voice that was not her own.

Bramble gasped and fell back a step or two as a sudden brilliant light filled the dark gloom of the chamber.

"It is the sword of the Law," said Granny, "that Erinoult carried of old. Gruff has read me long passages about this. I would know it anywhere. And there are the others, carried by his clan leaders. They slew many dragons in their time, during the hard first years of Erinoult's reign. And they have slain many enemies since. But now they have lain long asleep in the quiet of this chamber. Perhaps they were waiting for us."

"I shall have that," broke in Blackpaw. "I am the only badger of age, and being the oldest, it is mine by right."

"I think we'll let Granny carry it for now," said Bramble, his voice very flat and calm.

"She's old and feeble. She'll do no good with it if it comes to a fight."

"Perhaps more use than you imagine," replied the old she-badger.

"Where are the others, Granny? Let's have them all ready so that we'll have them close to paw if a need arises."

"Here. And here is another."

Granny handed short, stubby swords in sheaths to both Bramble and Blackpaw. The same brilliant golden light burst forth as Blackpaw drew his from its cover, and Bramble found the same light blazing from his own.

"Are there more? For Stump, and Morley, and Basil?"

"We won't need one for Morley," came a voice, out of breath, from the shaft door. "He has been caught by that filth from the north."

"Basil!" they all cried together, and sprang forward to help him bring Stump, who was limping badly, into the inner chamber.

"What happened? I heard nothing," said Bramble.

"We left you at the edge of the glade, as we planned, and split up, each of us to scout a small way, and to see what we could of the lay of things. Morley was to go along the edge of the deep forest to the north, and myself to the south. Stump chose to scout to the east, and you said you would go along west, to see what was to be seen."

Basil stopped, and ran a paw across his eyes.

"We hadn't been gone from our meeting point more than a few minutes when I began to hear a lot of strange noises in the brush around us. Not so much noise, as the way something sounds when they're trying not to make any noise."

"Give him a drink, Granny, and let's have a look at Stump. It seems he's got a nasty bite on his hind paw."

Bramble eased the wounded mole onto the smooth flooring, and handed a water pouch to Basil, who gulped at it greedily.

"I knew it was the killer wolves, but I was determined they shouldn't have all of us. I set out at a fast pace, hoping to find some water, so I could lose them. They may know about fire, and have a crude language, but I doubt they can hold their own in the water with a beaver."

"You mean you were trying to lure them away," said Beryl, holding tightly to Cabbage. "How brave."

"Not very bright, you beavers," huffed the mole, who had begun to feel better after a drink.

"Hush, Stump," chided Granny gently.

"And I see he was not so bright in lugging you all the way back here," put in Branch, teasingly.

"He had to. He forgot the way," replied the mole.

"But Morley? What happened to Morley?"

"As I said, I was trying to lose the wolves by doubling about, and in hopes of finding a bit of water, when I heard Morley, right in front of me, ambling along as if he were out for a Sunday stroll, gathering strawberries. He hadn't the least notion where he was, or the danger he was in, and before I could call out to him to run, three of those beasts were on him, and it was all over. I cut back into the trees, and came back along where I knew Stump would be, and we were making a break to come back here, when two more of them set on us. It was a bit thick for a while, and I began to doubt we would make it, until we hit on a hole of sorts, and we were able to squeeze in, and thereby squeeze out of the wolves' supper pot. Stump did a fine piece of digging, and we escaped clean, except for the dirt on my coat, and Stump's hind leg, which was almost a goner. One of those beasts got a grip on it just as we went down the hole, but I gave that rude fellow a good strong beaver bite, right on his nose, just the same as I would give a piece of pine bark, and he let go quick enough."

"Poor Morley. Dear fellow never knew about the seriousness of it all. I feel badly about that. I should have warned him it was a dangerous thing we were about, and not an outing to pick berries."

"He said Blackpaw said it was safe," said Basil, looking hard at the badger.

"It wasn't my fault," snapped Blackpaw. "I'm sure those wolves would have never found out we were here at all if you bungling animals hadn't gone out looking for trouble. Now they know we're around, and I'm sure they'll even come looking here, now. I tried to warn you, but you wouldn't listen."

Bramble's temper flared, as he thought of the innocent Morley Muskrat, ambling along in the woods, without a thought in the world to danger. He just hoped it had been over quickly.

"You have caused directly, or indirectly, a death, Blackpaw. Morley was not the brightest of sorts, but he was a good animal, and trusting, and if someone held a strong belief about an issue, he would always agree. We can't blame you or hold you responsible for your faith in your Erinoult and this glade, or bring Morley back by accusations, but I can say I don't much like your behavior."

"That's your affair," said Blackpaw coldly. "And your friend would be alive if you hadn't been such an ass, and gone out looking for trouble "

Bramble bit back his anger, for he felt somehow responsible for Morley, and a nagging doubt had begun to plague him that perhaps Blackpaw was right, and that they would have been safe in the sacred glade of Erinoult.

MORLEY ONCE MORE

Granny Badger had found an ancient oven in the old chamber of Erinoult, and she, Branch, and Beryl set about making a meal while Bramble and the others examined their new weapons.

Bumble and Cabbage were enthralled with the wonderful swords, and hounded their elders over and over to show them again how the blades burst into a glowing white light when they were removed from their sheaths. The older animals did so sorrowfully, for they were just beginning to truly realize their loss, and everyone had liked Morley Muskrat's good-natured kindness, and his slow wit.

Beryl had difficulty holding back her tears.

"I can hardly believe it," she said, her voice quavering. "It was only yesterday we were all at Granny's house to decide about what should be done to prepare for the winter, and now here we are in this strange place, with all our homes gone, and Granny's house burned, and poor Morley . . ."

Her voice failed, and she could not go on.

"There's no good dwelling on it, child," soothed

Granny. "It never does any good, and it only makes the burden greater. We must learn to release our loved ones. And it's not such a strange business, when you look closely into it. I suspect we will find that out whenever we've done our lessons well enough."

"I know, Granny, but it is disturbing, still. I'm sure you must have felt it when Gruff went."

The old she-badger stopped her work, stooping before the oven, which glowed cheerfully, releasing the good smells of fresh loaves which began to hearten the little company.

"It was hard, at first. I thought merely of myself, and that I'd been deserted, and what a hard time I'd have of it, going on alone. That lasted only awhile, though. I've found out that we never really are alone."

"When do we eat?" chirped Bumble, nosing his way next to his mother, and staring hungrily at the oven door.

"Soon. You and Cabbage see if you can find us something to use for a table, and while you're about it, see if you can't find us some dishes and spoons. I'm sure there must be some about."

Granny turned back to her baking, gazing into the fire, and going on with her answer to Beryl.

"So, after a while, something happens, and you know a certain way, hard to explain. But it comes."

Blackpaw, still glowering and hurt, stalked over to the oven from the corner he had retreated to.

"A bunch of superstitious old hags must have raised you all," he snorted. "The black sheep is just what it is, and no more. Nothing to fear or worry about. And your friend has served his purpose well, and ended in a supper pot, which is what I'm after. How much longer before we eat?"

"We don't need your help in the kitchen, thank you,"

snapped Granny angrily. "And you'll eat when it's ready."

"There's no need taking out your guilt on me. I'm not the one that suggested the scouting party, you'll remember. If you'd listened to me, your friend would be here waiting for his supper with the rest of us."

Basil and Bramble put away their new weapons, and came to stand near the fire.

Blackpaw had strapped on the sword he'd been given, and swaggered about.

"I think we shall have to make new plans, now. The wolves will probably have figured out that we are somewhere about, and be searching for us soon."

"And we shall be long gone by the time they do," answered Bramble shortly.

"Can't we stay until morning?" asked Acorn, who sat with her two small babies asleep against her side.

"I'm afraid not. By then those brutes will be hungry again, and they'll be sure to discover the glade, sooner or later."

"All thanks to you," growled Blackpaw.

"I have a suggestion as to the next menu for our friends from the north," said Stump, raising himself on his back paws stiffly.

"There'll be no next victim from our ranks if we travel quietly and quickly," said Bramble. "We are armed now, and can carry our own weight if it comes to a fight."

"I would as soon have some of my own brothers, if we get to a fight of it," sneered Blackpaw. "I'm not sure how readily handy with swords you are, or how stout your courage, if put to a test."

"One more word from you, you young upstart, and I'll turn the back of this frying pan to you. I've had enough of this nonsense, and I think it's time we dropped it, and were thinking about what we are to do next. If there is to be any safety, it is going to take all our efforts. By bickering, and dividing ourselves, we only lessen our chances of ever getting out of this glade with our hides intact."

"Well said, Granny," snorted Stump. "And I'd suggest we all put our hackles down, and our good sense to work."

"I'll agree to that," said Bramble. "And here's my paw on it."

"And here," added Basil, extending his own paw as well.

"Go on," said Granny to the young badger, who was glaring balefully at the other animals.

"You, too, Ash. You've said nothing, but I know what you're thinking. This has to be all for one, or nothing. And I don't think any of us would be fond of going it alone here."

The squirrel straightened his fur, and strode to the badger, extending a stiff paw.

"We'll go on together, then. I have the wife and babies to consider."

"You needn't force yourself if you don't want," Blackpaw growled. "I know there's no love lost between us. But I agree with this old baggage in what she says. We need each other for the moment, and I shall do my part to pull my weight."

"You might begin by finding time to keep quiet. I frankly find it easier to mind my own affairs when I'm not being insulted."

"If that's what you think, I'm sure your opinion is your own, and welcome to it. I have spoken only the truth, and I need make no apologies for that."

Granny Badger slammed the oven door, and turned on the startled animals. When she was angry, she looked a good deal bigger and younger, and quite a lot like Gruff.

And badgers, when they are angry, can be very frightening indeed

"We'll have no more of this talk. Bramble, you and Stump, and Basil, and you, Ash, I shall say this only once. This is an end of it. As for you, my good cousin, I've seen better manners among those louts out there from the Northerlands. I don't know how you spent your weaning, but I'm sure your elders would be appalled to hear this drivel.

"Now, I want no more of it, and we are going to sit here until it's agreed, what's done. is done, and past. We need each other, and we are going on now from where we are, and no more said.

"Do I make myself quite clear?"

The animals had fallen quiet, and no one of them had ever seen Granny really angry, and no one said a word, but all nodded. Even Blackpaw was somewhat stunned and subdued, and he inadvertently nodded along with the rest of the company.

Just as suddenly as she had exploded, Granny straightened herself, turned back to her oven, and went on with her baking, as if nothing had happened.

Bramble pulled himself together first, and motioned to Basil.

"Let's you and I go keep watch. I have an uneasy feeling."

"That might be a good plan," agreed Ash. "After all this shouting, I'm sure those brutes would have to be hard of hearing not to know that something was afoot in their area."

"Can I go?" chittered Bumble.

"Me, too!" shouted Cabbage.

"You two will do nothing of the sort. Where are my dishes? And my table?"

Granny Badger glowered at them over her spectacles.

The pups knew this was no time to cross the old she-badger, and they touched their paws to their forelocks, and said, "Yes, ma'am," and went on in search of their tables and dishes.

Bramble and Basil passed out of the shaft cautiously, and sniffed the darkening woods, testing every breeze of wind, and every sound that reached their tingling ears.

They had trotted along a short distance toward the edge of the glade when an odd noise caught their attention. It was more a shuffling than a sort of noise, and it came with growing regularity, as if it was getting nearer to where the friends crouched beneath the darkening shadows at the beginning of the thick outer woods.

They looked at each other, with a question in their widened eyes, but neither of them could quite make out what it was that was the cause of the strange sounds.

It came nearer and nearer, and Bramble was on the point of retreating back to the shaft, and making their stand there in the narrow opening, where the wolves' greater numbers would not help them, but Basil touched him urgently, and pointed away in the direction of a thick stand of trees not far from where they stood. There was a faint motion there, made more indistinct by the gloom of the twilight.

Hackles raised, Bramble put his paw to the new weapon hanging at his side.

A dim figure began to outline itself against the darkness of the deeper shadows, and Basil drew nearer his friend.

"I don't think it's big enough for a wolf," breathed Bramble, without taking his eyes off the strange figure.

"No, I don't think so."

As Basil finished speaking, the shadowy form wobbled

out of the concealment of the trees and fell forward onto the ground.

"It's Morley!" cried Basil, and was leaping away to where the wounded animal lay.

Without warning, two lean killer wolves sprang from the underbrush behind where the muskrat lay panting, and a third lunged at Basil from the dense undergrowth where the glade ended. Without thinking, Bramble had drawn and brandished the gleaming sword Granny Badger had found and given him, and he bolted forward, uttering his horrible war cry that was almost forgotten, for it had been many turnings since he had used it.

Basil, fallen upon from front and side, had drawn his weapon and lashed out clumsily with it, but the blade had bitten deeply into the muzzle of the nearest killer wolf, and it set up such a horrible howl of pain, the others checked their attack just long enough for Bramble to reach his two friends. Holding the two terrible blades before them, with the white fire dancing dangerously, the friends held the two remaining wolves at bay, lifted the wounded muskrat between them, and began backing slowly toward the chamber where the others waited.

"Why aren't they trying to finish it?" asked Morley, covered with dirt and blood, but otherwise seemingly not seriously injured.

"They aren't through," said Bramble between gritted teeth.

"They knew if they saved me, someone would try to get me back. They are cunning, these louts," gasped Morley.

"More so than I thought at first," hissed Basil.

"They are dangerous. More dangerous than I think we have realized. And there's something behind it all, but I can't place my paw on what."

The savage, lean wolves had crept closer, but remained out of range of the terrible bite of the glimmering white-hot blades.

"Look to yourselves!" cried a voice behind them, followed by the wailing howl of a fatally wounded killer wolf, whose death rattle gurgled horribly, like a dry wind shaking old bones.

Blackpaw was suddenly beside them, and helped the friends hoist Morley quickly to his feet, and without any further attacks, they started for the safety of the narrow opening of the cave.

"I am indebted to you, Blackpaw," said Bramble. "I shall bury my part of this grudge. It was well done, and you have my thanks."

The young badger nodded slightly.

"It is as Mother Badger says. We shall all be lost if we don't strike together. We shall leave our differences here, for now."

Before Bramble could reply, their attention was drawn to the center of the glade, for there, beside the wolf Blackpaw had slain, was the figure of another. This wolf was gigantic, and his coat a grizzled silver color, tipped with a dirty white. He let out a long, low wailing howl, which was answered from all parts of the wood, until the air was full of the terrible din.

Their hearts turned to ice inside them, the animals watched, horrified, as a pack of killer wolves descended upon their fallen companion and devoured him, raising their dripping jaws, and snapping the air when they were through with their grisly feast.

"We are waiting for you," called out the huge wolf as the pack began to depart.

He turned, and faced the trembling friends.

"You may have those things that sting, but we will

have your filthy hides yet. Now we go to sleep on our hunger."

And almost as if there had never been a wolf in the clearing at all, the last golden rays of twilight were gone, and the glade fell into a silent darkness.

FIRE IN THE WOODS

Helping the badly shaken Morley along, the animals went over their narrow escape.

"If it hadn't been for these weapons, we would have all ended up in a sad fix," said Bramble. "And if you hadn't come to our aid when you did, Blackpaw, there would have been one less otter about this sundown."

"The weapons Granny found were from the ancient armory of Erinoult. They have slain worse foes than these filth. They were used in the campaigns against the Dragon Hordes, and were cast in secret places by Masters. It is no wonder they bite deep."

"I didn't know I had it in me," stammered Basil. "Why, I've never had such a thing in my paw before today, and I don't know anything of fighting, or that sort of goings-on. I'm a peaceful sort, and have no business doing anything outside of my dam building."

"You were handy enough," said Bramble. "I guess you may not have any practice at it, but the sword seemed to handle itself."

"That is part of the wonder of these weapons," went on

Blackpaw, who seemed well versed in the doings of his ancient forefathers.

"We'll have to ask Granny more about these. It did seem as though all I did was take mine out of its sheath and it was almost a live thing."

"Where on earth did you get those things?" gasped Morley, finally catching his breath, his eyes wide with fear.

"Granny found them in the old shaft," replied Basil.

"They are the ancient swords of vengeance," said Blackpaw, "given to Erinoult to drive out the Dragon Hordes from his lands."

"They seem to work well enough on wolves," said Morley, breathing heavily. "And I'm much obliged for that."

The animals were almost at the shaft entrance now, and in the dark, had to go more slowly to pick out the opening against the deeper shadows. They stumbled with Morley, making a good deal of racket, and immediately there was a savage hissing sound, and a brilliant gleam of light drew an arc through the air dangerously near them.

"It's us!" barked Bramble, angry and frightened, for the blow had come close to his ear.

"Oh," mumbled Ash Squirrel. "You should say so. Granny sent me out here after Blackpaw left, and we heard all the howling, and a horrible lot of noise. I didn't know what you were, stumbling along like that, all doubled over. You nearly scared the wits out of me."

"And you almost trimmed my whiskers for me," shot Bramble, letting go of Morley so he could walk unaided.

"Morley!" cried the squirrel in alarm. "Is that you?"

"At last count, but I've been pawed and chewed so, I'm not sure."

The squirrel dropped his sword, sheath and all, which

clattered noisily onto the floor of the entrance to the shaft, and darted away into the darkness, bumping twice into the wall, but hurrying on ahead of the others.

"It's Morley, it's Morley. They've found Morley."

"If those louts outside had any doubts where to find us, they won't any longer," grumbled Blackpaw, stopping to look behind them at the still, dark glade.

It was difficult to make anything out, and beyond, where the dim shapes of the trees began, all was a wall of black silence. But it was an unearthly quiet, and it set the animals's hackles to rising.

"I'll stay here on watch," volunteered Blackpaw. "Whenever you've eaten, then relieve me. We'll keep someone here through the night."

"And we'll try to see what our plans will be now," replied Bramble. "It seems our good voice from the past wasn't taking killer wolves into consideration when he opened up this wall for us. I don't think I would like to try to get through these woods now, not even with our new weapons."

"There wouldn't have been a need for further flight if you had heeded my counsel," complained Blackpaw, taking advantage of having Bramble under his obligation. "All we would have had to do would have been to set up our settlement here."

Bramble, feeling elated at the discovery that his friend was not, after all, dead at the hands of the killer wolves, checked his sharp reply to the badger, and instead answered in a more even tone.

"That well may have been, Blackpaw, but there is no going back now. However, I find, to my great joy, that my friend Morley has suffered no worse than a mauling, and however much a mistake our scouting party may have been, it has, after all, had a happy ending."

"If you call it a happy ending to be trapped in a wood full of killer wolves, who would have never known of our presence had you not announced it with your ill-advised outing."

A sharp note crept into Bramble's voice as he spoke.

"I agree with Granny that we have had enough discussion of the merits of my scouting party, and I think we will be wise to drop it, and concentrate on what we are to do next, rather than going over again what's been done. I am much in your debt, Blackpaw, for surely saving my life back in the glade, and I would like very much for us to get on better than we have been. I, for one, am for burying the past, and beginning anew."

The badger was silent for a moment, then held out a paw to Bramble.

"We'll leave it then, for now. I hear them calling for you. Go on. And don't forget to send someone back to spell me here."

From the inner cave, Branch was calling out to Bramble in a loud whisper.

"Are you all right? We heard that terrible fight, and that awful voice."

"I'm in a piece, but scared half silly, and starving," replied Bramble, hurrying along to where he could make out the outline of his mate against the fire behind her.

"Come on then, we've filled Morley. He's in need of a bit of rest, and I'm sure he won't forget the jawing he's had from those louts soon, but I think he's going to mend nicely. A few holes in his old hide will give him a reminder of his big adventure."

"And let's not forget the holes in mine," grumbled Stump. "I had all the attention here for a while, but now I guess I'm playing second best, since my well-chewed muskrat associate has seen fit to come crawling home."

"You old dirt hog, you leave Morley alone. He's had a time of it, and I don't doubt but that he could use less of your comments."

"Oh, I'm glad enough to hear him prattle, Granny. I wasn't ever expecting to hear his nonsense again."

"You see? Even the good muskrat knows what I'm saying is true."

At this moment Bramble entered the snug chamber, and laid the weapon that Granny had given him aside. He went to the fire and took a piece of the fresh loaf that lay there.

"How fare our warriors?" asked the old she-badger, nodding her approval at him.

"Not much the better for the wear. And I'm not so sure a war makes a warrior of one. These swords of your sires are strange enough, though. Basil thought so, too."

The beaver was on the other side of the fire, sitting beside Beryl and Cabbage. Between mouthfuls, he agreed.

After another slice of the loaf, Bramble turned to his friends, and wrinkling up his whiskers in a serious manner, he cleared his throat.

"I'm sure you all heard what went on out there in the glade a short while ago. There is a dreadfully big killer wolf, who seems to be the leader of these louts from the north, and it seems they have taken a liking to us, which spells no good, no matter what.

"This brings up a problem. If they are waiting in the woods, where and how is the question. It will be too dangerous to try the woods, for there are many of them there, and even armed, we would stand no chance."

"But Erinoult, or whoever, gave us the road, Bramble," said Ash. "That could not be clearer. Otherwise, why would we have found the opening to the outside?"

"A good question," said Granny. "I know you and

Blackpaw have had a disagreement about the wiseness of
scouting ahead in the woods, but I favor your original
plan, Bramble. I don't know about the killer wolves in the
woods, but I do know we have no choice. The shaft ends
here, in this chamber. There were other tunnels in this set
long ago, but I've found them all blocked. Some of them
run on awhile, but every single one comes to a blocked
passage, and the only other way would be to return the
way we came, which is blocked, too."

Bramble scratched his head.

"I don't think it will be possible to go through the
woods, Granny. There are too many, even though we
have these new arms."

"There was a reason we were shown this, and I'm sure
we'll find the solution soon. We'll go on making our plans
as if nothing were before us but a nice holiday outing."

"Hoorah," chittered Bumble, always glad of a holiday,
and he and Cabbage danced a quick little jig before the
fire.

"What about the children?" asked Beryl, her voice
quiet and strained. "Are we going to take them into such
danger?"

"Exactly," agreed Acorn. "We can't be expected to
take the babies out among those horrible things."

Stump growled, and hobbled over to stand beside
Bramble.

"I lay my side with Granny, Bramble. Armed, I think
we might stand a chance, uneven though it may seem.
These things come from a long line of strange beings and
powers, and I think there may be more to this picture
than meets the eye. And we all agree that this wall was
split as if we were supposed to use it. Otherwise, why
wasn't one of the other shafts that Granny talked about
opened? It would have been just as easy."

"I'm not sure," replied Bramble, pacing to and fro. "But I do know this. If we are to go through the woods, there will have to be something happen out there to take those louts' minds off us. There must be a hundred or more, not counting that giant."

"You're not talking of leaving here?" came Blackpaw's voice from the shaft as he entered the chamber. "You can't possibly be thinking of going on."

"Who is watching the glade?" snapped Bramble.

"It's quiet enough. And I smelled the food, and then I heard you talking about this nonsense of leaving the safety of the glade."

Granny nodded to Basil, and the beaver angrily left the warm circle of the fire to go out into the shaft to keep watch.

"It seems we have another disagreement as to how we shall proceed," shot Stump. "This begins to interest me."

"There's no disagreement," said Granny. "I think our path is already marked out for us."

Blackpaw had taken a huge slice of the loaf and devoured it in a bite.

Bramble turned to Morley and Stump.

"If we decide to try the road through the woods, will you be able to keep pace?"

"There is never a quicker mole than one that finds a wolf upon his track."

"I think I'll be all right, once I get the stiffness worked out," agreed Morley.

"Then let's see if we can't organize our move. Granny, will you be able to bake us up some travel loaves to eat? There's no telling when we'll be able to find shelter again, or fresh food."

"Branch and Beryl can help me. I have an old recipe from Gruff's journals on how to make a good travel loaf.

He used to take them with him whenever he and Greystone went."

"Good. Then we'll take the rest of these arms, one for each of us, and we'll see what else we can find here that might prove to be of some use."

"You're making a big mistake," complained Blackpaw, between bites. "This is sheer folly to talk of trying to get out into the open among such a number of wolves. The only reason I reached your settlement from my own was the fact I had found these old shafts, and could go undetected. Aboveground, you'll all be lost."

"Granny has said none of those shafts run any farther than here," said Branch.

"How did you get all the way underground, anyhow?" asked Ash.

"We've already passed those tunnels he came by," said Granny. "But it would have done no good to go back by them, for he said the reason for his coming was to seek safety. The killer wolves were in his settlement already."

The young badger was cutting a third piece from the loaf when Basil, out of breath, and stammering, rushed into the chamber, pointing wildly back toward the glade.

"Come quick, everyone. There's something going on that I can't make out. It's a fire of some sort, and it looks like the whole woods is going up."

The small company raced down the shaft to the entrance outside, and stood dumbfounded at the sight that greeted them. Out of the darkness of the woods, there leapt great reddish-orange tongues of fire, and the heat and noise of the flames were already grown so intense that it was uncomfortable to the animals. Great shrieks and howls of terror and pain began to erupt over the roaring of the fire.

"Do you think this is one of their tricks?" asked Basil, looking at the fire, then to Bramble.

A more distant sound was heard, indistinct, but growing closer, of a steady popping noise.

A new fear was wakened in the animals, which was even deeper than that which the fire had aroused. These new sounds were sounds of mankind, and that was the most dangerous sound of all, for it meant that their most dreaded enemy of all was upon them.

The fire roared nearer, and branches near the animals jumped and swayed from the heat caused by the inferno of the burning forest, and soon even the trees at the glade's edge were consumed with the terrible fury of the flames.

NO WAY OUT

In the woods beyond the ancient, sacred glade of Er-inoult, the king of the badger clans, the blazing inferno roared out of control. A constant, popping din filled the small band of animals with terror and confusion, and the air became so parched and hot that even their fur became singed on their backs.

"Quickly, children! We must find our way into a deeper part of this shaft," cried Granny Badger, gathering her senses.

"But we won't be able to breathe," shouted Basil, coughing and gasping, and clutching at his throat.

"If we go deep enough, we will," reassured Granny. "Our sets are not so stuffy as to have no fresh air supplies brought down from above."

"What if it's under the fire?" asked Bumble, beginning to feel the least bit afraid, after watching the fire roar on unchecked.

"We'll see to that. Where we want to go, the fire won't be able to reach, for it stands under this mountain hill, which as you have seen, is all stone. There are no trees that grow upon it."

"Let's move on then, or we won't have any need to move at all," mumbled Stump, sneezing.

Granny Badger led the animals back down the shaft that they had come in for a way, then turned off abruptly to the left, winding downward until they felt cool stone steps beneath their feet, and then they sensed that the walls had changed from earth to solid stone.

"I began remembering things that Gruff read to me as we baked," said Granny. "It has been so long ago, it was slow in returning, but I finally began to recall a little that was said of Erinoult, and the Grotto of the Sacred Dome, and how that was where the arms lay that had slain the dreadful dragon beasts, before the times we have now. And when I found those, all the other things began to come back, and I remembered the chamber that was mentioned that held the High Clan's council when they finally decided to leave these worlds and once more seek their own havens."

"Is there going to be any treasure, Granny?" asked Cabbage, holding tightly to his father's paw, but his curiosity overcoming his fear.

"I don't know," she laughed, and the incident seemed to break the closeness of the danger the animals had been feeling, and the farther they were away from the blinding heat, noise, and flames, the easier they felt.

"If there's any treasure, can we take it?" asked Bumble.

"Only if it's the kind of treasure we can eat, or drink, or protect ourselves with," replied Stump. "I have no fondness for lugging around anything that's not going to either feed me, or quench my thirst, or keep me out of the reach of those louts outside."

"And we may not have to worry about them any longer," said Bramble. "The fire may have rid us of them for good."

"And replaced the wolves with mankind," Stump reminded him. "That fire was man-made, and from anything I've ever read or heard tell of, anytime you run on their kind, you've got more trouble than you'll know how to handle."

"It sounded as if they might be fighting among themselves," went on Bramble. "In my own lorebooks, I remember reading about all the sad things that happened after the times when all kinds lived together, and no one struck a blow against a brother. It seems that mankind split from everyone else, and then they even began to split from each other, until at last, they were warring among their own."

"Shameful!" snorted the mole. "What would happen if we animals started that nonsense? Why, the whole thing would be down around our ears in no time."

"But that's just what's happened, Stump. Don't you see? These wolves aren't being very brotherly in what they're doing. It's going against the Law. They are given the sick, and weak, and old, and are to do their part in the Purpose, but this is unnatural for them to be wandering about in gangs, slaying anything that lives. And even eating each other!"

Bramble made an unpleasant face.

"Yet here we are, and I've read of these things happening before," said Granny. "Gruff always said it all goes in cycles. First you start at the top, then you go on around, until you're at the bottom, then on around until you're at the top again. I have to agree with him, although I could do with a bit more of the top."

As she spoke, she poked the guttering torch ahead of

her into the darkness to clear away some old cobwebs, long deserted.

Stump shuddered.

"Even the spider folk got tired of this drabness, it seems."

"Moved long since now, I shouldn't wonder," said Basil.

"It was their own undoing if they did," broke in Blackpaw. "It's not every living kind that would be lucky enough to live in the Sacred Dome of Erinoult."

"Well, you seem chipper enough again, my young friend. Perhaps you have some more to tell us about your hero," Granny said.

"I've done much study on the High Clan, and all those that came after. I'm not ashamed to say that there were no finer realms than those under the reign of Erinoult and his kin."

"No, I guess you're not," agreed Bramble.

"Did they have a lot of treasures?" chittered Bumble.

"What ever is all this to do about treasures, youngster? All you can bother your head with lately is treasures. Isn't there enough excitement for you?" his mother asked.

"Oh yes, ma'am. But I just wondered about all the treasure. Since we've been down here in this old cave, and talking about all these old kings and things, I was just wondering where they kept their treasure. If you were a king, you had to have a treasure, or you couldn't be king."

"A sound argument, Bumble. But it took a few brains to be a leader, too, you know."

"Oh, kings had to be smartest of anybody. But if you didn't have a special place where you kept your treasure, you couldn't really be a king at all."

"And you had to have a big house," put in Cabbage, "with a lot of windows."

"Then we certainly aren't going to visit any king's house down here," remarked Beryl.

"Well," mumbled Cabbage, "maybe there were some kings that had special houses."

Before anyone could reply to the small beaver, Granny had turned a corner and entered an immense room, and the torch flickered and jumped, hissing in her hand.

"There you are. You see? It's as I told you. Our sets are airy, even if they are belowground. There is fresh air reaching us here, and I think we'll just stay and explore here while we're waiting for the fire to burn out in the wood."

More torches were lighted, and Bumble and Cabbage raced off in all directions, calling out to the others and poking their noses into anything at all that remotely might resemble the treasure they were searching for.

Upon examining the room closer, the animals found it was one large chamber, with a great domed ceiling that corresponded to the hill above it. The walls were smoothed, and cool to their paws, and there were many scenes of badgers everywhere, some in strange-looking armor and fancy lace, and others in golden and silver battle helms, with fierce-looking eyes that glowered and smoldered, even in the pictures. They spent quite some time wandering about the room, looking at the history that stretched out before them in the picture stories, and had gotten so enthralled by the wonderful and strange things that they forgot for a time why they had come there.

A sudden echoing howl of a killer wolf tore them from their explorations and jerked them back into remembering their danger.

"That was in the shaft we just left," cried Bramble,

drawing his blade from its sheath, watching. It burst into a brilliant white light all along its keen edges.

"They must have found the entrance in the glade, and come in to get away from the fire," shouted Basil, running toward the entrance to the chamber they were in.

"We must hold this. Quickly, Blackpaw! You and Stump and Morley, and Ash, look alive. You ladies stand behind us, and see to any of them that get through," ordered the otter, and dashed to position himself beside the door.

The entrance to the room was low, and slightly more than one animal's length wide, and since it had been built by badger folk for those of their own kind, it was not quite so tall as other doors might have been, and neither were the shafts that ran in the set, so the killer wolves, being taller and wider, were having some difficulty in moving about in the cramped quarters, and that had led to the howl which had drawn the other animals' attention back to their immediate predicament.

"It doesn't sound like they're having too keen a time of it," gloated Stump, thinking of his own injury at the mauling of the wolves, and taking a keen delight in the panic-stricken howls and yowls that erupted from the tunnel beyond.

A moment later, a wolf, his fur singed, and flecks of foam frothing from his huge jaws, wriggled his way into the room, and the waiting animals struck the startled beast before he ever had time to think of warning his companions who were following along behind him.

Another came, and then another, and after each wolf was slain, the animals quickly dragged away the carcass of the dead wolf, so that the others following behind never discovered their fate until the moment they reached the chamber door, where the friends waited, grim and determined.

The tunnel had grown quieter, and the animals had begun to hope that there would be no more of their enemies coming through the low entryway. They were weary with their work, and saddened and frightened at the sight of the still figures of the eight slain wolves that lay stacked in a heap beside them.

As Bramble turned and was about to give the all-clear signal, a heavy, growling voice loomed out of the dark shaft.

"There you, friend. I knows you is in there. Let's us has a jaw about this."

"It sounds like the big wolf we saw," whispered Basil. "The one that we saw last in the glade."

"What do you want of us?" called Bramble.

"Nothing, friend. But I knows you has gutted them worthless louts that was in here with me. They wasn't going to lets me in, but I killed any as was to bar my way. I sees now it was good I was last."

"First or last, it is no matter. You are at our mercy now," replied the otter. "It will be quick with you. Our blades are sudden."

"Oh, I doesn't worry none about that, friend. I is sure they is quick enough. I didn't hear no warnings, so I knows them lumps every one went right on to their business without no doubts that they was going to find another way out of that fire trap, and them two-leggers that come on us outside."

"You mean mankind?" asked Granny, coming forward to stand beside Bramble.

"I does indeed, ma'am. They is all up and down outside now, and they is hot after one another, and we would have had us a fine feast, if them devils hadn't a torched off the woods. But they is getting stewed, too, curse their weak hearts."

"And what is your plan, now that you know we're here?" asked Bramble.

"Why, I think us had better do some jawing, or we is both going to be stuck down here a mighty long spell."

Bramble turned to Granny.

"Is there any other way out of here, Granny? At the other end?"

The old badger shook her head.

His mind raced as he tried to think of what plan to follow, or what action to take, and he glanced helplessly around at his friends.

"Does you see my point?" asked the low, snarling voice from the darkness of the shaft.

"We're talking about sealing this door off and leaving by the back way. Our problem is we don't know whether to slay you now, or risk leaving you in this tunnel alive."

"You doesn't slips nothing like that by me. I knows they ain't no way out but by me. And I is a big one, isn't I? If you does slip out here and chop me with one of them sharp sticks you has, then how is you going to move me? I is fairly well wedged in here now, and they isn't no way you is going to unjam me, if I can't move under my own juice."

Bramble recalled the size of the giant wolf and knew it would be impossible to move him; in the close quarters, for the friends to get by the dead carcass would be beyond hope, and there was no room to spare either in the height of the ceiling or the width of the walls.

Bramble turned, his face fallen.

"What'll we do, Granny?" he asked, his voice breaking.

Granny, her eyes dancing, smiled.

"We'll invite him to the Council Table of Erinoult," she replied simply, and brushed the otter aside.

A DESPERATE STRUGGLE

All the animals stared dumbly at the old silver-tipped badger.

"You mean we're going to let him in here?" asked Acorn, holding her babies close to her.

"Granny's right," said Bramble at last. "There's nothing else for it. Not if we want to get back out of this shaft and into what's left of the woods again."

"It's too dangerous," said Blackpaw shortly.

"But we don't have to let him stay alive, once he gets here," finished Basil. "Is that what you're thinking, Granny?"

"He may have that figured out in his head. He knows we won't have any reason to leave him alive, once we get him out of the shaft."

As if the wolf knew what they were thinking, he called out to them again, his rough voice strangely gentle.

"I know we is at odds, but I think we is going to have to strike a bargain here, or we is both going to be feed for the worms here."

"You'll see what kind of worm lives here soon enough, you foul heart," cried Blackpaw.

141

"That is as it may be," replied the huge wolf, and this time, Bramble noticed that the voice came from much closer.

He was just beginning the words of warning to the others when the great beast from the north exploded into the room like a shot, and before any of the stunned animals could strike a blow, he had knocked them aside and wheeled about, fangs bared, in the center of the chamber. A grisly light shone in his black, empty eyes, and yellow froth licked at his drooling jaws as he spoke.

"Now we is on more even terms, we is. I can sees you hasn't treated none of my brave lads none too fairly, neither. Just likes you'd like to treats me, I'm after thinking."

Bramble, Basil, and Blackpaw formed a line on one side of their mates and babies, and Morley, Ash, and Stump stood guard on the other, blades drawn, and faces grim. They knew in this open space, there was a good chance the wolf would slay some of them before they could strike a fatal stroke, for the grizzled gray beast was more than twice or three times the size of an ordinary wolf, and his head was so large that his jaws could have held any of the animals without effort.

The blades of the swords gleamed a deadly rainbow, and it was those stinging barbs the great wolf feared. He hungered after the death of all the cowering animals he saw before him, but he knew that they were dangerous, even though they were small. The pile of carcasses of members of his pack proved to him the grim fact that they were not to be dealt with lightly, as long as they had the shining sticks. A new plan began to turn over in his savage brain, and he once more soothed his voice, and began to cajole and whine.

"We has our outs, but why doesn't we just has a truce,

and you can go on, and then I is coming along after. It ain't right to think of how we is going to kill each other, seeing as how we is all friends, now."

"No friend of ours, I'm sure," said Basil, and Bramble had raised his sword in a menacing fashion, pointing it straight at the great wolf's chest.

Bramble was not fooled a second time.

"Granny, you and Branch, and Beryl, and Acorn, get the little ones, and start back down the shaft."

"Now, don't goes getting spooked up," crooned the wolf. "I isn't going to tries nothing more."

"Basil, you and I will let the others start back, one by one, and then we'll go."

A great yellow-fanged smile broke across the grim muzzle of the killer wolf.

"Now ain't that going to be interesting? I wonder if you all is going to live to sees daylight again? One at a time, that's how it's always best."

"He'll tear us apart," whispered Basil, under his breath.

"It's only to give the others a chance to get clear. We'll see if we can't think of something to do, once the others are free."

"I don't like that plan," said Stump. "What if the womenfolk and pups go on back, and then all of us see if we can't figure something to do about this overgrown lump."

"That ain't no way to talk about your new friend," said the wolf, and as he finished, he began bunching his muscles for a spring, but Bramble was ahead of him, and before the wolf could move, the otter had leapt forward with a high-pitched war screech, and sliced the air a few feet in front of the great beast's nose, throwing him off balance, and making him retreat a few feet.

"Go on, Morley, Stump! Take Blackpaw. Granny and the ladies may need protection outside."

Bramble's voice carried conviction, and this time the old mole lumbered hurriedly into the dark shaft, followed by Blackpaw, and lastly by Morley, carrying a torch.

"Hurry!" shouted Bramble, then turned to face the huge wolf. His heart beat heavily in his throat, and the great beast was beginning to pace slowly now, making a circle in front of the two friends.

Basil got into a position closer to Bramble, so they could talk under their breath without being overheard.

"I don't know if we can hold him off long," hissed Bramble, "but we may see if we can't lead him for a little chase around here for a while, to give the others time to get clear."

"We might even trap him down here," agreed Basil, squinting his eyes and peering into the gloom that stretched away behind the wolf.

"Okay, let's go then. I'll go down one side of the hall, and you the other. I see some pillars toward the back there. And take a torch with you."

"Maybe we could lose him in the dark, and get away before he could find us."

"That might work. But how would we find our way back to the shaft entrance? We'd be as much in the dark as he would."

"But now we is all in the dark," howled the wolf, and he flung himself savagely forward, and swatted away the friends' torches, knocking them sputtering to the floor.

The huge, dripping jaws snapped viciously, and Bramble felt the hot, vile breath of the wolf right in his ear, but he lashed out with all the strength of his small, muscular body, and felt the sharp blade in his hand strike solid against flesh. It jarred him to his shoulder, and he almost let go his grip, but he bared his teeth, and bit down as hard as he was able, and whirled away from the smothering closeness of the wolf. His mouth was full of foul-tasting fur, and his paw was numb, but he spun and flashed back at the struggling heap behind him.

On the far side of the room, by the light of the flickering torches, he saw Basil, eyes wide, and stunned.

Without waiting longer, Bramble gave out the old war cry of his kindred, and lunged forward again, swinging the gleaming blade with all the strength left in his tiring body. Again, he felt it bite home, and heard the howl of agony from the wolf, and before he could recover his balance, he was sailing through the air, all the breath knocked from him. A sudden dull pain in his left forepaw hit him, and at the same time he landed heavily against the cold stone of the wall. His head was spinning, and his eyes could only dimly make out what was happening, for the torches had begun to go out.

He heard Basil cry out, but could not understand the words, and the next instant, he heard the gasping grunts of the wolf's breathing, and felt the awful force of the heavy paws as the wolf sprang. Almost in a dream, Bramble tried to lift his paw, and he felt the leaden weight that was there, and he didn't feel he had the strength to defend himself any longer. And he found, too, that the pain in his left forepaw was caused by a bite, and he felt the blood trickling slowly through his fur. The wolf had gotten hold of him and flung him, almost as if he had been no weight at all.

The light began to flare, then dim, and Bramble felt that this surely must be the end of him, for he could not seem to make the sword in his paw raise to protect himself, but just as the torches went completely out, he thought he saw another figure, outlined by the gleaming flame of the blade, although he could not understand it, for the figure seemed to be on fire too, with the white-hot blazing light that was coming from the sword. As he watched, the figure stood before him, and upon its head was a gleaming golden battle helm, and silver light reflected from the strange armor it wore, and at first, Bramble thought it was Blackpaw, for the nose beneath the helmet looked very much like the stout line of a badger, but then he remembered Blackpaw was gone already, and there would have been no time for him to dress in the manner this warrior was dressed.

There was a great, long, hideous howl, followed by long snarls, and terrible noises of grim jaws locked and unlocked, and growling, worrying noises that rose to high-pitched cries of great agony and pain.

Bramble had scooted himself back flat against the wall, holding his dangling forepaw carefully, for the gleaming figure had taken his sword. Flashes of light, blurred by swirling, contorted shadows, confused his vision, and he could only think of trying to find the shaft door, and to make his way back into the glade, and the safety of his friends.

His paw hurt a great deal now, and although the bleeding had stopped, he could not move anything below his shoulder, and his vision kept blurring, making it difficult for him to see anything in the chamber except the flashing white light that brightened and dimmed as he watched it.

Just at that moment, Bramble stumbled, and as he went down painfully onto his chin, he felt something go over the top of him, and his head was pushed down hard onto the cold floor by a huge paw. Above the pain, his anger came, for no matter how much his effort, he and Basil had been unable to keep the evil thing back.

His hackles raised, and he tried to call out to the wolf, but his strength left him, and his last impression was one of the white figure in the golden helm kneeling beside him, laying down the gleaming sword by his injured paw.

He thought sadly of Basil, and that he would never see Branch or Bumble again, and then all light and sound passed away into a whirling cyclone of spinning forms, and he knew only silence, as when one falls away into the final long drop into the dark pool of sleep. There were brilliant stars then, and a sweet music that made his heart glad.

JOURNEY THROUGH A RUINED WOOD

A dark gray sky was filling with a crack of reddish light when Bramble Otter blinked open his eyes and tried to remember what had happened to him, and why his fore-paw throbbed and ached, and why his head burst with a dull pain that made it difficult for him to look at the faint light of the dawn. Slowly it all began to come back to him, and he tried to sit up, but a thousand needles of hot pain ran through him, and he had to lie back and settle for taking in his new surroundings from flat on his back. After a moment of resting, he started again, very slowly and stiffly, and managed to sit, although with a great deal of discomfort.

He was in a burned-out hollow of what had once been a thick forest but now was reduced to blackened stumps and smoldering ground. For as far as he could see in the early morning light, the same sight greeted him, with nothing but endless blackened stumps and drifting gray smoke.

"It's not much to look at, is it?" asked a voice beside him, startling him, until he recognized his old friend Stump.

149

"What's happened, Stump? And where are the rest of us? And how did I get out here?"

The mole laughed softly.

"Gently, lad, we'll get to your questions. You've had a nasty brush, you and Basil. I don't think I know any luckier animals, at least not any that have lived to tell of crossing paths with a killer wolf the size of the one you were dealing with."

At the mention of the wolf, Bramble remembered his last angry thoughts and the helplessness he'd felt.

"Did the wolf get away?"

"He got free of the cave, and we were afraid that some horrible harm had come to you. But he didn't even stop long enough to set on us. I've seen terror upon the face of a lot of kind in my time, but I've never seen the likes of what I saw written across that wolf. Every hair on his coat was straight out from his body, and his eyes were as big as cakes, and bone-white. I'd give a lot to know what you two did to frighten him so."

"And Basil?"

"There's nothing that will harm that animal. He's about the same as you, bruised and chewed, but all in all, no worse for the wear than any of us who have had dealings with those louts from the north."

"Are Bumble and Branch all right?"

"Fine, and sleeping, I would imagine. We spent most of the night finding you two and lugging you out of the cave to here, where we've made camp to get our bearings and set our course."

"You carried Basil out, too? I thought I saw him slip out, just before I was set upon."

"He was in the shaft. We had to carry you both out, one at a time. And it was a time of it, I don't mind telling you."

"Did you see the other one?" asked Bramble, suddenly recalling the glowing white figure that had attacked the wolf.

"The other one?" asked Stump.

"The one with the golden helm who attacked the wolf. I'd been knocked down and mauled, and I was trying to lift my blade to defend myself, when this fellow stepped in front of me, took my sword, and set on, just as that beast made his death lunge."

Stump shook his head slowly.

"There was nothing in the cave beyond two stunned animals. We gathered you, and all the arms, and everything else we could find a use for, and crossed the glade, and made as far as we could, hoping to get beyond the reach of the rest of those nasty fellows, or those others, who have fired the woods."

"Mankind?"

"They've fought all night, away down in the direction of our old homes," replied Stump, pointing in a general way toward where the sun was beginning to rise over a distant range of low foothills.

"I think it's as well that those louts from the north came when they did, for if they hadn't, we'd all as like as not be caught up in that man business there, now."

The otter shielded his eyes with his uninjured paw, and stared away at the low hills for a long moment.

"The woods have all been burnt away," he sighed at last.

"And up in the direction we should be going, too," added Stump. "It's not going to be easy, keeping to cover when we're traveling. At least not until we get beyond that next ridge or two."

A digging, sudden warmth next to his side told

Bramble his pup was awake, and giving him a very pain-
ful, powerful hug.

"You're up awfully early," he said gently. "Is your
mother awake?"

The sleepy pup nodded.

"Did you kill that old wolf?" he asked.

"No, he got away. But I don't think he'll bother us
again, not for a long while."

"Cabbage said his dad did it, but I know it was you."

"We both did it together, son. Basil was very brave,
and he stood right up and set on the wolf, then I got into
the fray, but the fellow was too much for us, and he took
to his heels. I suppose he didn't want anything more to do
with our new weapons that Granny found for us."

"Oh my," said Branch. "All my balms and herbs are at
home, in the kitchen. I don't have a thing here to bind up
those cuts with."

Her brow was knitted, and a worried cloud passed over
her eyes as she looked at Bramble's wounds.

"I'm sure we can find some new source," said Granny
Badger, who had come up unnoticed, and not bent to in-
spect the otter's wounds.

"I saw a wormheart root that was undamaged back a
piece. I'm sure if someone will get it for me, I'll have
these scrapes all dressed in no time."

"We'll get it, Granny," chimed Cabbage and Bumble
together, and were racing away before anyone could tell
them otherwise.

"Don't get too far," coaxed Beryl, although the two
pups were too busy chasing themselves to hear her advice.

"We can keep an eye on them," said Morley, yawning.
"I remember seeing the wormroot. I guess I noticed it because it wasn't burned like everything else."

"Come on, then," scolded Stump. "Let's go see if we

can't keep track of those two youngsters, and get the dressing. I'm sure Bramble and Basil would like less jawing and a little more action. Those wolf bites need the wormroot, and not all our gabbing."

And so saying, the mole and muskrat set off after the two youngsters, the muskrat nodding his head in agreement with something Stump was explaining.

"Where are we, Granny?" asked Bramble, as the old badger sat down next to him and began to clean his forepaw.

"As best I can tell, we've come in the direction that Gruff used to describe as being toward the Falls. It's harder, now that most of the Wood is burned, for most of the landmarks I remember Gruff talking about were old trees, but there is still that, and I don't think it would be easy to mistake."

She pointed to a mountain peak in the distance, with the snows already glistening on it. To the right was another peak, in the rude fashion of a hedgehog in outline, also covered with the snow that was beginning to fall in the higher altitudes.

"Those will guide us as far as the Falls, and I'm not sure what lies beyond, or if we shall need to go there. Greystone and Gruff would never say exactly what they saw there, or anything much about that part of the trip."

"It'll be enough just to get beyond these borders, and away from whatever is left of the wolves, or mankind."

"Maybe they'll take care of themselves," suggested Blackpaw, speaking for the first time since Bramble had been awake.

"That would certainly be a handy solution, but I don't think we can count on it," said Granny. "Most likely, they'll be on each other's track, back and forth, but I don't think the wolves have the courage to openly attack

a man camp. They'll just follow along after the battles,
and find the easy prey."

"So our plan is simply to make for the high peaks,
then?"

"Yes, Bramble. There doesn't seem to be another
direction we can take. We don't dare go back toward our
old settlement, for the wolves are still there, and now
mankind, and they've burned the Wood, so that there
would be no real point in that move. The same holds for
going toward the Upper Weir, or the Glen, beyond Wide
River. You can see that those directions all lie toward
where the wolves are coming from, and now we have the
added danger of this fresh invasion from mankind. They
have never been in these parts for as long as I can
remember, and I don't think they've been here since Gruff
was a pup, and probably not before that. But now, for
some reason we don't know, the wolves from the north
began to go beyond their rightful hunting grounds, and we
find them far from the realms where they have been
known to flourish. So going in either of those directions,
I'm sure, would only spell disaster and grief."

Granny paused, letting her words sink in.

"So the only place left for us to try is in the direction
of the Falls."

"Old Bark is there somewhere, too," added Bramble,
almost as an afterthought.

At the mention of the bear's name, Blackpaw stiffened
and snorted.

"You'll find no solace from that renegade. If anything,
you might find yourself suddenly a part of his dinner
fare."

"You've heard of Old Bark, then?" asked Basil.

"I've heard well enough what trouble he has caused
among all the places he's ever been. Stories of animals

disappearing, and all other strange goings-on, such as it is. It's not so strange when you come down to the fact that bears do turn renegade once they are too old to hunt."

"Wherever did you get all that?" asked Granny. "It sounds as if someone has been spreading tales, and doing a wonderful job, as well."

"These are no tales. I've come across stories of him in the lorebooks I've studied, and there are many tales among my clan about the dreadful bear that sets upon does and pups, and even eats the flesh of the dead, not to mention having no respect for territory, or any of the other laws we try to abide by."

"Well, it's plain to see you've bought the whole bill of goods," replied Bramble. "There's no use trying to argue with you, but perhaps we might hear Old Bark's piece, if we ever reach him. I think he has been made into an unwilling villain, and I, for one, would be anxious to see him, and find what counsel he has for our troubles."

Blackpaw snorted.

"Humph. I'm sure he could give you wonderful counsel, right enough. The solutions to all your problems will be the solution to his own, and that will take care of his supper dish for as long as we last."

"Have you any other suggestion?" asked Granny.

"Well," the badger stammered, "it's as well that we set off in the direction you've given, mother, but I think we should alter our course before we come into contact with that brute of a bear."

A feeble voice followed as Blackpaw fell silent.

"I think that the best of all ideas would be to have a little something to keep up one's strength, then maybe another nap."

"You'll have that, Basil," answered Granny somewhat

more cheerfully. "We did find more stores there when we went back for you after our friend had fled."

"That was the strangest thing," began Basil slowly. "I could have sworn I saw some sort of animal in a golden helm, with something all over that shone silver. After the wolf had knocked me down, I tried to reach my sword, and saw that he had turned on Bramble. Then I saw Bramble lunge, and then everything was so confused, but there was a lot of howling and screeching, and then this flashing white light."

"That was Erinoult," cried out Blackpaw. "His battle helm was golden, and in the fashion of a hawk."

Bramble's eyes widened.

"It did look like some sort of a bird, with its wings opened out."

"This is a strange thing," said Basil. "But then not so strange, either. I guess it's only the beginning. We've all been much too close, and too smug in our cellars, to really notice anything much."

"Too smug indeed," said Granny, taking a piece of wrapped loaf from Acorn, who had spread out a small tablecloth on the ground. "But I don't think so smug that we won't all be thankful for this breakfast."

As the companions prepared to sit down for their meal, they heard a cry from some distance away, and looked up to see the two pups, followed closely by Morley and Stump, hurrying toward them through the ruined, blackened woods.

A GREAT EXODUS

As the youngsters neared the gathered friends, they both fell into excited chitters and jabberings, and no one could make head or tail of what they were so desperately trying to say. Only when Morley and Stump arrived a few moments later, limping from their still fresh wounds, did the story become clear.

"There's a migration moving this way," said Stump, pointing back in the direction they had just come. "You'll be able to see the dust soon. I couldn't tell who all was in it, but it is a large number of different sorts. From the fire, I would imagine."

"This doesn't look good, Granny," said Bramble, frowning, and looking away toward the distant horizon, which had, as Stump said, begun to be clouded with the rising dust from the movements of a large band of animals. "If we can see them so readily, I'm sure every killer wolf in these parts, and every other hungry mouth in humankind, can, too. I wonder that they haven't split into small groups, so they could go more secretly."

"I never did think the animals that lived in this wood were too bright," offered Blackpaw. "I have been in these

157

woods, on the other end, and it seemed they were full of silly rabbits, or giddy deer, who were all leaping about, chasing each other, or playing games with each other that made no sense. My clan once wintered in that part of the woods, or a place very similar to it, and we all agreed it wasn't the best place of all for a permanent shelter. There was nothing really wrong, except that I got the feeling that the animals that settled there were not really, well, animals at all. They spoke a very plain language, and I don't think they used fire at all, and had more or less gone back to their wild state."

"That's a very serious thing," agreed Granny slowly, "if they have forgotten their beginnings and are reverting back to their old ways."

"It seemed as if that's what I remember," replied Blackpaw. "My sire only kept the clan there for the one winter, and we moved on to where our settlement was, until I left to find safe haven just these last few days ago."

"Do you think your clan might be among these folk who are migrating?" asked Granny, addressing the young badger seriously.

"I don't think my clan would be traveling in a herd like that. No one would who had any thought to their safety."

"Then we had best see what we can do to get out of the path," urged Bramble. "We'll have to detour one way or the other, and remain out of sight until they get past, or until we can tell for certain which way they are going."

"It didn't look like they have any direction," said Morley. "I think they're just running, and they go in the direction of whoever's in front."

"That seems to be about the best I could make out," agreed Stump. "There wasn't much sense in it, but there never is when you get so many together, following first one, then the other. Most likely as not, there'll be a lot of trampled animals, and a lot of running, but no one will be really getting very far. I've known herds like that to run in circles for three days, and just end up right back where they had begun, only hungrier and more tired."

"That's exactly what the killer wolves are after. First they scare their victims into a panic, then just wait until they've run themselves down. Nothing to it," said Morley. "And I should have reason to know."

"Then let's set to it. If they keep on coming this way, we'll have to go either north or south far enough to let them pass. I don't think we'd be wise to set off in our direction toward the Falls now. In the state of mind these chaps are in, they'd just follow right along, and then we would just as well leave a map for our friends from the north to follow."

"We might try talking to them," suggested Basil. "I hate to think of just leaving anyone to a fate like mankind, or the killer wolves. We might try to reason with them, and convince them their best path would be to split up into small parties and go on toward safety in that manner. Everyone would have a better chance then."

"That's easier said than done," grumbled Blackpaw. "I haven't ever been able to reason with a rabbit, or those silly deer. They don't seem to do well outside of a group. Always have to have six dozen or so animals around them, and I've never heard of any of their sort making a sensible decision and sticking by it. Oh, they may start off with the best of intentions, but they never seem to last long. At the first signs of danger, or the first pretty flower to be sniffed, off they go in every direction, and all their high-flown plans are left in a heap."

"I'd still feel easier if we would at least try to warn these animals. It doesn't seem right to just leave them to their fate, without even trying to tell them there is danger here," continued Basil.

"You're right, of course," put in Bramble. "We can at least try to warn them that it would be best if they would split up and travel on in the direction we are going toward the Falls. That way, with any luck, and much prudence, we would all stand a better chance of arriving there all in a piece."

"We can leave the signs," said Granny Badger. "It might be easier than trying to deal with a mob. And it looks as if they're coming this way, right enough."

The hanging pall of black dust spread over the sun, darkening the sky, and the air seemed to grow colder. It was plain to see that the leading edge of the churning storm was advancing directly toward where they stood watching.

"There seems to be a great many of them," said Morley. "More than I first thought."

As the animals watched, the vanguard of bolting, terrified creatures became visible. Between the gentle slopes of an old stream bed, the first wave of the frightened herd poured out, their eyes bright in shining fear and their nostrils flared in panic. And at the same moment, the companions saw a dozen killer wolves charge down upon two of the leading animals and drag them aside, free of the rest of the herd.

"They'll pick them apart, until there's none left," said Bramble, a sick feeling in the pit of his stomach.

The attack turned the herd back upon itself, for the ones in the front saw the new danger, and tried to change their direction. After many chilling and horrible cries, the huge mass of the herd turned, like some crazed thing, and thundered away in a direction that would eventually lead them back onto the exact trail they had just covered.

"So much for a warning," grumped the mole. "I hardly think they'd have listened to us anyhow. I imagine we'd all have ended up mashed to pulp for our trouble."

"There's no reasoning with a lot like that," snorted Blackpaw. "I think we're lucky that they turned when they did. At least we'll have a head start on them."

"I wouldn't be so sure," said Bramble. "It looks as if they're coming back this way now."

Over the din of the thundering herd, there were cries and howls from the killer wolves, and the friends watched, unable to move, as the great horde of fear-crazed animals raced back at breakneck speed, on a path that would once more carry them directly over the ground where they stood.

"Get the supplies!" barked Bramble, taking his young pup under his arm. "Let's move on up here to higher ground. They may not turn, and I don't think there's a hope of stopping them, and I think they see the danger they're in."

The companions hastily grabbed their small belongings, and followed the scurrying otter, upward now, toward a broken patch of blackened stumps, where an old stone wall still stood, charred a dirty brown, but offering at least some shelter from the dangerous hooves of the fear-blinded herd.

"Quickly! Help Granny, Blackpaw. Lend a hand. You, take the babies from Acorn," commanded Basil, as he helped Beryl and Cabbage over a low and broken portion of the wall.

The companions had barely gained safety when a hundred or more frenzied animals of the stampeding herd rushed headlong at them, and had it not been for the haven the tumbling stones afforded them, they would have surely been badly injured, or even killed.

"That was a close one," breathed Morley. "I think the poor chaps have lost their senses. They don't seem to have any idea where they're going, or even if they're going in the right way to get away from whatever they're running from."

"No doubt," muttered Stump. "But I don't like lagging about here at the whim and fancy of a pack of animals that seem to blow whatever way the wind is blowing."

"We'll soon be free of them," assured Bramble, in a tone more confident than he felt. "I don't think they are going to be able to hold out long at the pace they're traveling. And it doesn't seem as if any of them has thought about food, or where they're going to get water, or find a safe place to sleep."

"They'd last, all right, if they'd follow out until they hit the end of the fire. There's sure to be food and water there."

"I agree, Ash. They would do better to get hold of themselves and try to think out their move."

"That's easy enough said, Stump, but I guess they must have had a rough go of it during the fire. And we don't know what all has happened to them since. We were lucky, having a hole to dodge into."

"Bramble is right," agreed Basil. "These poor creatures may have been so hard pressed, the only thing they could think of was to fly."

"Here come more of them! Get down!" shouted the mole.

The ground beneath them began to tremble, and in another moment, great clouds of dust enveloped them, as hundreds of feet flew over their heads, and all about them swirled an endless procession of heavy-breathing animals, large and small, running hard.

A shriek of absolute, raw terror filled the animals' ears,

and right before them, in the quiet eddy behind the wall where they crouched, a young deer, his feet kicking the air, fell heavily to the ground, landing with such force all the wind was knocked out of him. He had hardly touched the ground before a grayish-brown form appeared beside him, drooling jaws opened to deliver a back-breaking, killing blow.

Before the killer wolf could slay the fallen deer, Basil and Stump had fallen on the surprised wolf, and felled him easily with the gleaming blades. The deer, his eyes rolled back in his head, trembled and shook, senseless in his fright.

Stump, wiping his sword blade on a piece of tattered cloth he had taken from his belt, tried to reassure the frenzied animal.

"Here, here, old fellow. This won't do. You've got to get hold of yourself. You're going to be all right, now."

Sputtering in fear, the deer focused on the mole. Flat on his back, he surged up a bit, but seemed unable or unwilling to move.

Basil patted the animal on its side, trying to soothe it.

"You can do it. And you can travel with us, if you like. We're heading for the Falls, where there is plenty of food, and clean water."

"There's nothing up that way," bleated the deer, finding his voice at last. "No one lives up there but a renegade bear."

"That's true enough, except the renegade bear part. Who told you this?"

"Owl Wing. He says we are to find new grazing beyond the Four Oaks."

"Is that where you're all bound now?" asked Basil.

Glancing around him in growing confusion, the deer staggered to his feet before answering.

"We must get away from the fire. It's burned all our winter forage."

"And don't overlook the killer wolves," reminded Stump.

"Killer wolves?" echoed the deer.

"This fellow here," said Basil, pointing to the still figure of the slain wolf.

The deer's eyes rounded and turned black with fear, as if he were seeing the new danger for the first time. Without another sound, the deer leapt away, clearing the far side of the stone wall in a single bound and running hard toward the distant herd.

"Well, you tried," said Stump. "I don't think these fellows are too bright."

"It doesn't seem that way."

"Come on," called Granny. "Hurry!"

The beaver and mole scurried back to the knot of friends, and picked up their meager packs.

"We've done our best to warn these nits," said Basil. "I don't think they know what they're up against, and I don't really think they listen to anyone, except maybe their leader. What was his name?" he asked, turning to Stump.

"Owl Wing, I think he said."

"Well, if we ever chance across this fellow Owl Wing, we'll see to it he is properly warned, so he can act accordingly."

"Leave the signs," instructed Granny. "There may be other animals who are following along, who might read them, and save themselves from the dangers here."

"Let us, let us," cried Bumble and Cabbage. "We know how to do it."

Bramble frowned down at his young pup.

"Can you do it quickly, and get it all right?"

"We know how," insisted Cabbage. "We've done it before."

"I know," said Morley. "I almost had the wits scared half out of me last spring when I came down to Mill Pond, and there they were, all around my watering hole. From the way I read them, there must have been at least eight hungry bobcats, and a wild boar on the loose."

Bumble blushed a deeper gray, and looked down.

"We didn't mean to really scare anyone. We were just practicing."

"You should be ashamed of yourselves," scolded Branch.

"No time now for that," corrected Granny. "You do those signs again now, you two, and do it just like you did. Don't leave anything out."

"Yes, ma'am," the pups muttered, and set about their work in a somewhat subdued manner.

"This is all we can do for now," said Bramble, "although I doubt if anyone will have time to read them, much less pay any attention, if they're with that herd."

"You never know," said Branch. "You'd be surprised at what might go on when you're hard pressed."

"You're right there," agreed Granny. "I have a feeling the signs won't be wasted on everyone that might chance along this way."

And Granny's belief turned out to be true, although she would lament the fact later, much higher up, and near the path that led over the Wild Pass to the Falls.

THE WOOD OF THORN

FOLLOWING THE SIGN OF THE MOON

Moving as quickly as they were able, and keeping to what sparse cover they could find, the small band of friends crossed through the burned woods. Twice more they were forced to avoid being trampled by large, terrified herds of animals, and once, Bramble thought he had spotted the leader, Owl Wing, the deer had mentioned, but there was no time to try to warn the frightened creatures, and the companions were nearly crushed underfoot before they found shelter from the flying hooves.

Stump, straightening himself from a close brush with a large deer, had grumbled bitterly.

"I don't mind so much being mauled or chewed over by those louts from the north, but you'd think these folks would be a little more civilized, seeing as how we shared the same wood all these years."

"They don't have much sense when it comes to dealing with things like this," replied Bramble.

"Don't think we do, either," answered the mole. "But I don't go around stomping innocent animals to an inch of their life, or scaring the wits out of half-grown pups."

"Oh, we like to see all the deer, and all the others,"

169

shot Bumble and Cabbage together. "They must be having a good time."

"Don't know about any good time ever come of a fire, or killer wolves, or mankind," mumbled Stump.

"It does give us an advantage," said Blackpaw, looking beyond where they had made their camp for the night. "It means the killer wolves and mankind will be busy with that lot, and we'll be able to travel on unnoticed."

Granny Badger stopped in the midst of handing out the rations of travel loaf.

"It seems that's so, although I don't feel any too good about it. We did try to warn them, though. May get another chance, if we keep crossing paths this way."

"If we're not mashed to pulp first," snorted Stump.

"We won't be," assured Bramble. "But we are going to need to decide soon which way is going to be the safest, once we reach the end of the burned part of the woods."

"I saw what must be the beginning of good trees," offered Acorn, chewing his food hungrily.

He had been the afternoon scout. The animals had taken up the habit of keeping a lookout posted ahead of them, and Acorn had been the last before the camp was made.

"How far?" asked Granny.

"Another day, perhaps even less."

The old she-badger frowned.

"We shall find our going harder, once we get there."

"Why?" asked Beryl. "Won't it be easier? We won't have to be so careful, and there'll be plenty of cover for us, so we won't be noticed."

"What will hide a beaver will hide a killer wolf, or mankind, just as easily," replied Granny. "We'll have to go more slowly, and a lot less noisily. We are also going to have to be very careful that we don't get lost in these woods, if I'm not mistaken."

"Erinoult said he would give us charts," snorted Blackpaw. "Didn't we bring along all the things from the cavern?"

"There were no charts there," Bramble snapped shortly. "We were lucky to find these weapons and what little food there was, much less a map of a wood that no one is quite sure of."

The young badger bristled.

"If the chart was not brought along, I'm sure it was the fault of a careless animal. Erinoult distinctly said he would provide us with food and a chart to our destination."

"I remember that," agreed Granny. "The Master did say just that."

"Then where is it?" asked Basil, a worried note in his voice.

"Maybe it's a chart to the treasure house," chimed in Bumble. "I'll bet it's a chart to tell us how to get to where he had all the treasure hidden."

"Hush, Bumble," warned his mother.

"Is there anything in these supplies that looks like a map?" asked Bramble, taking off his small knapsack and searching through the contents.

The others followed his lead, and soon the sacks were all emptied and spread out before the disappointed animals.

"There's nothing here of that nature," moaned Morley. "No map, no clue, no nothing."

"Someone must have forgotten to take something," said Blackpaw, looking accusingly at the muskrat.

"Nothing was left behind," said Granny Badger. "We went over it all again, and after we got Basil and Bramble

out, I went myself to make sure we were leaving nothing
we would need later on."

Bramble leapt suddenly to his feet.

"Could that lout of a wolf have taken something when
he left? I mean, could he have gotten it?"

Beryl and Ash moaned aloud, but Granny silenced
them with a stern glance.

"The wolf had nothing on his mind but to get away
from where he was. And I searched through the stacks of
things that were there, looking for these swords, and there
was no chart or map of any kind."

"Then your Erinoult was wrong," sneered Basil, bitterly disappointed, but trying to conceal it.

"He wasn't!" cried Blackpaw, his hackles rising.

"Hush, you two!" scolded the ancient animal. "I think
I may know what Erinoult meant. It wasn't that he was
going to give us a new map of where we were to go. I
don't think he meant that at all."

Granny Badger opened out a worn, old volume of lore
from Gruff Badger's study.

"I've kept it safe here under my apron. I couldn't stand
to leave our old home without something, and this was
what I took. But I think I know what Erinoult had in
mind when he said he would provide us with a chart of
where we were going."

As she spoke, she carefully laid out a small page that
was neatly folded into the center of the book. Across its
brown, crinkled surface ran glyphs and ancient signs, all
in the high, flowing hand of Gruff Badger.

"He used to copy maps into this book from time to
time, sometimes from places he and Greystone had been,
and other times from some story he had read in his
studies, or that someone had told him of. He was very
careful about those sorts of things, and always said there

was nothing half so interesting as a good map to a place a fellow had never been before."

"What good is one of Gruff's old maps going to do us?" asked Morley.

"Not one of Gruff's old maps," corrected Granny. "A map Gruff copied out of an old lorebook."

She had spread out the brown parchment chart, and now the others crowded around her to look.

Bumble and Cabbage squirmed their way into the group, chattering loudly.

"A treasure map. The old king hid his treasure, and drew a map to find it."

None of the others were able to convince the two pups that it was not so.

"What is this, Granny? Or rather, where is it?" asked Bramble, trying to decipher the small, neat handwriting, and puzzling over the intricate markings and symbols that were fading with age.

Granny Badger smiled.

"You are looking at one of the places marked here," she said, pointing away to a V-shaped valley that showed between the gentle slopes of the distant foothills. "There." She pointed to a spot on the chart, and moved her finger in a line along the paper, then stopped and tapped it. "And here is where we came from, the Glade of Erinoult."

All the friends leaned closer, trying to see where Granny was pointing. The writing was so thin, and the drawing so faded, none of them could make much of the dark blue spot Granny pointed to.

"How do you know?" asked Blackpaw. "I can't make anything out of this. And you said yourself, this old chart came from your mate, not the chamber of the Master."

"Oh, it came from the chamber, well enough, but a good deal earlier than our trip."

"Impossible," snorted the young badger.

"Not when the travelers were Gruff and Greystone. He had spoken about this once, in a roundabout way. It only made sense after I'd seen the chamber myself, and come upon Erinoult, and heard the stone speak."

"Then where do you make us?" asked Bramble. "And where do we have to go to reach the Falls?"

"Are you going to accept this chart as true?" asked Blackpaw, turning on the otter.

"We'll have to, friend. Or else wander about here, with no direction, until the killer wolves get us, or until we're trampled down by another lot of hysterical animals who've lost their good sense as well."

"It's folly," glowered the badger. "We may as well go on toward the unburned wood, no doubt, but we don't need this foolish scribbling of a map to guide us."

"No, but we shall need it once we're there," said Granny calmly. "This wood is very thick, and according to Gruff, very dangerous. There are quicksand pools, and poisoned trees, and thorn brakes, as well as the other dangers that we are more familiar with lately."

"Where are these things, Granny?" asked Basil, screwing up his whiskers, and trying to detect the symbols for the things the old badger spoke of.

"Here, and here. And here is the opening that will take you to the path that goes all the way through the wood. The other trails all end inside. If one has followed the wrong turning, there's no hope of a return."

"You mean there's no way out?" asked Beryl.

"There is a way, for those who know the secrets."

"What secrets?"

"The secrets of Thorn Wood," replied Granny simply.

"And we have the map here that will take us safely through if we are able to find our way there and can manage to pick the right path to take us."

The other animals gathered closer to the old badger, and peered harder at the chart spread before her. Finally, after a long time looking, Bramble made out the neat scrawl of ink over a large, dark splotched area on the brown paper, and it read in the high language of all animaldom:

> This is the Wood of Thorn.
> There are many dangers here.

Below that, Gruff Badger, on some faraway day long ago, had penned a further note.

> Greystone and I have gone safely
> through. Follow the sign of the
> trine moon.

And in a flowing, neat hand, there was the symbol for the trine moon.

Also there on the map, in tiny print, making a weaving line that looked like a coiled snake, was a trail marked from one side of Thorn Wood to the other. Surrounding the path that was marked on the chart were Gruff Badger's symbols for danger, and they seemed to fill the wrinkled page, until after further study, Bramble thought only the most desperate of animals would ever venture into a wood so full of fearful peril.

He looked about him at his mate and pup, and his friends, and Granny, and even Blackpaw, and hoped that the old she-badger was right, and that Gruff Badger had marked his trail well.

Before he could finish his thoughts about traveling through the strange, forbidding forest, he became aware of another noise that meant danger for the friends, and one that was nearer than the dangers of the wood. The regular thump and racket of mankind erupted from all about them, and with no further time for plans, the animals gathered their young and their meager supplies, and set out at a fast trot for the grim fastness of Thorn Wood.

BLACKPAW DEBATES

"I don't like this," huffed Stump, marching solidly along beside Bramble. "First it's those filth from the north, then mankind, then a fire, and now we've come slap up against a problem with even more stickers."

"Thorn Wood isn't a problem if you know what you're about," answered Granny, although the mole hadn't addressed her directly. "Gruff spoke of it with great hesitation, and I've almost forgotten, but it all begins to come back now."

Blackpaw turned and snorted.

"It's always easier to make up anything you want to hear and expect it to be believed when you're beginning to have a little gray at your muzzle."

Paying no attention to the young badger, Granny went on.

"Gruff and Greystone had a great deal to say about how one acted when afraid. All sorts of unpleasant thoughts, and snapping at each other, and first one thing, then another. I must agree, and I think it's a bit easier for me to look at it all now in that light, and understand the story they told me."

Granny paused, and looked directly at Blackpaw.

"They had traveled almost the same journey we have made, except there were no killer wolves or mankind about then, and had begun in a direction we are following, leading off toward the Falls. They met a chap in these woods who seemed a nice enough sort, a distant relative of Gruff's some way, and another otter by the name of Lakewalker, who was kin to Greystone. This seemed great good fortune, for the two knew the lay of the country, and if I'm not mistaken, it was this very wood."

"Not much to it now," grumbled Stump.

The animals gazed around at the black, ruined wood and charred ashes, and tried to imagine what it was like at the time Gruff and Greystone had traveled here.

"The four of them went on without danger, and it was strange to Gruff, for he had expected trouble in some way. However, it was like a summer outing, he said, and Greystone and his cousin even had time for a short river expedition to look at a particularly fine weir."

"If there is a river, we could use the water, now," agreed Basil. "Our water supply is getting low, and if this Thornbrake or Thornstump is as dangerous as you say, then we'd better have as much as we can carry."

"I don't think any river has ever flowed in these parts," glowered Blackpaw. "Even if it had long run dry, there would be a stream bed or dry wash. And it's easy to see there isn't anything of that nature here."

"There are times when rivers go underground," said Bramble. "When you understand water, and study it as I have, you begin to have a feel for water in any form, or fashion, and I know there's water here. It's beneath us."

"Fine lot of good that will do us," sneered the young badger.

"It will serve us nicely, for we'll find where it touches the surface somewhere."

"More history? Are we now expected to believe you've been here, too? You seem so sure."

Basil broke in angrily.

"Your opinions are your own, Blackpaw, and you have as much right as any to your belief in them. But your whining and outright bad manners toward Granny are uncalled for, and whether or not there's a river here, it won't hurt to hope. Otherwise, we may as well all lie down now and refuse to budge. Or if you don't want to believe it, and would like to stay, there won't any of us argue with you."

"You'd like that, would you? Just forget Blackpaw, and one less mouth to feed and water. Make it a lot simpler for you if I did that, just balked and refused to go a step farther? Then you'd be rid of me, and there'd be nobody left who can see clearly what's going on. Well, I'm not staying behind, and there'll come a time when you're glad enough of Blackpaw's presence."

The young badger glared defiantly at the stunned animals for a moment, then marched doggedly on, head high, looking neither right nor left.

"Humph, well, I never," began Stump, but Granny cautioned him to silence.

Bramble watched the young badger, a puzzled frown growing darker.

"It may be so, just as he says. Still, I feel a sort of danger from him. Nothing I can quite put my paw on."

"I could have said that of you once, Bramble," said Granny softly. "You were not too unlike our friend, when you were full of what you believed truth, and were sure you had it, and all the rest of us were the cause of all the problems."

Bramble blushed a darker shade of gray.

"I suppose you're right, Granny. Just reminds me a bit of me. That's always uncomfortable."

Acorn and Basil had been about to speak, but had stopped.

"And you, too," said Granny, pointing at them. "You're a fine lot to be complaining of this fellow, after all the time Gruff and I spent listening to your goings-on about how the old ways would have to change, and that Gruff and Greystone would have to give over and let the younger animals run the community, and then there were plenty of times, too, when you as much as said you really didn't believe Gruff Badger when he said he'd been to the Falls. Oh, don't deny it, I heard you. You didn't tell him to his face. No one ever did that. But I saw it. You thought to yourselves, 'Here's this old animal hardly able to dig in his garden, now how could he ever have done all those things he says he's done.' "

Granny Badger smiled and shook her head at Basil.

"I know. That seems to be a thing we all pass through. A part of growing up, it seems. Always doubt everything, until proven otherwise."

"What happened to the story, Granny?" chirped Bumble, who had tired of all the other talk and wanted to hear more of whether or not there would be any treasure, or dragons. Grown-up talk did not interest the young otter pup, and he always felt as if they did it on purpose to try to cover up the important matters, or to avoid talking about anything interesting at all.

The old badger turned and patted Bumble.

"The end of the story came when these new chaps Gruff and Greystone had met went with them into Thorn Wood."

"You mean they were lost?" asked Basil.

"Oh no, nothing of the sort. They went into Thorn Wood quite easily. Found the proper path, and in those days, I think the old runes were still plainly marked for any and all."

"Was Thorn Wood a dragon lair, Granny?" asked Cabbage.

"I don't know. May have been at one time, but it was certainly a long time before the story I'm telling now."

"I think I remember something about a great battle fought there, between the dragons and an army of mankind. I think there was something of elves, too."

"Your lore, Bramble, is quite a lot like my own. That was from another time, long before the time we're discussing now."

"I want to hear about the dragons," chittered Bumble.

"Me, too," agreed Cabbage.

"Let Granny finish her story," scolded Branch.

"There's not too much to the story," laughed Granny. "Gruff and Greystone were going through Thorn Wood, and felt sure they would find a way. The two strangers who traveled with them doubted, and they turned back halfway into the journey. They never saw the other side of Thorn Wood, nor did they ever see the Falls, or any of the other places in between."

"Or Gruff Badger, or Greystone Millweed?"

"Gruff made a point of that story every time we would be in a tight place and there wouldn't be any sure end to what we were doing. It might not be anything more of an adventure than planting the winter crop of turnips, but there would always be the animal who would come by to assure us that we were in for a spell of dry weather, or that the birds would get the seed, or that it would be next to impossible for the piece of ground we'd planted in to produce anything but weeds. You all know the sort.

Seems to make them feel better to always be thinking of the grim side of things."

Stump shot a sidelong glance at the old animal.

"That's half the sense in living, being able to see what's wrong with things, so you can fix it."

Granny touched the mole's paw gently.

"Bless you, Stump, yes. That's exactly the way of it. You do have to know what's wrong with a thing so you can know what's right with it. But there is a point that's passed, and then the dark side just begins to look darker, and there doesn't seem any need in going on."

"Sort of like where we are now," said Acorn.

"Exactly. We have our work cut out for us, and we know where we shall have to go, but we don't know exactly how we are going to get there."

"One thing for sure, we know how *not* to," put in Stump, motioning back toward the burned-out forest behind them.

"Our way does seem to be fairly clearly marked in that way, indeed," said Granny. "And that's away from the killer wolves, and mankind, and the ruins of the fire."

Bramble, glancing ahead as he walked, realized that he had been vaguely uneasy in something he had seen.

Or was it something he hadn't seen?

As he started to ask Granny a question about Thorn Wood, it struck him suddenly that the badger, Blackpaw, was nowhere to be seen.

AN UNSEEN RIVER

As far as the companions could see, there was nothing but a vast expanse of fire-gutted wood, and nowhere, in any direction, was the familiar form of a badger.

Bramble's heart sank.

"What ever could have happened, Granny? Do you think he has taken us to heart, and just disappeared?"

The old she-badger shook her head.

"I don't rightly know what to think, Bramble. Blackpaw is strange enough, that's no mystery. First he's for us, then against us, and then he's saved your life. It's as much a puzzle to me as to anyone, and yet I should be the one that would understand him best."

"Well, he can't go far without us seeing him, sooner or later," added Stump finally. "You can see everywhere, and if there's no hiding for a mole, there's sure to be none for some lug of a badger."

"Do you think he would actually leave us?" asked Beryl. "I mean, out here, with nowhere else to go, or no one to turn to?"

"There's always the killer wolves to turn to, don't forget," shot Basil. "Or mankind. They're supposed to make lovely sorts to visit with."

"Not all of them are bad," said Granny. "There were some in the older times, and I expect there's quite a few now, that hold by what's right, and the Law."

"I would love to meet those sorts for a while," put in Acorn. "Seems as if all we ever run across are the ones who are hungry, or just mean."

"Then our luck is bound to change, sooner or later," said Bramble.

"I wouldn't count on it. What would any decent soul be doing way out here, or in Thorn Wood?"

"Oh, Stump, you are always on the dark side of everything. Besides, you're overlooking us. I think we're decent sorts, and here we are."

"Looking on the dark side is never disappointing," countered the mole.

"But you're a hoax, all the same. I've known you since you were a kitten, and for all that black talk you do, there's nothing more to it than just trying to get someone's dander up."

Stump mumbled, and looked away.

"Well, someone has to look at the truth of the matter. All sorts of trouble to be gotten into, and it's always sure to happen, if everything isn't taken into account."

Bramble's voice was tight as he spoke.

"But what of Blackpaw? Are we to leave it as it stands, or search for him?"

"Neither," replied Granny. "We won't leave it as it stands, for we can't wait here for him to come back, even if he has any plans to do so. And as for searching, we'll stand just as good a chance of finding out what has happened to him by going on."

"Do you think he ran off because he knows where some treasure is hidden, Granny?" asked Bumble.

"Oh boy," shouted Cabbage, "I'll bet that's what happened. He didn't want to have to share it with his friends, so he's hiding until we leave."

Branch Otter shook her head.

"I don't know where you get this treasure business. Reading too much of the old lorebooks has certainly put odd ideas into your head."

"I hope it's someplace around here so we'll get to see it when we catch him," chittered Bumble.

"Is he a bad animal?" asked Cabbage.

"No, not bad," replied Granny. "I think he's just a little young, and a little too sure of himself. That's usually because an animal like that is scared to death, but doesn't want anyone else to know."

Morley, shading his eyes and gazing at the dim outline of Thorn Wood far ahead, exclaimed, "There's something coming this way, Granny. I can't see anything but a dust cloud, but it's moving straight for us."

All thoughts of the vanished badger disappeared. The companions strained to make out what the dust cloud concealed, if friendly or dangerous, but the distance was too great. Of one thing they were sure, and that was there was definite movement, and if the direction held, they were on a collision course with whatever, or whoever, it was.

"Is it another herd?" asked Morley.

"I think not. Too organized. Much too much order for any of those frightened beasts we've run into so far."

"I think Bramble has a point," agreed Basil. "It's almost as if whoever it is is marching all in order."

Stump cleared his voice loudly.

"Mankind marches like that. Seems as if they like that sort of thing."

Bramble tried to pierce the thick, dark cloud that hung on the horizon, straining to make out the forms or shapes it hid from his view.

"What would mankind be doing coming from the direction of Thorn Wood?"

"I don't know," answered Granny.

"Could it be different than what you said, Granny? Could it have changed up so that it wasn't all full of those things that might keep everyone out of it?"

"It could be. But I don't think so. This bunch, if it is mankind, might be returning from there because they were unable to get through. They may have tried, and been turned back."

"I'd just as soon they would have gotten on through," grumbled Stump. "We have plenty to deal with now, between starving to death, and keeping out of reach of the killer wolves."

"Do you think these men could be friendly?" asked Acorn, hopefully.

"Now there's a squirrel's thinking for you," snorted Morley. "Muskrats may be a bit slow, but I've never heard of a muskrat yet who's been caught flat-footed like that. One thing, then another, then it's, 'Oh, look, they're leaving nuts,' and then it's all up, but a stew made of gullible squirrel."

"Hush, Morley. There are some men who have belonged to the clans of animaldom in their time. They were welcomed, and esteemed by many of the Great Ones."

"I'm sure that was so, but that's all over now."

"It might be changing back to the old way," said Bramble, still squinting at the distant cloud. "Beginning with a dragon winter, things start to change, for better or worse. Or both."

"You don't change bad habits and evil ways so easily," replied Morley.

"No, but then that's all supposed to be. But it does take a good deal of time."

"More than we have," snapped the mole. "We're sitting here with no cover, only a few weapons, gadding about the if's and wherever's, just watching while mankind is fixing to march right over us, and all we can do is have a quiet chat about whether or not it might hurt."

"And what about that cousin of yours?" asked Bramble, remembering the young badger again.

"He'd have to be blind to not see that," said Granny. "And there's nothing we can do, at any rate."

"Leave the signs again," offered Branch. "If he comes back here, or tries to follow, he'll know what we're going to do."

"What are we going to do?" asked Bramble. "If we knew, I'd be all for it."

"What if we continue on as we are, and keep whoever it is in sight, then try to pass them in the dark?"

"That's as good a plan as any, Basil. And we won't have to delay getting into Thorn Wood."

"If there was a delay that could cause that, I'd be for it," huffed Stump.

"Then it would be just that much more delay to your getting a rest and a long nap."

The mole looked long at the old badger.

"In that case, Granny, and if you promise me a pan of your wild apple tarts, I'll be in favor of going on with this little venture."

"Leave the signs, Bumble," ordered his mother, "in case Blackpaw tries to find us."

"Go on ahead, Morley. We'll keep a sharp eye out from here on. We may need all the warning we can get, if this new threat turns out to be mankind."

"I wouldn't look too heartily at them if they turn out to be killer wolves, either," grumped the mole. "If they've learned about fire, and a language, they may have learned how to march as well."

"Whoever they are, what we need to know before we meet them is if they are friendly or not, and then what to do once we know."

As the companions were loading their small supplies and preparing to continue on, a familiar voice called out to them, although no one could see where it came from.

"You were right, mother. There is a river here. Or was."

"It's Blackpaw," gasped Beryl.

"But where is he?"

"Here. Can't you see me now?"

A dark snout and two ears appeared behind the charred remains of an ancient oak. A moment later, there appeared the forepaws, then the thick shoulders, and then the rest of the stout badger's form. He was dripping wet.

"I found your river, right enough," he laughed. "Walking along, and sploosh, there I was. Never saw the hole until I was in it, and didn't know if I was going to ever find my way back out, but I think something has changed the river bed, and I hit a dry bank, and I saw light coming from above me somewhere, so I found it, and here I am."

Basil laughed.

"This is the first time I've ever seen a badger with his coat wet. I can see why you fellows stick to the deep woods."

The young badger stiffened, and his hackles began to rise.

"That's enough, Basil. I don't think all that water has done your sense any good, either. We have found our friend back, and if I understood him rightly, I think our water problem has been solved, as well as where to hide, if we need to."

"We've discovered a new danger," explained Bramble, pointing away toward the cloud of dust.

It appeared to the animals that it had moved much closer.

"What is it?" asked Blackpaw.

"Who is it, is more like it," corrected Morley.

"The thing that matters now is that we have a hole to dodge into if we need it, and a drink of water if we get thirsty."

"The thing we need to do now is explore this discovery of yours, Blackpaw, and see if we can find out which way this old river runs," said Granny.

"Wouldn't it be on your map?" asked Acorn. "The one Gruff and Greystone did?"

"I don't know. I don't remember seeing anything about an underground river. They may have traveled through a part of the forest without a river, and therefore, it wouldn't be on their map. There is a river that runs through Thorn Wood, and it's the only one you can drink from safely. The others are dangerous. Some of them change your form, and others are poison. It is good to know what you're drinking before you put water to your lips in Thorn."

"Could this be the same kind? I mean dangerous?"

"I think not," said Blackpaw. "I drank enough of it when I fell in. It doesn't seem to have harmed me any. Sweet, too."

"Then let's get on, before we waste any more time here," urged Basil.

"I think if we watch closely, we can follow the trail of the river from above," said Stump, pointing to the ground. "See? All the large trees here? They go to there, then the small trees start. And look. It goes on. A regular road, marked by the large tree stumps. The big ones seem to have tapped into the river."

"That's good thinking, Stump. We'll be able to follow along easily."

"How will we be able to get into it if we need to?" asked Ash, holding her babies closely to her side.

"We have two good diggers with us," replied Bramble. "A mole and a badger should be able to give us a door to anything we might want underground."

"I hope we don't need it in a hurry," grumped Stump.

"We won't," said Granny, "if we think ahead a bit."

As the animals prepared to follow along the underground river, Bumble and Cabbage ran to Blackpaw.

"Were there any jewels or dragon hoards there?" they chorused.

A strange light flickered in the young badger's eyes for a moment, and he at last replied slowly, and under his breath.

"No, but I know where there is a dragon hoard. We'll find it together, if you like. But you have to keep it a secret. No one but us must know."

"Can I tell Granny?" asked Bumble, almost beside himself with excitement.

"No one."

And sworn to secrecy, and too full of their new secret to hold it in, the two pups raced ahead of the others, their minds filled with kings and dragon treasures.

Following along behind at a slower pace, Bramble Ot-

ter frowned to himself, and wondered what Blackpaw had
said to his young pup. He was relieved, in a way, that the
badger had come back unharmed, but there was something deep within him that felt odd, as if something were
not exactly as it should be, but he could not express it, or
explain it to himself.

He turned his mind away from the vexing thought, and
began to concentrate on following the path the unseen
river made, its broad swath traecd aboveground by the remains of the once great trees.

And looking up, he saw the ominous black pall
growing nearer, and his thoughts were turned away, to a
nearer and more pressing danger.

TRACES OF MANKIND

After traveling uneasily all night, guided by bits of a late trine moon breaking through the clouds now and then to show them their halting progress, the companions found themselves dangerously close to the area where they had last seen the mysterious dust cloud. It was as dark as the bottom of Granny Badger's hole, for the most part, and it was only with the help of the ragged sliver of moon that Basil peered into the dense black shadow before them and discovered they were directly in the middle of some sort of ruins that smelled faintly of mankind, although the scent was very ancient, and the fire in the woods covered almost everything with a burnt musty smell that confused the senses.

"Is any of this on that map of Gruff's?" asked Bramble, feeling very nervous about being in the middle of where mankind had once lived.

"We'll have to wait for morning to study it," she replied. "I don't think there was more than a mention of some places where an ancient clan of mankind lived. It was on the road to Thorn Wood, and it was said that at one time the animals in Thorn, and the humans in this

193

settlement, were very friendly, and had the best of friendships."

"That must have been very ancient times, mother. I've never heard of any lore of that sort. Always the end of everything is marked by the betrayal of the furless ones. They are always the forerunners of doom."

"There is a good deal of truth to what you say, cousin, but there is more truth than I think you know of. What we see is often only the tip of our noses, and we are in dire trouble if we are on our way into a pit, and need to see where our danger lies."

"Were these men kind?" asked Branch, wondering what they could have been like, and if they were tall, or short, or dark, or fair.

She had only read and heard of mankind, and never actually seen those furless beings who went about most of the world upon two legs, and who had such a terrible reputation among animaldom. Branch was a true otter, and always had a great desire to know all there was to know of a subject, and although she often pretended she didn't, she would encourage Bramble or Bumble to find out for her, and in that way, she always knew as much as there was to be known about whatever was about to be known of or sniffed out.

"I expect some of them were," replied Granny. "There is a whole history of some of these clans who fought side by side with the old Masters in the wars of the dragons, and later, too."

"I'll bet we could find a lot of things here, Granny," chirped Bumble. "I'll bet there's lots of bones, and gold, and all sorts of things we could use."

The old she-badger snorted a curt laugh.

"I'm sure this place has been picked over proper long before now. It's been a long time since these walls were whole, and a lot of years have passed when no one but killer wolves, or worse, have been roaming around here."

Morley adjusted the weapon at his side, and kicked over a crumbling doorpost.

"Doesn't look as if this place has had any visitors, good or bad."

"Seems only as it should be," mumbled Stump, who was exploring a shallow hole that ran under a fallen pile of rubble that had once been the main wall of some sort of building. "This seems to have been dug by them. Never did see or hear tell of any diggings that were anywhere near good quality."

"They're not too handy at digging," explained Bramble. "But they seem to have had a fair number of dwellings in this settlement."

"No roots," replied the mole. "That always seems to be their problem. Here today, gone tomorrow. Almost as bad as some animals I know."

In the dim light, Morley saw the mole looking directly at him. He had opened his mouth to reply, but was shushed by Granny Badger.

"Shhhh!" she warned, and all the companions fell quiet.

Holding their breath, and not daring to move, they strained their ears, suddenly on the alert. A long time passed, and Acorn was getting ready to stretch his paw out to his mate to take their smallest baby, when a distinct sound was heard, not as a noise, but as what it sounds like when air moves against air. The moon had set a few minutes before, and the total darkness made the animals' hackles rise, and as their eyes grew accustomed to the blackness, they sensed, rather than actually saw, what appeared to be shadowy forms moving toward them from the other side of the ruins of the old man settlement.

"Quickly!" hissed Granny. "We just find hiding."

Acorn, trying to help Ash with the little ones, brushed against a pile of rocks and sent them clattering noisily all about. Almost at once, a dark shape loomed out of the darkness and fell upon Morley and Stump. There was a low growl, and then the metallic noise of their blades being drawn.

As the ancient swords came free of their sheaths, a pale white light brightened the area where the animals stood. In the wavering halo of the swords' glow, the companions saw the dull, ugly eyes of killer wolves reflect back at them, and with no further warning, they were set upon by half a dozen large gray beasts.

Yellow fangs snapped hungrily, and the drooling jaws reached out to devour Bramble, who fell back a step and swung his weapon with all the strength he could muster. His paw numbed at the shock of the blade striking home, and the noise began all about him. Howls of pain and anger went up from the wolves, mingled with shouts from the friends, and cries from the babies.

"Watch out!" cried Basil, struggling to keep his feet as he tried to keep a large wolf at bay.

"Here! To me!"

Granny Badger brandished her blade in a menacing fashion, watching sharply for a chance to strike to best advantage.

"Form a circle!" shouted Bramble. "All you ladies and babies in the center!"

Blackpaw leapt to stand beside the otter.

"We can hold, if they're no more than this."

"Quickly, then, the circle. We'll see how long we're able to hold, once we know exactly what we're up against."

As Bramble finished speaking, the wolves lunged in upon the friends, great jaws drooling, fangs bared.

Cutting and slashing as well as they were able in the dim light, the companions formed up a rough circle.

"Here's one down!" called Stump.

"And another!" echoed Morley.

They were answered by more vicious snarls, and another savage attack was pressed upon the tiring friends.

"How long until dawn?" cried Bramble. "We have to hold them until then, so we can see if we can find cover or an escape."

"You isn't going to sees no sunlight, you woodscum," growled a low voice from the ring of darkness that lay at the outer rim of the halo of light from their swords.

"No, indeeds they isn't. You is going to be bare bones by the time this night here is over."

"Fancy talk for fellows who are dealing with the heirs of Erinoult," shouted Blackpaw, his voice full and brave, raising the hopes of the other animals.

"Are we all right?" called out Basil, trying to count noses.

"I've been chewed, but not any more than I've been used to," answered Morley. "Seems as if muskrat must be a rare treat for these louts."

Branch hugged her pup closer to her side.

"We're all right. Where are Beryl and Cabbage?"

"Oboy!" whispered the young beaver loudly. "I'll bet these wolves are trying to protect some treasure house for the old king who used to live here."

Branch jerked Bumble's paw before he could reply.

"I suppose as long as we're worrying about the old king's gold, we're still all right."

"Let's close up our defense," suggested Granny quietly. "I don't think these fellows are through yet."

As she spoke, a huge form flew directly at her, and before she could strike a blow, she was buried beneath the hot weight of the killer wolf.

"Granny's down!" called Bramble, trying to get closer to the old she-badger as she struggled with her attacker.

In the dim light, he saw the red eyes of the wolf open wide, and heard the bone-crushing jaws snapping shut, again and again. He was hoping against hope that none of those bites had found Granny, and at the same time he was trying to direct a blow at the dirty gray form of the beast from the north.

A sudden brilliant burst of dazzling light blinded everyone for a moment, and a loud voice, deeper even than the voice of the wolves, but speaking in their tongue, called off the attack.

In the next instant, the companions were left, battered and stunned, and wolves, light, voice, and all were gone.

Bramble was first on his feet, and recovering from the shock, he ran to Granny Badger's side, his heart pounding in his throat.

OLWIN THE RED

Bramble Otter felt a catch in his breath when he knelt beside the mate of Gruff Badger. She was breathing, but in short gasps, and her eyes were closed. There was blood covering her muzzle and chest, and for a moment, Bramble was unable to go on. The other animals had all crowded around, none of them daring to speak, or to ask the otter how Granny was.

Stump put out a paw and patted the old animal gently.

"No killer wolf can be the end of Granny Badger," he consoled himself aloud. "Why, she's seen more trouble than most of us ever dared dream of, and I'm sure this is no more than afternoon cake and tea, to her way of thinking."

"Why wouldn't she get in the circle with the rest of us?" wailed Ash. "She insisted on staying there to fight."

"It's not in Granny's heart to remain long away from danger. She's as much at home with a sword as she is in the kitchen."

Blackpaw, who had remained silent, sat down beside the injured animal.

"There may be something we can do, or perhaps there

isn't. Yet as the next heir to Erinoult, I now claim my right to carry the Master's sword."

And so saying, he reached down to take the gleaming blade from the old she-badger's paw.

Bramble and Basil had moved to stop him, but the strange light flashed again, and the same deep voice thundered out, this time in their own tongue.

"Do you have one who is hurt?"

Not knowing what else to do, Bramble stuttered out a weak reply.

"Then bring them here, to me," came the voice.

A brilliant orange light, with a deep blue core, suddenly burst forth from the ground behind a ruined wall. The animals were drawn toward the light helplessly, and began to sway to the sound of an ancient music that seemed to fill the air until it was difficult to breathe.

"Bring them here," ordered the voice. "Closer."

Almost in a trance, the companions carried Granny toward the voice, unable to do anything but obey. As they reached the place where the center of the light came from, it dimmed, and the sound of the music faded.

They were face to face with a man, dressed from head to foot in a deep red cloak.

Terrified, but unable to fly, Bramble found his tongue.

"Granny is hurt. I'm not sure how bad."

The voice came, but softer now, and the man bent over the injured animal.

"It is nothing more than a blow, I think. Your friend should find her senses soon."

"But all the blood," began Bramble.

"If I'm not mistaken, it is from a fatal blow delivered to one of her enemies."

The otter's eyes opened wide, and for the first time, he

saw that the sword still clutched tightly in Granny's paw
was stained a dark black color.

"Well, I never," replied Stump. "The old baggage
didn't need any help at all. She'd already taken care of it
all herself."

"She has hit her head in a fall," went on the man,
standing once more, and pulling the hood back, revealing
handsome, even features, and a long, red beard.

Feeling better knowing that Granny was only stunned,
Bramble turned to this new stranger.

"Might we have the pleasure of your name? I'm unsure
about the custom of meeting with men, although I've read
somewhere of it."

"You speak well, otter. And I am called Olwin the
Red. I am familiar with all kinds, and all speeches."

Basil looked startled, and backed away from the tall
man.

"He's speaking in our manner," he sputtered.

"Of course, friend. It is nothing so unusual to converse
with all manner of brothers in my line of work."

"And you told the wolves to leave!" added Morley.
"You were speaking in their tongue, too."

"They are an unfortunate lot," replied Olwin, turning
to the muskrat. "They are usually found only in the far
northern lands, and life there is harsh, and no pleasant
things to enjoy, such as you have in these softer
climates."

"Harsh is hardly the word for that pack of ruffians,"
snapped Basil.

"They are indeed a hard lot, and rightly so. To exist
where they do, only the strongest survive."

"No offense, sir, but you sound as if you're defending
these louts," said Stump. "I'm sure they may finally end
up as good sorts, after a few more turnings, but I'd say

that the way they are now is not exactly the best of all ways to be."

"Stump has a point," agreed Bramble. "I know that sort is part of it all, and they are there by right of the Law, but it doesn't make me fear them any less. And I don't get any pleasure in being forced to kill them, or be killed, either."

"As you say, little brother, they are a part of the Law, and therefore must be respected in that light. However, they are gone now, and I don't think we need worry more about them for the moment."

"How do you come to know so much about them and their doings?" asked Blackpaw. "I would think there would be many more enjoyable lores to read than that of those rogue killers from the north."

Olwin studied the badger for a moment before answering.

"I can see you are an animal who thinks deeply on matters. That is good. We all are better off for thinking things through, it seems. But to answer you as to why I've spent my time on the lore of the northern folk, I can say simply this. Until we know and understand the why and wherefore of it all, down to the most unpleasant of things, we can never know a thing completely."

"As I always say," put in Stump, pleased to find an ally, even if he were a human. "You can't know what's good with a thing until you know the bad of it."

"Well said," smiled Olwin. "Well said, indeed, Master Mole. Whether or not a thing is good or bad, you must explore it for yourself, and see how it fits with whatever you believe. My study of the northern folk has been carried out in exactly that manner. Now I have some power over them, as a result of those studies, as you have discovered tonight. It was my command that caused them to call off their attack."

An odd thought struck Bramble as the man spoke, but he said nothing aloud of his doubts.

"Then you're the one who made the lights, and all the music," piped Bumble, pushing his way to stand at the feet of Olwin.

The man smiled, and reached down to give the pup a pat.

"Yes, my little friend. That is another lore that I have studied long and well. It is upon the nature of things, and very handy to know."

"Indeed it must be," grumped the mole. "Does it include fixing supper for starving moles, or bandages for an old baggage of an animal like Granny?"

Olwin laughed, tossing his red hair loosely about his shoulders.

"It does, indeed, Master Mole. We shall have a feast such as may even tempt your appetite, if I'm not mistaken about certain things I know of moles."

Again, Bramble felt a certain uneasiness at the speech of the handsome man, but he couldn't exactly say what it was. A vague restlessness in the pit of his stomach, but more than that, he wasn't sure. And that, he thought, might well come from the fact that he suddenly remembered his hunger, and the fear, when they had been set upon by the killer wolves.

Appearing before the animals was a long table, covered with a red cloth, with many dishes upon it. It had come from thin air, accompanied by the music of a reed pipe, and as suddenly as that, there were chairs of just the right size for all the animals there, including the two pups, Bumble and Cabbage.

Before anyone could speak, Granny Badger sat up slowly, looking about her in dazed wonder.

"Granny!" they all cried in unison, and fell upon the old animal, hugging and pawing her, until she regained her senses somewhat, and sent them scurrying for safety to avoid her feeble cuffs.

"What's all this? What's happened? Where is that lout who attacked me?"

"Slowly, slowly, mother," soothed Olwin, who had taken over the role of leader quite naturally, and in such a way the animals had hardly noticed.

"Who are you?" snapped the old badger, showing no fear of the human who stood before her.

"Olwin the Red," he replied easily. "I have set up your feast table, and scattered your enemies, so that you may rest and dine in peace."

"He can make all sorts of sounds come out of the air, Granny, and tables and chairs just as easily as anything. Look!" chittered Bumble, dancing around in his excitement.

"I'll bet he's one of the old kings," shouted Cabbage, jumping onto a chair, and opening the lid of a dish that was shaped in the fashion of a large bird with a brightly colored plume.

"You seem well read," beamed Olwin. "Yes, it all has to do with the ancient kings, and with the ways of power."

"Is there a treasure here?" blurted Bumble, unable to contain himself.

"Treasure? You mean precious stones, or metal?" asked the tall man, his flaming red beard standing out before him.

"Or whatever it was that made up the hoards that those old dragons kept."

"The dragons were the ones that kept the trinkets," replied Olwin. "They had no idea of the real treasures when they overpowered those ancient kingdoms. Being the sort they were, they kept the bright, gaudy things, and left the rest. There were some of the dragon lords that knew the real secrets of the treasures, and they were the ones who were the most powerful and dangerous of all."

"What secrets were those?" asked Basil.

"The secrets of power," replied Olwin. "Gold or mithra or gems don't make treasures. That's merely things from the earth that glitter, or cut, or look well on the necks of high ladies. The real secret of a treasure is the knowledge of power that it gives you."

Again, Bramble's hackles began to tingle, but he could not, no matter how he tried, define what it was that was wrong.

"You're right there, my good sir," said Granny. "All through the years of trouble in those olden years, it was never the trinkets that mattered to any degree. It was always the lure of power, of control, that led to the downfall of those early kingdoms, and to the ruin of many a soul, of animalkind as well as all the others."

"It is only unfortunate that there was no one who could have brought all the warring factions together," went on Olwin, motioning for the others to join him at the table. "All the unnecessary violence could have been avoided, and peace brought to all, in every realm."

As the animals sat down to the red-covered table, a flute began to play softly, and one by one, the lids of all the dishes removed themselves.

"Eat well, my guests. It is a feast you have well earned. After we are refreshed, perhaps we can become better acquainted, and exchange our news."

Bramble sat next to Branch and Bumble, and while the

others were eagerly exploring the delights of the table, he turned and whispered under his breath.

"Do you feel anything amiss?" he hissed, pretending he had dropped his spoon.

Branch gazed into his worried eyes.

"Do you?"

"I'm not sure. It could just be I don't find mankind familiar, if Olwin is a man. I've read of these sorts, wizards, or magicians, or tricksters, or what have you. They were not all of them to be trusted, from what I gathered."

"He saved our lives," said Branch, struggling to remain fair.

"He called off the killer wolves, right enough," agreed Bramble. "But what I would like to know is, did he set them upon us to begin with?"

Branch's eyes widened, but they had no further chance to speak, for Olwin was addressing a question to Bramble, smiling kindly at him over the long expanse of the heavily laden feast table.

THE TRUE KING

"I believe Olthin was the sire of your kind, was he not? And a very powerful king indeed, in times of old," said Olwin.

"He was a great leader, and in his prime, he was a friend of all, except the Purge. I think that's what they called the dragons then."

"It was so," replied Olwin.

"Have you seen any dragons here?" asked Bumble, eyes wide.

Branch tried to restrain the pup, but he struggled free.

"There have been no dragons here for a good many years, I shouldn't think. At one time, I suspect this was a nest for them."

"Is that why this old settlement is ruined?" asked Cabbage.

"Oh, this was left long after the dragons were no more. I think the people deserted this settlement for a better life on the shores of Over Sky."

"We had to leave our settlement because the killer wolves came," chirped Bumble. "And my dad says it's all because it's a dragon winter."

"He does, indeed?"

Olwin's eyes narrowed for a moment, as if he were deep in thought.

"We were forced to leave our old homes because of an invasion of that rabble," said Granny, feeling somewhat better after cleaning herself up and having some food. "I thought it was a band of renegades, until we had come a bit farther. Now I see it has spread all over."

"It has spread everywhere," replied Olwin, pouring out a drink from a flask he took from within his cloak. "And it will continue on. The last sign has shown itself, and the hordes from the northern realms are pouring across all lands. The time has come for the True King."

As Olwin talked, his beard became redder, and his voice rose.

When he had finished speaking, he stood up from the table and lifted his cup.

"I propose a toast to the True King. Will you drink it with me?"

Blackpaw was up first, lifting his paw, then the two pups.

"I knew we'd find a king sooner or later," chittered Bumble.

"And I'll bet the True King has a lot of treasures and dragon hoards hidden all over."

Bramble was slow in rising.

"No offense, sir, but those matters have nothing to do with us. Whoever this king is, I wish him all success, if he is just. Our travels are only to get us beyond the realms of the killer wolves and mankind."

Olwin drained his drink.

"Do you know anything of the True King?"

"No. I am poorly read in any lore but my own."

"Then you shall hear the story of this affair, and decide who you shall march with."

Stump spoke up from his end of the table.

"Marching! I've got no business marching with anyone, least of all a fellow as fancy as a king. And those sorts always have a great tendency to be at war with someone or other. I think I'll keep to my own, thank you."

"I've never heard the story of this king you speak of," said Granny. "My lore is not so complicated as many, and I'm ignorant of what else has been going on all this time. Let's hear your story."

"Thank you, madam. It is good to see an animal who displays so much wisdom."

Olwin bowed to Granny.

"No wisdom, just common sense," she went on. "I have never heard of any of the lore much beyond our small settlement, and I think it wouldn't hurt to be forewarned about some of the kinds we may chance across in our travels."

"I haven't had a chance to ask," said Olwin, "of your travels. We have become so taken with other things, I'm afraid my manners are somewhat lax. I've yet to find out from where you're coming or where you're bound for."

Blackpaw stood as he addressed the strange human.

"I come from below Four Oaks, near Granite Falls. My settlement was set upon by killer wolves, and I went seeking aid, or safety, where I ran into my companions."

Bramble tried to catch Blackpaw's eye, but the badger went on.

"As for where we're bound, that remains to be seen. We are going in the direction of Thorn Wood, but that's only because we seem to have no other choice."

"Thorn Wood," Olwin said softly. "That is a dangerous

place. Very dangerous for man or animal. More than a few have been lost there."

"We have what we think is a chart of it," went on Blackpaw. "I'm not too sure of its worth, but if it's what it's supposed to be, it should see us safely through."

Olwin smiled quickly.

"A chart, you say. Wherever would you find a chart of Thorn Wood?"

Bramble joined the conversation.

"It's an old chart handed down by a friend. It may or may not be of use. And we've not really decided that Thorn Wood will be our road. If there was another choice, I think we'd all welcome the chance to forget trying to get through so dangerous a place."

"That would be well advised," agreed Olwin.

"Are you saying you don't think Granny's chart is good?" sneered Blackpaw.

"Maybe, maybe not," replied Bramble. "All I say is this. It's just as well to have more than one basket for the eggs."

"Do you have any clues as to what other way we might take?" asked Basil.

"There are a hundred roads you might take," laughed Olwin. "To find the one you want is another story."

"We're trying to get to the Falls," said Morley. "I don't know why. All I know is that's what we decided way back there when the wolves attacked us at Granny Badger's house. That was decided then, and no one has said anything different since, so I think I'm right in saying that's where we're bound."

Olwin looked thoughtfully at the muskrat.

"Why the Falls?"

"Old Bark," said Granny simply.

A queer light played across Olwin's face, and he covered it quickly with a smile, but it had been there for a brief moment, and Bramble had seen it. It was a look of intense hatred, and fear.

"Have you not heard the news, then?" asked Olwin, having regained his composure once more.

"What news is that?" asked Stump.

"The Falls have been overrun, and Old Bark gone. No one knows where."

"Have you heard of Old Bark?" asked Acorn. "I wasn't ever so sure it was much of an idea to begin with. There are a lot of tales of how he's gone rogue, and murdered a lot of innocent animals."

"There are those rumors," agreed Olwin coolly.

"You say the land below Thorn Wood has fallen to killer wolves?" asked Granny.

"Those, and mankind, too. There have been many battles there, and the mountains are full of renegades, as well as Thorn Canyon."

"Let's stay here," shouted Bumble. "We can find the old king, and we can have plenty of good things to eat, and Cabbage and I can help Blackpaw find the dragons' hoard."

The badger looked angrily at the otter pup.

"Staying might not be a bad idea," he said, trying to keep his voice calm.

"I've heard no one say anything about us being welcome," said Beryl. "Goodness knows, anything would be better than lugging our belongings around on our backs, being set upon by wolves and mankind. I'd welcome the chance to settle down awhile."

"That does sound inviting," agreed Ash shyly. "I haven't had a chance to hardly get my breath since we left Granny's. And the babies are tired and cranky from all this constant moving."

"Again, my apologies," offered Olwin. "I make a sorry host. My meager hospitality is yours for the taking, for as long as you'd like."

"That's very kind, I'm sure," said Granny Badger. "And I think we'll accept it, at least for tonight. I don't think I could go two steps on my own, after the mauling that lout gave me."

"Granny!" said Bramble, springing to her side. "Of course we're not going to let you try going anywhere, but to try to get some rest."

He helped her remove the sword of Erinoult, and laid it on the table as she tried to rise.

"Bring her here," said Olwin, and he motioned toward a loose pile of stones.

In the next instant, there before the animals was a golden-colored tent, with red awnings and a tall canopy which twinkled and shone as if stars were trapped in the weave of its cloth.

Acorn and Ash took the babies, and Beryl gathered Cabbage to go inside.

"This is really very kind of you," said Branch. "I'm sure Granny needs the rest."

"You don't have to worry about your sleep being interrupted here," assured Olwin. "You may stay as long as you'd like."

After struggling with Bumble, who did not want to go to bed, Bramble finally coaxed the pup into going inside to protect his mother.

"I'll need a sword to do that," he insisted, and became so stubborn about it that Bramble at last gave in, and after giving Bumble strict instructions to not play with the weapon, he went to get the sword from the table.

"May as well let him sleep with it," he said to himself. "I'm not sure what it is that's wrong here, or even if anything is wrong, but I'd feel better if we hadn't run into this fellow."

He thought a bit longer. If they hadn't run into the strange, red-bearded man, then they would certainly have had a harder time with the killer wolves, or worse, been unable to escape. But his mind kept running back to the fact that Olwin, if that was indeed his name, had spoken to the wolves to call them off.

"I'm sure I must be being unfair," he mumbled to himself. "Here my life has been saved, and I'm casting doubts at the one who did it."

Still, he had wondered at the look that had crossed the man's face at the mention of Old Bark, and why he had made a point to tell them the Falls were overrun, and no longer safe. It could quite possibly be as he said, but Bramble felt that vague uneasiness inside again.

That feeling had been there ever since they had met Olwin, and as kind as he had been to them, and as concerned as he seemed for their safety, there was something about it all that continued to bother the otter.

There were a dozen questions that nagged him that he could not answer to his satisfaction. Why, for instance, had Olwin been so interested in hearing that Granny had a chart of Thorn Wood? And how had a man come to hear, or know, of Old Bark? Bramble had thought it strange that a man would be familiar with the name of the bear, although it was no stranger than this man's powers, producing food from nowhere and a sleeping tent from thin air. It wasn't as snug as a cheery holt by the river, but it began to look better and better to the tired animal.

"I must be exhausted from it all," he thought to himself. "A fine animal I am. I'll probably feel better in the morning, when I have a fresh outlook on everything."

Reassuring himself, he felt somewhat more cheerful,

and even smiled when he saw Morley and Stump asleep on their paws, stretched out on the long feast table.

His smile faded quickly when he realized that Blackpaw was in deep discussion with Olwin, talking in low tones he could not overhear. They stopped when they saw him, and the man beckoned him to join them.

"Thank you all the same, I've just come for Granny's sword. I don't think I'd be any more company than my friends there."

He indicated the sleeping mole and muskrat.

Striding to Granny's place at the table, he picked up the sword that lay there, and bidding his host and Blackpaw good night, he returned to the tent. His eyes were heavy, and his bones ached, and he realized how truly tired he was as he lay down beside Branch on the soft cloth pillows.

Bumble woke up from a light sleep, although he had insisted that he wasn't tired a few minutes before, and wanted the sword he had been promised. It was only as Bramble handed it to his young pup that he noticed the sword he had brought from the table was not the sword that Granny had worn.

He forced himself to sit up and examine the sword closely.

Even in his confused mind, there was no doubt that the sword he held was the one Blackpaw had been given in the chamber of Erinoult. Angrily, Bramble made an effort to rise, but decided it would be time enough to confront Blackpaw in the morning, when he was fresher. And there were many questions he wanted Olwin to answer, if he would.

As Bramble drifted into a troubled sleep, he thought he dreamed, or remembered it as such, that the man Olwin entered the tent where the companions lay, and Blackpaw was at his side. Dangling from the badger's belt was a strange sword, not of an ancient make, and covered with glittering stones at the hilt. The simple mithra-worked sword of Erinoult now hung barely showing beneath the cloak of Olwin.

It was at that moment that Bramble suddenly realized the sleep he felt coming on him was not natural. The image of Morley and Stump came back, and his own drowsiness, and now he needed to be alert, but could not.

The last thing Bramble remembered as he slid under the black surface was Olwin and Blackpaw laughing. The sound of it turned the otter's heart cold.

OLWIN AND BLACKPAW

Bramble, in a nightmare which seemed to go on, saw the badger Blackpaw and the strange, red-cloaked man Olwin take all the swords that had come from the cavern of Erinoult. One by one, the man put them into a heavy leather sack, and having gathered them all but the one Bumble slept with, he stepped toward the sleeping pup.

With all the remaining strength left in his reeling body, Bramble staggered up and tried to ward off Olwin.

"Here, here, old fellow. This won't do," said Olwin, soothingly, and pushed the otter back onto the sleeping pillow.

"He's the most stubborn of the lot, besides the mole," said Blackpaw. "I've had the worst trouble from him."

"Then we shall see if we can't arrange something that may tame him a bit. Perhaps a muzzle might do the trick."

"That would certainly take the fire out of him."

The badger leered at Bramble.

"He has caused me a lot of inconvenience, to say nothing of the insults he has handed me."

"It is nothing to me what he does or thinks. What is

217

important is the chart the old baggage has. If it is in truth a guide through that infernal piece of witchcraft called Thorn Wood, then all the rest of my quest shall be easy."

"Has the wood caused that much change to your plans?" asked Blackpaw, striding out of the tent beside Olwin.

"It has forced not a change, but a complete halt." Olwin smashed a fist to his palm. "I had all in readiness, and struck with good timing, and have turned to rout everyone who has dared stand against me. All my armies are victorious, and all have claimed complete control in every realm, except the territory below that cursed Thorn Wood. There is no way through it, and I was beginning to despair of ever taking the Falls, or Thorn Canyon, or the lands beyond, until you mentioned there was a chart. It is an answer to my problem, and a stroke of good fortune only the gods can have sent me."

Blackpaw took a deep bow.

"Don't forget their servant."

Olwin turned sharply on the badger.

"You are nothing to me but a tool. If you serve well, you shall be rewarded more than amply. If you grow useless to my plans, you are expendable, just as those filthy things from the north. They have done their part admirably in some cases, but their worth lessens now. I must have an army that is capable of more than wanton slaughter."

"How did you gain control of the killer wolves?" asked the badger, hoping to earn a more secure place with the strange, frightening human. Blackpaw had learned well that flattery was often a useful ploy to gain a hold over someone.

"It was no easy task," replied Olwin. "I had spent years in the study of various lores, and had gotten nowhere, until I came across a curious volume from an ancient ruin below Over Sky. It told of power to be had, and the secret of that power, so I began to study in earnest. I learned all there was to learn from the book, then sought out a teacher to fill in those places that were empty. I found a great scholar who was pleased to have so eager a student. He taught me all he knew before he realized what object I was after. Naturally, he tried to stop me, but he was old, and the strain on his heart was too much.

"Since then, I have gained control of the north by the power I have over the wolves there. They are a stupid, loutish bunch, and the simplest display of the most ordinary powers were enough to cower them, and bend them to my purpose."

"You mean the lights and noise that you can do?"

"Those things are but child's play."

"Could I learn to do them?" asked Blackpaw.

Olwin laughed a short, harsh laugh.

"I said they were child's play. An animal might find the exercise too difficult."

Blackpaw's anger flared, but he said nothing, for he feared this man greatly.

"You might perhaps learn some of the simpler conjuring tricks, I suppose," Olwin added. "It depends upon how easily you learn."

"I have knowledge of all animalkind, and have studied the secrets of Erinoult," huffed Blackpaw. "It is from that Master that the chart of Thorn Wood comes."

"Then we shall see how the venture goes. If this chart gets us through Thorn Wood, then I may reconsider about your worth, and that of your ancestors."

Olwin had begun emptying the sack onto the table where the drugged food had been laid out, and searching through all the items there carefully, he came across the worn volume of lore that Granny Badger had carried away from her old home, and which had held the wrinkled chart of Gruff's that marked a safe passage through the dreadful Thorn Wood.

"That's it," said Blackpaw, pointing to the ragged volume.

"This?" sneered Olwin.

"Inside. Here, I'll show you."

Blackpaw eagerly took the tattered lorebook, and began leafing through it.

"Well?" demanded Olwin, his great red beard bristling out before him.

"It was here. It's got to be here."

The man snatched the book from Blackpaw, and tore out page after page, until the table was littered with the scattered parchment. But there was nothing there that resembled a chart of any kind.

Olwin's face darkened.

"You have lied to me, earth hog. My punishment shall be swift and harsh."

Blackpaw trembled, but held his ground.

"It's here. We must search the old badger. Granny has it hidden somewhere on her."

"We shall search once more, then," glowered Olwin, his voice as deep and menacing as it had been when he spoke the savage language of the killer wolves.

The two hurried back to the sleeping tent where the drugged animals lay, Blackpaw trotting along ahead. His mind was racing, trying to remember where he had seen the chart last, and who had had it. All he could remember was that he had seen it in the book that Granny Badger had taken from under her apron, and that it had a clearly

marked passage through the dangerous wood, and that
was what the red-bearded man wanted above all else.

And now, the badger thought to himself grimly, it was
what he wanted above all, too, for if the map were not
found, he didn't like to think of what might be in store for
him.

His thoughts turned bitterly to the council of elders in
his old settlement, and the decision to exile him from the
clan.

"There'll be more than exile for me, if I don't find the
chart this man wants," he told himself.

Blackpaw was not a coward, whatever else he was, and
he began to try to formulate a plan that would save his
hide if the map were not to be found.

"Curse that old baggage," he mumbled under his
breath. "She'll be the death of us all if she's done something with that chart."

Entering the tent once more, Blackpaw began methodi-
cally to search each animal's meager belongings, while
Olwin tore back blankets and rolled aside the heavily
sleeping friends.

As the badger tried to search Bramble, the otter
opened one eye slightly, and whispered urgently.

"You won't find the chart. I've hidden it. After you left
the first time, I took care to put it where it won't be
found by the likes of you or your friend."

Blackpaw looked hurriedly over his shoulder to see if
Olwin had heard the otter's whispers. Satisfied that he
hadn't, he made an extra amount of noise in pretending to
search, and answered Bramble without looking at him.

"It is all our lives at stake, you fool. If Olwin thinks
there is no map, we are all in the same stew. He has plans
that won't be tampered with. He controls the killer
wolves, and he wants the lands below Thorn Wood."

The otter listened silently, pretending to be still asleep. He was again thankful he had been too worried to eat or drink more than a bite or two of the food from the table of Olwin. His suspicions about those with strange powers had proven to be true.

Blackpaw turned a knapsack inside out.

"We've got to come up with something to stall him. He won't be put off."

"Tell him that it must have been stolen by the killer wolves that attacked us. One knocked Granny down, and there was another one there with him. They would like to be able to get through Thorn Wood, too, I'm sure, to find all the helpless animals there for food."

Blackpaw paused a moment.

"That might hold him off long enough for us to plan an escape. And remember, any escape we could hope for entails getting safely through Thorn."

"What a lot of mangy louts," snarled Olwin, becoming more enraged by the moment.

Blackpaw finished going through the mole's knapsack, then turned to Olwin.

"I don't find it here, either."

He paused, as if deep in thought.

"Do you suppose one of the killer wolves could have taken it? During the attack, one of them knocked Granny down. There was another one with him that escaped her blade."

Olwin stopped short in his search, and stood abruptly up. He shook his head.

"They don't have the sense to find value in anything but something to stuff themselves with."

His brow furrowed, and his eyes darkened.

"They might have gotten it without knowing," suggested Blackpaw. "They snap at everything. One of them may have bitten into what he thought was Granny, and just held on to whatever it was. They'll devour anything when they're in a frenzy."

Olwin threw aside a knapsack in disgust.

"I think the old badger has that map committed to memory," went on Blackpaw. "I've heard her talk about it enough on our way here. She's a lot sharper than you would think, seeing all the gray in her muzzle."

Olwin flung back his cloak, revealing the blade of Erinoult, which hung at his belt. On the man, it was the perfect size for a long dagger.

"I should do away with the lot of you now. I would give you over to those sneaking curs from the north, except that what you say has a ring of truth to it. If they've destroyed that chart of Thorn Wood, they'll pay dearly for it."

"Between us, we could make the trip," offered Blackpaw. "The old one can lead, and we can mark the trail, so that you can return and bring back your armies."

Bramble, through half-closed eyes, saw that the wily badger had struck up some note of interest in the tall, red-cloaked human. He grudgingly gave Blackpaw credit for devising the plan which had, in all likelihood, saved their lives.

BUMBLE AND CABBAGE

A great pillar of fire and smoke swayed wildly above the heads of the companions, and a thunderous noise crashed and roared about them. Olwin, draped in a blood-red cloak, his beard and hair the same color as the fire, stood surrounded by six large killer wolves. At his right hand, and slightly behind him, was Blackpaw, now cloaked in the same fashion as the man.

The fire and noise increased until the ears of the animals rang with the savage din, and they put their paws to their heads.

Nearer Olwin, the dirty gray forms of the killer wolves howled and snapped at the air.

Olwin raised his voice above all the terrible noise.

"Your lives have been spared that you may help me overthrow the tyrant of the Falls, and below. You have this mercy shown you because I am a just man, and as True King, I do not strike without cause. If you serve me loyally, you will be richly rewarded. If you fail me, or my cause, a death more horrible than this will be yours."

A tremendous clap of thunder sounded, and a blazing hand of fire erupted from the inferno and devoured one of

225

the snarling killer wolves before anyone could move or blink an eye. The wolf's companions whined and rolled on their backs, setting up a great, pitiful howling.

Stump, standing beside Bramble, tightened his jaws.

"If he hadn't taken my sword, I'd show that lout a thing or two," he hissed, tears welling in his eyes.

"Olwin is too sly to attack that way," whispered Bramble. "That's how he keeps all these poor beasts under his control. He thinks if he slays one like this, they will fear him too much to turn against him."

"Those wolves aren't anywhere as big as that one in the cave," said Basil.

"No, they're not. That must have been one of the leaders."

Bramble did not turn his eyes away from Olwin as he spoke.

The man threw back his cloak, and drew the blade of Erinoult that he had taken from Granny Badger. Its blade was a dull gleam.

"Look! It's not shining," said Morley. "It's almost gone out."

Granny, standing motionless, her old eyes full of tears, spoke so softly that the companions could hardly hear her.

"Its flame is dying in the hands of the darkness. The sword of the Master has never been held by any but those of the Law, until now. I have betrayed the trust."

"Nonsense," scolded Branch, patting the old animal reassuringly. "You've done no such thing. We were tricked, and drugged, and there was no fair fight. This Olwin is a powerful man, and we are but simple animals. There was nothing we could do against his likes."

"And we're not through yet, Granny," added Basil.

"The damage is done," said the old animal. "The

sword is in the hands of a stranger, and one who intends only death and destruction."

"Not if we can help it," put in Bramble. "Blackpaw has sold us out, and our position isn't the best, but he did come up with an idea that may be our salvation yet."

"Are you going to believe anything he says?" asked Morley. "He's given us all over to Olwin, and now he's up there prancing around in that silly cloak, looking like a lapdog for that fellow."

"I don't think much of Blackpaw's actions," replied Bramble, "but he has come up with a plan that may work. We're dealing with a magician who has only power and control on his mind, and any way he can achieve his ends he will use. Look at the risks he takes in dealing with the killer wolves. Those chaps can be very nasty when they have a mind to. When they're in packs, they are as dangerous as any enemy could be."

"Blackpaw is in good company, then," snapped Acorn.

"Better than he deserves, if you ask me," added Beryl.

"Still, he's the one that has saved us," said Bramble. "His plan includes us all, and it is the only reason we have lived out the day."

"What is this plan that scoundrel has, and why has it saved us? Were you awake?"

"I didn't have much of an appetite," explained the otter, "so I didn't eat or drink as much as the rest of you. And I was awake when they came into the sleeping tent looking for the chart. I remembered Granny dropped the book just as I was helping her to bed, so I picked it up. That's when the chart fell out. I thought I'd study it awhile before I went to sleep, so I stuck it under my pillow. I didn't last that long, though, and the next thing I knew, Olwin and Blackpaw were talking, and I heard them say they were looking for the map of Thorn Wood. That's when I hid it."

"But where is it? And what is this plan of Blackpaw's?"

"Give him time, Morley," cautioned Branch.

"Blackpaw told Olwin that Granny knew the map by heart, and that the chart was in her head."

The old badger jerked around, coming to her senses.

"I don't know any such thing," she snapped. "I've hardly looked at that map."

"I know, Granny. But we have to make Olwin think that you know it by heart."

"How are we going to do that? He'll be right with us all the while, so even if we do have the chart hidden, we won't have a chance to study it without him seeing it. And if he sees it, he certainly won't need us anymore."

"Do you remember anything at all about where Gruff said to enter the wood?" asked Bramble. "If we can just get that far, we may have a chance to escape into Thorn. If we have the map, we have a better chance than Olwin, even with all his power."

"It's the only chance we have, Granny," agreed Stump. "I don't like our odds, but it's better than suffering the blowings and goings of Olwin."

"Can we sneak a look at the map? I'm not sure if I remember or not," said Granny.

"Perhaps after Olwin is asleep. We'll wait until late, and then try."

"Will you tell that traitor cousin of yours about our plan?" asked Basil, turning to Granny.

"It's his plan to begin with," she said simply. "He knows the map is still safe, although I'm not sure he knows of its whereabouts."

Bramble answered the old she-badger's questioning look.

"He doesn't know where I've hidden it, and I don't think I'll take him that far into my confidence."

"Good. The less he knows the better, for the moment. I'll try to bluff Olwin, and see if I can't recall some of Gruff's map. Maybe with a little peek I'll be able to carry it off."

The companions fell silent, and watched Olwin's fireworks for a moment. Great geysers of sparkling green and red were flowering up from the earth, and a harsh, howling wind sprang up suddenly, and swept all the flames into a whirling caldron of dirty orange flames. It hovered dangerously near the small company of friends, then touched the fur of the wolves, leaving them smoldering and whining in pain, and as quickly as it had come, it was gone, leaving the clearing where they stood in silent darkness.

A small, dim green light burst forth around Olwin and Blackpaw, and the man strode to confront the friends.

"Well, my good beasts, you see how useless it is to resist me, eh?"

He snapped a finger, and the remaining killer wolves ran quickly away, their tails between their legs.

"I much prefer dealing with men, but I make use of all kinds. You should consider yourselves fortunate to be included in my schemes."

Stump made a strangled noise low in his throat, but Bramble held the angry animal back, and he stepped forward, bowing low.

"Oh, True King, we are yours in your cause. We feel great pride in being able to do your duty by you."

Blackpaw sneered from beneath his new red cloak.

"Well spoken, Master Otter," replied Olwin. "There might be merit in you, yet."

Olwin turned on his heel, and made a sign in the air. Immediately, there was the table once more, laid out as it had been when the animals had been drugged.

"Come, let's refresh ourselves. Have no fear, there is no sleeping herb here. I have use of you in other ways than to clutter my pillows. We have a long march tomorrow, and Thorn Wood to cross."

Olwin motioned for the animals to sit.

"We need to discuss our approach, old one. Where are we to make for, so that we can enter the wood safely?"

Granny Badger wrinkled her brow as if in deep thought.

"That depends upon where we are now."

"We are near where Dark Hollow used to lie, not far from the edge of the old wood, before it burned."

"Then we shall make our way as we can to the east, or as near east as is possible."

"There is nothing between here and Thorn Wood that will bar our way. It is only beyond that accursed wood that you'll find that blackguard Old Bark, and his meddlers."

"I thought you said he was gone," piped Bumble, before his mother could stop him. "And I want my sword back, too. Granny didn't tell you to wear it. I was taking care of it."

Branch grabbed the small pup before he could go on.

Olwin had begun to scowl, but Granny Badger interrupted.

"I have given Olwin full consent to wear the sword. It is as it should be. Only the rightful king shall bear it for long, and I'm simply an old animal. It would be no good for me to wear it now."

Olwin's red beard jutted forward, and his eyes sparkled.

"It is as you say, old one. The rightful bearer shall be king, and I shall endure over even that renegade Old Bark, and all his clan."

"How come you to hate the bear so much?" asked Stump. "What sway could an animal hold over so great a man as you?"

Olwin blinked, and turned a blank look on the mole.

"Bear? What has a bear to do with Old Bark?"

"He *is* a bear," replied Stump.

A small shadow of understanding spread across the man's face.

"So he has those powers, too, does he? This shall indeed be interesting and amusing. I begin to see why all my plans there have gone awry."

"Shhh," hissed Bramble, looking hard at the mole.

Olwin threw back his head and uttered a deep, harsh laugh.

"So this is the way of it. No wonder I have had such a time of it. Those louts from the north won't go near that blasted part of the wood, and my armies come crawling back complaining of rivers that disappear, and trees that march."

"Oboy!" shouted Cabbage. "That sounds like grand fun."

"And we'll make good soldiers out of you two," smiled Olwin, patting the pups kindly. "You shall have your own weapons, and march beside me."

Bumble and Cabbage raced around the table shouting and pushing each other.

"I'll get to lead," cried Bumble.

"No, me!" shot Cabbage.

Granny Badger finally managed to catch the pups' attention, and frowned her most disapproving frown, upon which they both sat quickly down, subdued.

Bramble's heart beat in his throat, and it was hard for him to keep his spirits up, for he knew the wily Olwin had outwitted them, by having the pups near him as they began the trip to Thorn Wood. With the youngsters at his mercy, the animals would be unable to try to make good their escape. They were hopelessly bound to Olwin, to do as he would have them.

Branch gripped his paw hard, and Bramble tried to reassure her with a smile, but tears welled up in her eyes, and she kept looking at her young pup frolicking around the table. She glanced at Beryl, who was also finding it hard not to cry.

"Ah, but you mustn't worry," called Olwin, seeing the two friends. "There will be no trouble, will there? Everything will go smoothly, and your little ones will stay as sleek and healthy as they are now."

He smiled, but the threat was there, although unspoken.

Bramble's paw gripped the edge of his chair so hard he thought it must break, but he said nothing. He was powerless at the moment, and knew he would have to wait for the proper time to strike.

A HAZARDOUS MARCH

At the first light of dawn, the companions were ready to march, packing and putting their small belongings in order. The sun rose slowly, for the summer was beginning to wane, and although it was not yet cold, there was a promise of a chill in the air.

Bramble stood on a knoll overlooking the burned-out wood. Branch came to stand beside him. Row after row of foothills rolled away toward the distant horizon, where the dim, foreboding smear of darkness showed Thorn Wood to be.

"We have a good march to reach it," said Bramble. "We may find our chance sooner than Thorn Wood."

Branch squeezed his paw.

"There will be no chance, so long as he holds Bumble and Cabbage. He knows that. He is an evil man."

"I don't care for him much, either," agreed Bramble. "I'm not so familiar with mankind as to know if it's just because he's a man, of if he's unusual. I'm sure some of mankind must be of the right sort."

"I don't think I'd care to explore around to find out," put in Stump, joining the two otters.

"I don't think that's for me, either. But did you wonder at what he said of Old Bark? I mean, he didn't even know he was a bear."

"I don't know. We talked that all out last night. It seems as if Thorn Wood is the last boundary that Olwin has to cross to capture the Falls, and whatever else lies there. Old Bark evidently has an army of some sort that keeps Olwin at bay."

The otter looked away in the direction of the dark line of the wood.

"It seems as though our friend has been trying to get through that wood for some time now, and then we show up, talking about a map. Awfully convenient for him, I'd say."

"And worse luck for us," said Stump.

"Was it his armies who set fire to this wood?" asked Branch.

"I'm sure it must have been. The chaps who lived here wouldn't want to burn their own homes," answered Bramble.

As the otter finished speaking, they were joined by the rest of the companions, except for Blackpaw, who stayed with Olwin.

"We finished up packing what little we have," said Granny Badger. "It's not much, and we've little food or water left, and no weapons."

"Maybe we can get our swords back," said Stump. "We might tell this fellow we won't go into this strange place without them."

"A fine lot of difference that would make," grumbled Basil. "Just one less mole for him to worry about. And I'm sure the killer wolves would find it very much to their liking if you stay behind unarmed."

"I don't think he's going to give us back our weapons,

Stump," said Bramble. "It would be too dangerous for him. He's not the sort who does things without thinking them out. Anything that would reduce the chances of our escape you can bet he'll do. Like keeping the pups with him, and getting them excited about being soldiers and all."

"He does think in a very sly way," said Granny. "Like some animals I've known."

"Mostly stoats," snapped Morley. "You never could trust one of their kind. Always shifty-eyed, and waiting for you to turn your back so they can rob you blind."

"I've known a stoat or two in my time that were decent enough," argued Basil. "I think they're probably just not used to living much around others."

"Deep-woods animals aren't," said Granny. "Us badgers are more used to being alone than with a community, and Gruff and I used to live pretty much to ourselves. Still, we never had any trouble from the stoats that came around, looking for a handout, or wanting to borrow a spade for their garden, or some seed for winter turnips."

"Doubt you'd ever see anything again," mumbled the mole. "Not from that lot."

"If I remember rightly, I think you borrowed a rake to clean up your forecourt last spring, and I've yet to see that back where it belongs."

Stump cleared his throat loudly, looking quickly away from the old animal.

"Do you think Old Bark knows about this man?" asked Basil.

"I'm sure he must," replied Bramble. "If Olwin has been trying to get through Thorn Wood all this time, I'm sure everyone on the other side must know."

"I wonder where he keeps his armies. I haven't seen anything but a few killer wolves."

Beryl held Cabbage closely to her, stroking the squirming pup.

Bramble wrinkled his whiskers, and thought for a moment.

"You know, that is strange. I haven't seen anyone else, either. And except for all this business of tents and tables appearing and disappearing, I haven't seen anything of a regular sort of camp, either."

Before the otter could go on, Blackpaw strode up the ash-covered knoll to stand beside him.

"Greetings, soldiers. I see you've gotten all in readiness. Are the youngsters ready to march with their king?"

Despite their mothers' efforts to hold them back, Bumble and Cabbage pulled away and ran to the waiting badger, still dressed in the dark red cloak.

"Will we get one of those?" chirped Bumble.

"And a sword?" cried Cabbage.

Blackpaw laughed.

"You'll have both, my good pups. And what grand soldiers you'll make for the True King's armies. I am to be Grand Marshal of all the animal forces that march under his banner, and when you're older, you can be my underlings."

He patted them both, and turned to the others.

"Olwin says I am to give you your instructions, and to lead. You give me full obedience, and all will be well. Granny, you tell me how we are to direct our course, and I'll take that information back to Olwin."

"Isn't he going with us?" asked Acorn, suspiciously.

"He says there are dangers in Thorn Wood, and that

he will guide us from a safe point behind the advance group."

"Hrumph," snorted Stump. "For all his hoopla he's still nothing but a stoat at heart."

Blackpaw glared at the mole.

"You'll find those sentiments may be very inconvenient to you, Master Mole. Fortunately, I am the one who heard, and not Olwin. I shall overlook it this time. But don't count on my kindness more than once."

"I wouldn't count on anything from you," shot the mole. "You're a disgrace to any decent animal sort, carrying on like that, and wearing that silly cloak, trying to look like a man."

Blackpaw pulled the cloak away from his side, revealing the sword he wore.

"There was a time I had to abide by your insults, but I am in charge now. Another word from you, long snout, and I'll save Olwin the trouble of dispensing with you."

Bramble restrained the mole with a paw.

"He's not himself," apologized the otter. "All the strain. He hardly knows what he's saying. Forgive him, Grand Marshal. He'll be a good soldier."

Blackpaw huffed up somewhat, and looked away.

"Very well. But no more outbursts. Now you two, come along," he said, motioning to Bumble and Cabbage.

Beryl burst into tears, but her pup was so busy trying to keep up with his new friend he didn't hear or see. Branch held tightly to her mate's paw, and her chin trembled, but she did not cry aloud.

Bramble squeezed very hard, and fought to keep his own eyes from filling.

"It'll come right," he muttered. "You wait and see, it'll come right."

"I'm sure it will," Branch managed.

Granny Badger watched the two pups go, scampering around the feet of Blackpaw.

"They'll be all right, those two. You've no need to worry there."

"Do you think Old Bark will know we're not on Olwin's side?" asked Morley. "If we're marching along through the wood, won't he think we're more invaders, and get us lost, too?"

"There's a good possibility of that," agreed Stump. "I mean, if we're out there in Thorn Wood, tramping around with the likes of Olwin, what else could Old Bark think?"

"Do you suppose Old Bark is a man, too?" asked Ash. "I was just thinking. Olwin seemed to think he wasn't a bear, until we said something about it. I think it was you, Stump."

"Bear or man, it's no matter," said Bramble. "He evidently doesn't get along well with Olwin, so I'll take sides with him, no matter what. As to what or who Old Bark is, I'm sure we'll find out soon enough."

Branch had wiped her eyes.

"Olwin may be in for more than he bargains for, trying to keep an eye on those two."

"He'll probably have had his fill in an hour or so, and send them both back to their mothers," agreed Morley.

"They are certainly active enough. Goodness knows they'll have six hundred and three questions for that Olwin, and twice as many games they'll want him to play."

"You're probably right, Granny. We'll worry about them when the time comes. They've been through enough already to know a little about taking care of themselves," said Bramble.

"Now what we need to see to is how to get to Thorn Wood."

"I can recall a little of the map, from the peek I got at it last night, but it was awfully dark," said Granny. "And my eyes aren't as good as they once were."

"Can we risk another look now?" asked Basil. "We can form a sort of ring around Granny, like we're repacking something. Then we could all take a look. It might be better that way, in case anything happens."

The old badger frowned and nodded.

"That would be the best. We don't know what we're in for, or if we'll be separated, or what. I think we should all have a chance to look at the chart, and to try to remember it as best we can."

Bramble knelt, and began fussing with a strap of his knapsack. He spoke without looking up, in a low whisper.

"All right, I'm going to lay out the chart here. Keep an eye out for Olwin or Blackpaw. I'll leave it here for a quick look. As soon as I'm through, you can take turns doing something to your packs. But be careful."

"You first, Granny," said Morley.

The old animal put down her pack beside Bramble's, and began to rearrange her apron. She laid it carefully down, then refolded it, and tucked it neatly into her pack. At the end of the long, careful maneuver, she had managed to get a careful look at the map, and had committed to memory most of the important details of the first leg of the journey through Thorn Wood.

"All right, you, Morley," said Bramble, getting up.

One by one, the animals studied the chart, pretending that they were doing various things.

It was at the very end, while Stump was having his turn, that a quick warning was whispered, and the chart disappeared once more into Bramble's hiding place.

Olwin, flanked by Bumble and Cabbage, and followed by Blackpaw, strode to the group in military fashion. The two pups were dressed in small versions of the man's cloak, and each had a finely carved wooden sword at his side. The pups were very grave, striding around swishing their cloaks, and looking darkly at their parents.

"We are ready now. You, old one, and the others, lead on. My Grand Marshal shall bring me all the news, and we will follow along behind to mark the trail for my armies."

"We're his aides," said Bumble stiffly, trying to keep the chin strap of his gilt helmet out of his way as he spoke.

"We're going to be generals when we get big," added Cabbage.

Blackpaw looked sternly at Bramble.

"We've wasted enough time here. Let's be on our way."

The animals formed up, Granny leading, and the young badger bringing up the rear. Branch and Beryl were in the middle of the little band, and kept turning around as they moved off.

At their last glimpse of the pups, Bumble had drawn his tiny sword, and was chasing Cabbage around Olwin's feet.

Branch would have smiled, had she not been so frightened, but she remembered the words Granny had spoken, and in her heart she knew they would be all right if they but held true to the Law, and did as they knew to do. She looked ahead, and over Bramble's strong shoulders, she saw the line of woods ahead, now greener in the broadening light.

In the sunshine, Thorn Wood did not look as bad as she had imagined.

THE DISAPPEARING FOREST

As the day wore on, the animals became aware that the distance to Thorn Wood was greater than they at first had thought. After marching until well after midday, they seemed no nearer than when they had begun earlier in the morning. Upon reaching the top of one foothill, they all would expect to find their destination a bit closer, but if anything, it only seemed more distant, as if they were traveling backward, or not at all.

Granny Badger began to tire, being weakened by the close call with the killer wolf and the long journey.

"Here, sit down awhile, Granny," ordered Branch. "We'll just have to take a break now."

"This is as good a spot as any," concluded Basil. "I'll swear I think we're farther away than when we started this morning."

"I've been keeping my eye to a spot that's off color in the wood," said Bramble. "I can't see that we've gone to one side off our path, yet we certainly don't seem to be reaching anywhere in a hurry."

Morley's eyes opened wide.

"Do you suppose it could be some sort of magic from the wood? Or Old Bark?"

"That's it," shouted Stump, blowing out his cheeks. "Wheew. I've walked my paws to nubs, not getting anywhere, and all along it must be some sort of fancy work from some lout like Olwin."

"Shhh," cautioned Bramble. "Blackpaw is coming for his report."

"Oh, cranberry custard for Blackpaw," snorted the mole. "He's all bluff and thunder, too."

"But he's dangerous, all the same," insisted Bramble. "And he does hold the upper hand for now."

"I wonder how his highness is taking to having those pups underfoot all this time?" asked Beryl, trying to sound cheerful.

"Most likely driven right out of his head, if they behave for him as they're accustomed to," grumbled Stump. "I've spent a lot more pleasant times than I'd like to admit chasing those little rascals out of my corn crib, or shooing them off my herb cellar roof. They can come up with a deal of mischief between them."

Branch turned to Granny.

"You don't think he would harm them, do you? I mean, if he were angry at their games?"

"He's not about to," assured the old animal. "If he hurt them now, they would be of no use to him, and he's not the sort to let a chance like this slip by. But here's his messenger now. We'll have a report."

Blackpaw had come to stand beside Granny, his sword hilt showing beneath his cloak.

"Olwin grows impatient. We've been on the march for six hours and over, and yet we've made no progress, it seems."

"Olwin isn't the only one who grows impatient,"

snapped Granny. "I'm old, and my paws hurt, and I don't have any business at all traipsing around the countryside like this. An animal my age should have good sense enough to stay at her own hearth, minding her own soup kettle, and tending to her own knitting."

"Olwin's not interested in your complaints. He's interested in crossing Thorn Wood, if we ever get there."

"You tell your precious Olwin that Granny is all in, and we're going to take a rest here," said Bramble. "We'll go on as soon as she's rested enough to travel."

The badger glared hard before he spoke.

"Is that an order you're giving? Or a request?"

"A request, naturally," replied Bramble. "We all have the same goal, and that's to reach Thorn Wood. Without Granny, none of us stands a chance at all."

Blackpaw studied the otter.

"I wonder what those plans may include, once we get there."

"They include seeing Bumble and Cabbage safe, first off," replied Bramble. "Then there's a question of whether or not we reach the other side of Thorn."

"And if that is successful?"

"You know as well as I what the answer is to that. How do we figure into the plans of Olwin once he has achieved what he set out to achieve?"

"You will fit in wisely, I'm sure," said Blackpaw. "There is room in the growing army of the True King. An animal can go far, if he behaves himself, and acts as he is expected. It would not be such an unpleasant life."

"Perhaps not," replied Bramble. "Still, we are dealing with a man, and there is no knowing his whims. What of those poor louts from the north he has terrified and forced to do his bidding? They were following the Law where they were. Now he's brought them behind him with his power, and their fear of him, and he's broken the boundaries they have known. And look at the rewards they get for their service."

"The killer wolves aren't animals," argued Blackpaw. "Not civilized animals, anyhow. Everyone knows there are the animal kind, and then the beasts."

"It isn't fair, and you know it," shot Morley. "I don't hold any glad will for those brutes, but I don't relish the thought of what Olwin is doing to them, either. It's not natural."

"What would a muskrat know of these matters?" snarled Blackpaw. "Other than growing turnips, and wandering about hedgerows, what sense is there to an overfed swamp rat?"

Morley bristled, but held his silence.

Blackpaw had thrown back his cloak, and swaggered around.

"Do you really believe all these things he tells you?" asked Branch quietly.

"His word is the Law. He's very powerful," replied the badger. "He can get things done. There's order to his aims."

"But what order?" asked Stump. "Whatever suits his fancy, that's for certain. And what's good for Olwin had best be good for his subjects, or else."

The mole made a motion of drawing a hand across his throat.

"The strong must rule. Look at how you silly animals were living before this. And my own clan, too. No order, no sense to anything."

"Didn't you like your clan?" asked Acorn. "How could you say there was no meaning to it all?"

"The silly fools were always yammering about this or

that, but they were never doing anything worthwhile, or important."

Blackpaw paced furiously as he talked, and gestured wildly. Small, ash-gray clouds of dust erupted from behind him at every step. He had grown very restless as he spoke, and Bramble tried to soothe him.

"So you think there will be more order under Olwin?"

"Of course. And more serious work done, and more plans to be made."

"Isn't just getting along, and having a roof, and enough to eat, and a nice sunset enough for you?" asked Basil. "There's plenty to this business, and I guess there are some who would feel better if they were in Olwin's shoes, heading an army, or always going around feeling as if they knew a lot more than anyone else, but I'm quite content to mend my dams, and patch my house, and see to the needs of my mate and pup, and my friends."

Something the beaver said seemed to put Blackpaw into a cold rage.

"That's as you say, you water slime. I wouldn't expect anything more from so simple-minded an animal. That's why we're all in such a mess today. It's good that Olwin has come along to set things to rights."

As the badger fumed, the small gray figure of Bumble, cloaked in red, waddled up to his mother.

"Bumble!" she cried, ignoring the icy stare of Blackpaw.

"He sent me up here to see where Blackpaw was. He wants to know why you've stopped."

The pup looked tired, and he carried the fancy helmet in his paws. The finely carved wooden sword was gone.

"Where's your weapon?" growled Blackpaw sternly. "You don't become generals by losing your weapons."

"He took it back," replied the pup. "I guess he got tired of me playing with Cabbage."

Bramble looked hard at the small gray figure.

"Are you changing your mind about being a soldier?" he asked.

Bumble's lip quivered, but he held back his tears.

"Oh, who wants to be a dumb old soldier anyway? They never have any fun."

"Is Cabbage tired, too?" asked Beryl.

"Cabbage has to not say a word for a whole hour," replied Bumble. "He told him if he did, he'd turn him into a black stump, and leave him behind."

Beryl put a paw to her mouth, and gave a little gasp.

"He was just teasing, he said. He said it's like a game we're playing. It's not much fun, though. You never get to say anything, or run after each other, or anything."

Bramble looked at the frail figure of the old badger.

"Are you up to traveling, Granny?"

She nodded, but didn't open her eyes. She remained seated beside Branch.

"I wish there were still some trees left," said Basil. "We could make her a chair lift."

"Maybe we could string two knapsacks together, and carry her between us," suggested Stump.

"I'll do no such thing, Stump Mole. Why, you're almost as old as I am. I don't fancy being lugged about like an old sack, either. I'll get where I'm going on my own two feet, thank you."

Her voice was strong, but she had to struggle to rise.

"Help her up there," ordered Blackpaw. "She's the most important of the lot of you."

"Little you care," snapped Beryl. "And besides, we all know the way as well as Granny."

Blackpaw glared.

"And how would you know that?"

He paced nearer, threateningly.

"How could you possibly know about where we're going, or how we're going to get there? Have you been looking at something? Something that was supposed to be kept concealed?"

"Granny told me," stammered the frightened beaver.

Blackpaw confronted Bramble.

"Have you shown everyone the map? Have you lost your good senses? What if Olwin had seen you? A fine kettle we'd all be in now."

"Well, for one thing, we'd all most likely be a good stew for some hungry killer wolf. Olwin has no use for any of us, except for the fact that he thinks we know a way through Thorn."

"Give me the chart!" demanded Blackpaw. "I'll hold it."

He held out a paw, glowering.

Bramble shook his head.

"I can't get to it now. And I think we've got company, to boot. We don't dare let Olwin suspect."

"And why are you so worried if your precious Olwin is so all fired hot on having you for his Grand Marshal? What would a little thing like a chart mean to him? Why, he's got a Grand Marshal to beat all Grand Marshals."

The mole could not keep the ridicule out of his voice.

Blackpaw's hackles rose, and he had drawn the sword before anyone could move to stop him.

A commanding roar from Olwin, who had arrived a moment before, brought the badger up short.

"I don't care what amusements please you, but you'll see to it your duties are performed first."

He turned to Bumble, who stood trembling before him.

"And you, you young waterwhelp! What's kept you so long?"

Bumble had stuttered, but no sound came, and Bramble answered for him.

"Granny was exhausted. She's had a near thing, and not enough rest, and now all this walking. It's been too much for her."

Olwin glanced past Bramble to where the old badger stood unsteadily behind him.

"Then she shall ride," he proclaimed, and moved his hand in an odd fashion before him, and there appeared on the ground a brilliant red and green pole chair, with a wicker seat and padded cushions.

"I won't get in that contraption," blurted out Granny, raising herself to her full badger height.

"You will, and you'll enjoy it," ordered Olwin. "Or otherwise, we might just be missing a pup or two by the end of the day."

"You leave those pups alone," said Granny, her voice as strong as Bramble had ever heard her. If she hadn't been all gray, he would have sworn the words had come from a young, more vital Granny Badger, as she had been long ago, when she and Gruff had first moved to their old wood together. "And I'm not riding. When I can't walk any longer, you'll just have to leave me."

Olwin glowered at the old animal.

"Very well. You've pronounced your own fate, then. When you're no longer able to carry on yourself, there will be no one left behind to help you. You'll be left alone. And you know what that entails."

"Then who'll guide you through Thorn?" she asked slyly. "Your Grand Marshal?"

Olwin's beard bristled out, and his eyes darkened.

"Your spirit may be your undoing yet, old one. My patience wears thin."

Stump Mole interrupted the two with a strange look, and a low mutter of amazement. He pointed toward the low foothills away and beyond them, where Thorn Wood had stretched a few moments before, seemingly a full day's march from them.

"They've moved," said the mole.

And moved they had, for not more than a stone's throw from the group were the dark shadows of the eaves of Thorn Wood. The branches of the tall trees moved, although the animals could feel no breath of wind upon them.

OWL WING

Olwin's face drained behind his beard, but he recovered himself quickly.

"What new prank is this?" he glowered, looking at the swaying limbs of the trees.

"I didn't think we were anywhere near this close when we stopped," breathed Morley. "And look at that. There isn't any wind blowing at all, but the trees are all moving."

"It's an ill wind of another nature," growled Olwin. "This has the mark of that rogue Old Bark."

"You mean he's the one that did this?" asked Bramble. "I know he was old and wise, but I never thought he'd be capable of anything like this."

"He's capable of anything," snapped Olwin. "And there's nothing he'll stop at to keep me from crossing to the Falls. He'll go to any lengths to have his way."

Bramble looked sideways at the man.

"That's been said of someone else I know of."

Before the man could reply, Cabbage came dragging up, looking tearful.

"I'm scared. I shut my eyes like you told me, and

251

counted up to a hundred swamp lilies, but then I was going to ask you something, and when I looked, I was all
alone, and there were trees all around me."

Beryl caught her frightened pup to her, and hugged him
until he quietened.

Bumble peered from behind his cloak.

"They're all moving."

"They are moving," agreed Stump. "I don't like the
look of this at all. It's not right for a wood to be going
about, first one place, then another. Trees aren't that sort.
Supposed to stay put, if you ask me."

Blackpaw had moved closer to Olwin.

"Do you think it's Old Bark?"

"What other reason would you give for a forest moving? It's that meddler, all right, but he's got more than he
bargained for this time."

The man turned to Granny.

"Does your memory tell you anything about this, old
one?"

Granny looked long at him before answering.

"What I have read, and been told, is that it is sometimes deceiving when traveling toward Thorn Wood.
Sometimes it looks distant, and sometimes it seems so
close you could almost touch it, but it is all merely part of
the wood's mystery."

Bramble turned to Granny.

"Let's see if this is really Thorn, or not."

"Be careful," whisperered Branch.

"I want to go, too," cried Bumble, dancing wildly
about.

"Hush! You can come with me. If it's the work of Old
Bark, or if it's just a shadow, we'll find out."

"I'll go with you," said Blackpaw, drawing back his

cloak to reveal the sword. "You might need protection."

Bramble smiled.

"It's not likely that sword is going to be of much use here," he said.

"It may," huffed Blackpaw. "And there may be wild things."

"No doubt, if all the stories about the place are true."

Granny Badger caught Bramble's eyes, and beckoned him to her.

"If you go toward the center there, where you see the red leaves on that tall tree, I think you'll find a door in the woods, if they really are there. They'll be thick everywhere else, and one could spend a week trying to go forward a paw's length. Repeat the old rune that Gruff taught me:

> Great Wood of Thorn
> O timeless born,
>   let me pass your cloak
>   of elm and oak,
>   and see the other side.

I remember that from the map, too."

"What if this isn't the real wood?" asked Morley.

"Then we don't have to worry with anything more than walking on farther."

Stump shook his head doubtfully.

"You'd better let me come along with you," he said. "I'm not so sure about all this conjuring business. Not natural, if you ask me. Woods are woods, and ought to stay put, like they belong."

"Should I go?" asked Basil.

"You stay with the others," ordered Blackpaw, before Bramble could answer. "And you," he said, pointing to

Acorn. "You and your mate keep your babies close to you, and out of the way."

Olwin stood silently, gazing into the wood.

"I think it's a hoax," he said at last. "It looks strange."

"We'll check it for you," said Blackpaw, and he motioned the otter to follow him.

They had gone only a few steps when the entire length of the wood before them disappeared completely. There was nothing where it had been but burnt ash and another low knoll.

"What infernal business is this?" hissed Olwin. "That cursed traitor is at his games with me." He slammed a fist into a palm, and glowered. "He'll dearly pay for his pranks, or I've missed my guess."

"It's right back where it was," said Basil, pointing to the distant smudge of green on the horizon.

"Do you have any way of telling how far away it really is?" asked Bramble, addressing the old badger.

"It may be where you see it, or it may not," answered Granny. "If I knew exactly where we were, it might help. But then again, it might not."

"I've told you where we are, old one. It would make no difference with this wood. This is the report I get back from the armies I send to destroy that foul thing. It's never where it ought to be, or disappearing before their eyes, or rushing forward, or back. I've had reports that it is sometimes mistaken for a river, with white plumes of water, and mad tides that sweep away all and everything that comes near it."

Olwin's eyes had turned a deep green as he spoke.

"But those were tales I never believed, until I had read the lore of other times."

His face softened for a moment, but the look didn't last long.

"That infernal meddler is responsible for this. We shall have a nasty surprise for him, though. He'll never dream that I've found the key to the wood."

Olwin threw back his head and laughed.

"All this time, I've been at a loss as to how to deal with him. What strange fate that he'll have his end served up to him through a pack of animals."

"I wouldn't be too sure of that," said Granny softly. "It's no easy thing, finding the proper way into Thorn."

"You just told your companion what to look for, and what to say. Won't that open the way?"

"Only if you're in the proper place," replied Granny. "It would never do if you were somewhere other than the one true door. It might open wide for you to pass, right enough, but it would soon turn you around so that you'd be lost in its wilderness."

"Then what's the secret of knowing, if you have reached the one spot you say is the true door?" asked the man, glowering.

"There is a sign," said Granny. "Sometimes it's one thing, sometimes another, but there is always a sign."

"Tell him what it is," ordered Blackpaw, sensing Olwin's anger.

"Well, it's hard to say, in words. It's more like you just know it. It will feel right, or it won't."

"There must be more to it than that," insisted Olwin. "I've studied lores of every kind, and there's always the secret of the power somewhere. There must be something. A sign, or countersign, or a rune to say."

"As you wish, then," said Granny. "Sometimes you'll hear the sound of running water, or it might be drums, far off. Or there may be a bright light that flashes."

"That's more like it. I knew there must be something solid to see the workings of."

"It's not exactly solid," went on Granny. "Those signs may be there, or they may not. That's what makes Thorn Wood so dangerous to those who would travel there. My Gruff said it was frightening enough to be there as he and Greystone were, simply on a journey, and with no other intention than that of getting home."

"I have more to my work than that, with all the other witless things wandering about getting through those infernal woods. It will surely come to pass that I will be able to break the fastness of Thorn."

Olwin had paced back and forth furiously as he spoke.

"Shall the plan go on as we had it?" asked Blackpaw.

The man didn't answer for a moment, and seemingly hadn't heard the question.

"I think I shall explore ahead a bit, and see what there is to see, and if that ragtag Old Bark is up to his tricks again."

And so saying, he turned the cloak about him, and where Olwin the man had been, there now stood Owl Wing, the stag. The animal was huge, and had great curving horns that gleamed dully in the sun. Olwin's voice came from the animal.

"Do not think I don't know what you're about. I won't be gone long, so don't fancy yourselves escaping. There's nowhere you can go that I won't find you."

With that final warning, the huge animal sprang away, and was out of sight in a few bounds.

"That was the animal we saw leading those herds in the stampedes," blurted Basil, his eyes wide, and still gazing in the direction the stag had vanished.

"That deer said their leader was Owl Wing. No wonder those herds kept crossing paths with the killer wolves. They were being led to the slaughter to feed the armies."

"Were those things true you told him, Granny? About the secrets of Thorn Wood?" asked Branch.

The old badger smiled faintly.

"When have you ever known me to tell you an untruth?"

Branch shook her head.

"Never."

"They were all true enough, as far as they go. And it is so that it was more of a feeling that Gruff described than any sort of plain sign that anybody could see or hear."

"I hope you haven't told Olwin anything that may anger him," said Blackpaw, staring hard at Granny. "He is not one you would want to displease."

"He will find out for himself that I have spoken the truth," said Granny. "Gruff and Greystone got through and back because they had no motives other than being lost and wanting to go home. That's why they returned safely. Your friend is a bit more ambitious, it seems. He has designs of overthrowing the wood and whatever is beyond, and obviously he has some quarrel with Old Bark, although I can't imagine why. There seems to be more to this than meets the eye. I was under the same impression that Bramble was, that Old Bark was simply a wise old bear who had lived to great age, and who kept his cave below the Falls."

"If Olwin finds fault, then there must be no good involved with the animal."

"Why do you insist on defending this man?" asked Beryl shyly. "You're an animal, too. Don't you feel afraid of him?"

"Of course not!" snapped Blackpaw, a bit loudly. "He's powerful, and a man, but there is nothing to fear."

"Look what he threatened to do to Bumble and Cabbage," reminded Branch. "I don't think he would find that necessary if he were the right sort."

"And don't forget the killer wolf," added Stump. "Fried on the spot, for no other reason than just because Olwin was feeling mean."

Blackpaw seemed to grow confused.

"There's no use in your trying to turn me against him. He's the only one that's been decent to me, or offered to give me my rightful place in the order of things."

"Great leaping toadwillows," snapped Morley. "You mean you feel like we've mistreated you because we didn't make you Grand Marshal? Of what? Potatoes? Whoever heard of anything so silly?"

"Silly to you," scowled Blackpaw. "Nothing is important to you, you simple-minded beast. But if one is going to get on in the world, it's necessary to put things in their proper perspective. There must be leaders, and there must be followers."

"Balls of rubbish!" grumbled Stump. "Just look at those poor beasts that were following Owl Wing, or Olwin, or whatever his name is. There they were, following their trusted leader, and all he had on his mind was to lead them into the stewpot of a pack of killer wolves."

"There must be an answer for that," argued Blackpaw.

"Come back to our side," pleaded Basil. "We need all the help we can to escape him. He's powerful and dangerous, but if you serve as our spy, we might be able to learn something that will allow us to make good an escape."

Blackpaw huffed up, and blustered.

"I'm not the sort of animal that just blows along with any way the wind is going. I'm loyal, and steadfast to my principles."

"You owe that loyalty to us first," scolded Branch.

"You are a badger, after all," said Granny gently.

Blackpaw looked about him wildly.

"You're trying to confuse me. My loyalty lies with Olwin. I'm his Grand Marshal."

"That's exactly what we want you to make him think," said Bramble. "Just go on doing what you're doing, and let him think you're on his side."

"And then we'll know what his plans are, and what to do if we get a chance to slip away," said Basil.

"You could take away his cloak," chittered Bumble. "I heard him talking to himself, and he said it real loud, but I don't think he thought I heard him. He took it away from an old, old man, and it gave him all the power there was, he said, except the power to get through Thorn Wood. He wants Old Bark's cloak, that's what he said."

Bramble stopped and looked at his small gray pup.

"You say it's his cloak?"

"I never thought of that," said Morley.

"How will we get it away from him? He wears it all the time," put in Beryl.

Blackpaw felt all eyes turn toward him.

"No, I won't do it!" he said, before anyone could speak. "It would be too dangerous, and I don't want to, anyway."

"What would be too dangerous, my good Grand Marshal?" came Olwin's voice, and the animals turned, startled, and were face to face with the red-bearded, heavily cloaked man once more.

THE REALMS OF
OLD BARK

A DARK WIND BLOWS

An unbroken stillness fell over the companions, and nothing was heard above their frightened breathing.

Olwin stepped nearer, towering over the animals, his red beard blazing, and the blood-red cloak drawn back revealing the blade of Erinoult that he wore at his side.

His voice thundered when he spoke, and a dozen killer wolves had appeared out of nowhere.

"Is there talk afoot of treachery?" Olwin boomed, fire raging in his eyes. "Have there been plans to desert the True King?"

"Oh no, sire," blurted Blackpaw. "We have been talking of how best to get through Thorn, and to deal with your enemies beyond."

Olwin glowered menacingly at the young badger.

"A pack of lies from a pack of cowardly animals."

"We have been planning our way through Thorn Wood," said Bramble, trembling, but his voice was steady. "And we are the only ones who know the way through. If you destroy us, you lose all hopes of ever gaining a door to Thorn Wood, or Thorn Canyon, or the Falls."

Olwin's glance settled on the otter.

"You seem to be the spokesman, Master Otter, so tell me the truth. Were you not planning an escape? Come, it will do you no good to try to lie to me. I know the nature of beasts and men. There is no good borne me by any kinds who oppose me."

Bramble looked evenly at the man.

"We mean no harm to anyone, even the killer wolves, if we can avoid it. All we want is to be able to live out our time in a quiet settlement, and raise our pups to do the same."

"Of what worth is that?" asked Olwin, his voice calmer, although the threat still remained. "What use can that be?"

"More use than burning woods, or setting killer wolves on helpless animals," blurted Morley.

"Or trying to get through a wood that would be better left alone," added Acorn.

"Those are things that must be done," replied Olwin. "That is the order of things."

"Why?" asked Branch.

"Because it's a waste, the way it is. No common tongue, animals at each other's throats, looting in the realms of mankind, and then there's the simple fact that I know all lores, and of all kinds. I can bring it all under one reign."

"That's all well and good, but it doesn't seem to be working out so well. Old Bark has thrown your plan for a loop, and it doesn't look as if that will ever change," said Bramble.

At the mention of Old Bark's name, Olwin scowled, and smashed a fist into his palm.

"That rogue won't keep me at bay long. I'll have his

precious wood, and Thorn Canyon, and the Falls. It's only a matter of time."

"How will you get through Thorn? Without us, you have no hope," said Basil.

"Without you, I'll be able to travel more swiftly," replied Olwin. "You are but a drag on my speed."

"And where are your armies?" asked Branch. "We've seen nothing but these killer wolves."

Olwin's face took on an ugly reddish color.

"You are full of questions today, aren't you? I don't like questions, especially from those who bear me only ill will, and who oppose the True King. There can be only one way to deal with those," said Olwin softly, the lines in his face tightening.

He stepped back a pace, and threw his arms upward, toward the sky. All at once the sunlight dimmed, and a howling wind sprang up.

Bramble held to Branch, and tried to find his pup, but could not see him for the whirling gray ash that filled the air. A cry from Basil rang out, to be swallowed by the wind, and then shouts from all directions seemed to fill the air. Ash bumped into Stump, and squealed, which scared the mole badly, but he quickly recovered, and tried to find his way to the otter.

Olwin had vanished in the shrieking gale, but the animals were all too aware of the presence of the killer wolves, and expected to be set upon at any moment.

"Let's try to keep together," shouted Bramble. "Here, Granny, Stump! Over here! We'll stand a better chance if we are together."

"Where's Bumble?" cried Branch. "Does anybody see Bumble?"

"Or Cabbage?" wailed Beryl.

The friends milled around in a confused knot, trying to

find the pups and keep themselves in a defense, should the killer wolves attack. Bramble could think of no other reason that Olwin would have caused the storm except that he was turning the wolves on them.

Squinting into the wind, and trying to keep his paw in Branch's, Bramble struggled forward, in the direction he remembered Thorn Wood to be.

Morley appeared out of the wind-blown gloom and fell into line, and then Stump and Granny joined them, but they saw no sign of the pups. Ash and Acorn appeared out of the gray darkness next, almost invisible in their gray coats, with their babies under their arms.

"Did you see Bumble or Cabbage?" shouted Branch. "We can't find them."

The squirrels replied, but Branch could not hear, although her heart sank when she saw them shake their heads.

"Watch out," warned Stump. "There's something there ahead."

Before the mole's voice had died away, a cloaked figure loomed in the darkness.

"It's Olwin!" cried Blackpaw, who had had no chance to go with the man when the wind appeared.

He tried to struggle toward the figure, but was stopped short by the appearance of a killer wolf, crouched and ready to spring. Blackpaw barely had time to raise his sword and strike before the wolf lunged.

"Good work," shot Morley to the badger. "Since you're the only one armed, we'll have to form our defense around you."

The killer wolf howled in pain, and loped away into the darkness of the wind.

Blackpaw's mind raced, and he was torn with indecision. The man had much power, and was able to get what he wanted, and had told him he would teach him the secrets of all the knowledge he held. Yet there was no doubt in the badger's mind that it was a dangerous game to play, and it was difficult to tell if you were in Olwin's favor or not. And if you were not, then there was no telling what the result would be.

On the other hand, he was with his own kind again, and they needed him desperately now, for he was the only one among them who was armed, and who could protect them from the killer wolves that lurked all about them.

He wondered, too, if this was the fate Olwin had doomed them to, to punish them for their plans of escape. It seemed Olwin not only had dreadful powers to create things out of the air, but he could also hear and see things when he wasn't there.

"There's another one!" called Stump, searching the ground about him for a rock, or any kind of weapon he could defend himself with.

The gaunt killer wolf leapt at Beryl, jaws drooling. Its weight knocked the beaver down, but before a killing bite could be given, Blackpaw had slashed the wolf and driven it off.

Bramble stood beside the young badger.

"When your arm gets too tired, we'll take turns with the sword."

"I wish it was Erinoult's blade," lamented Blackpaw. "That was a mistake, giving it to Olwin."

"We'll worry about that when the time comes. We have to see to our hides, now."

Bramble patted the badger kindly.

"It looks as if our differences have been settled for us. Olwin has a definite way of letting himself be known."

Blackpaw said nothing, for he was having a difficult

time letting go of his title of Grand Marshal, and all the dreams he had dreamed, which Olwin had encouraged.

"Here's Bumble and Cabbage!" shouted Morley.

"Where have you two been?" cried Beryl.

"And what's that you've got?" asked Branch.

"It's his cloak," chittered Bumble. "We got his cloak. Cabbage and I were standing right by him when the wind came, and I was trying to get away, but I tripped, and then Cabbage fell over me, and while I was trying to get up, I got stepped on by Olwin, and then the next thing I knew, he was on top of me too, and I was all tangled up, and couldn't get loose."

"Me, too," shouted Cabbage. "I was rolling around and around, and I kept getting stuck, and he kept hitting me, and then he pulled out his knife."

"And then he tried to stab Cabbage, but I bit him, and he dropped it, and then when I tried to run, this old cloak was all over me, so Cabbage bit him, and then the next thing I knew, we were by ourselves."

"And look, Granny, we got your sword back."

Cabbage held up the weapon to the old badger.

"We couldn't get the sheath. He was hanging on to that," chittered Bumble.

Granny's eyes filled with tears as she took the sword of Erinoult.

Its blade had begun to gleam more brightly, and as the old badger took it, the darkness of the windy gloom began to brighten, until at last it was hard for the animals to look directly at the blade.

"We can see, with that," said Basil, his excitement growing.

"And now we've got two swords," cried Morley.

"Watch out for Olwin. He won't give up his prizes so

easily," cautioned Stump. "We've got a head start on him now, but we'll have to mind our oats to keep it."

"Let's try for Thorn Wood!" cried Bramble. "We can at least hide there."

"Quickly, Granny! You lead with that light, and Blackpaw, you stand guard at our rear. We'll march in a line, in case the wolves or Olwin attacks."

"They'll sure be able to see us plain enough," grumped the mole. "But I don't think they'll want to tangle with Granny, now that she has that sword back."

The mole had barely finished speaking when a horrible scream filled the air. All the animals' hackles raised, and they looked about them, terrified.

"That wasn't a wolf," said Bramble, regaining his voice first.

"Olwin," said Granny. "He has lost his cloak and his sword. He may be having to deal with those wolves of his now, alone."

The otter shook his head.

"He has more ways than one to defend himself. The loss of this cloak or sword won't make much difference to him, except to make him angry. I think we've probably more to fear from him now than before."

"You mean we didn't help by getting his cloak?" asked Bumble, disappointment heavy in his voice.

"Of course you helped," reassured Bramble. "And you got the sword back for Granny. That was the best thing of all, and very brave of both of you."

"Shouldn't I be at the front?" asked Blackpaw. "If Olwin is more dangerous now, then it should be me to face the danger first, and not Granny."

"We need the light in front of us," said Morley. "Or we can't see which way to go."

"Then I'll carry Erinoult's blade," went on Blackpaw. "He's my ancestor, too."

"We'll let the sword decide," said Granny. "I think it has a mind of its own. And I'm sure that's how the pups were able to get it from Olwin. It does things sometimes without anyone doing them."

She handed the brightly glowing blade to Blackpaw, who trembled as he took it.

DANGER LURKS

In the middle of the howling windstorm, the animals watched breathlessly as Blackpaw took the sword of the ancient Master Erinoult. They all felt angry that the young badger was to be trusted after his disloyalty to them, yet they were also oddly relieved that he was among them again. And they would not need to pass judgment on him at all, for the sword would proclaim whether he was to be fully taken into their circle, or kept apart.

The badger's paws trembled again as Granny handed the gleaming blade to him. His face changed as he touched the glowing handle of the sword, and without any further hesitation, he held it in front of him, eyes shining. The light did not waver or dim, and a glad shout from the companions rang out.

The old badger took the sword Blackpaw had held, and gave it to Bramble.

"Here. You take turns with this, if we need it."

"It didn't dim, Granny," blurted Morley. "What happened?"

"Did you think it would?" she asked.

The mole shook his head.

"I didn't know what it would do."

"What does it mean?" asked Branch, raising her voice to be heard over the wind.

"He's been tested," said Granny.

Stump grumbled aloud.

"All fine and well, but if you ask me, we'd be just as well off a good piece from here."

"We're going, Stump. You get back there and keep an eye out for our friend and his louts. I don't think they've gotten through with us yet."

Even as Granny spoke, Acorn shouted, and Ash squealed.

"Here!" cried Acorn. "There's two of them here."

One dark shape loomed, then another. A moment later, the friends heard the snarl of the wolves, and their harsh breath came even over the noise of the wind.

Bramble's mind raced, for there was something familiar in the size of one of the killer wolves. Some faint alarm went off in the back of his mind, but in his hurry to protect Ash and her babies, he could not put his paw to what it was that worried him so.

Blackpaw, in a brilliant halo of light, led the way, and the dark shadows of the wind-blown gloom vanished before him. In another instant, he stood beside the squirrels.

"Where are they?" asked the badger.

"They were there," replied Acorn. "I could just make them out. They seem to be following us."

"They were there, and had every chance to attack before we could have fought them off," said Morley. "Why didn't they finish one of us off?"

"Get closer here!" warned Bramble. "We have to keep ready. They may have missed one chance, but I don't think they'll make that mistake again."

"I wish this wind would stop," fumed Acorn. "I can't see my paw in front of me. And all this burnt wood blowing around makes me want to sneeze."

"Why didn't Olwin just finish us off?" asked Basil. "He could have turned us into anything. There was no need for all this."

"Maybe he just wanted to feed his wolves," replied Stump. "Those louts stay hungry all the time. And outside of us, I haven't seen anything they might like for supper ever since we last heard those man armies fighting, right after we left the tunnels."

Bramble thought hard.

"I guess he feeds them the same way he fed us. Waves his arm around, and there would be something for them to eat."

"You know, just before this wind came up, I would have sworn Olwin looked surprised. Just as he was throwing his arm up," mused Granny, leaning close to the otter's ear.

Bramble remembered back, concentrating. That look might have been anger, or was it fear? It could have been either.

"Then he might have been going to disappear us, or do something bad, but didn't get the chance."

"Is this just a regular wind?" asked Basil.

"I don't think there's anything regular about these parts," growled Stump. "Nothing has been right since those louts from the north drove us out of our old homes."

"We've got his cloak," chirped Bumble. "Maybe he can't do anything to us."

Bramble patted his pup gently.

"I'm sure you did a good job there, but I'm not too

sure his power depends on his cloak. He's probably feeling a little lost without it, all the same."

"He can't hurt us with his sword anymore," shouted Cabbage. "I grabbed it and ran."

"You two!" fussed Beryl. "You're going to make enough noise so he'll hear us, and then we will be in a fix."

Blackpaw stood, staring away into the gloom beyond the light of the sword.

"I don't know why they aren't on us. I know they outnumber us badly. We might slay a few, but we have no hopes of standing against so many."

"No hope at all, and our only course now is to lose them, and Olwin, or Owl Wing, or whoever he is, while this wind holds."

Bramble stood beside the badger as he spoke, his brow furrowed. He was still trying to place that small, chilly feeling he had felt when he saw the figures lurking in the murk of the blown ashes.

"Let's set our direction toward Thorn," said Granny. "It's our only haven now."

"Olwin will be making for there, too, Granny. Shouldn't we try to go someplace he won't expect us?" asked Basil.

"I think Olwin knows we've got no other place to turn to. There's no hiding anywhere around, except for Thorn. And I don't think he was going to do anything more than to try to frighten us back there. He wants through that wood too badly to risk losing his chance by doing something silly like destroying the one who knows the way. I have a strange feeling that something else happened that he wasn't expecting, and it threw him off guard. I'm not sure this wind is of his doing."

"He'll be sure to be after us, then," moaned Morley.

"And once he finds us, there won't be any doubt about what's going to be the outcome."

"That would depend on whether we are on this side of Thorn or beyond," said Bramble.

"And if we get through without him catching us, then we're in trouble again, with Old Bark. If he's so picky about people getting through, he'll just think we're more of that scofflaw bunch, and get us lost, or worse," Morley said, dejected.

"Let's don't lose hope, old fellow. We've every reason to believe that Old Bark is at odds with Olwin, and if he knows we're of the right sort, perhaps he'll let us on through without trouble."

Bramble's tone was more cheery than he felt, although he did believe firmly that Old Bark was a fair and just animal. Except now, he found, from talking to Olwin, that Old Bark was a man, at least part of the time. It grew very confusing for the otter.

"Can you remember which way we were going?" asked Basil. "If we're going to head for Thorn, we should be on our way."

"We're steering right," said Blackpaw. "But it would help if this wind would let up enough for us to check ourselves."

"And then we'd have no concealment at all," snorted Stump. "So this wind blinds us a bit, it blinds those others, too. I'll travel on with it, although I don't like it at all."

"Here, you pups, you keep with us! We'd never find you if we lost you today," scolded Branch.

"And don't get so far from us. The place is filled with killer wolves," added Beryl.

Cabbage ran back to his mother, but Bumble went on

as if he hadn't heard. He wandered a bit farther, just to prove to himself that he wasn't afraid, then turned.

It was then that he caught sight of the gray-black form lurking not more than a few paw lengths from him. He opened his mouth to shout a warning, but stopped, for the figure had disappeared.

Wrinkling his whiskers as he had seen Bramble do when he was thinking, Bumble took a step or two in the direction the vanished shadow had gone.

Had it been a killer wolf?

He hadn't been able to see at all clearly, although he was expecting the shapes of the wolves, for he knew they were all around them.

Something in the way the form had lumbered away had caught his eye. It was not the slinking, skulking motion of the wolves, nor was it the way a human would walk, so it could not have been Olwin. Bumble knew the man could change his form into a huge stag, but this was not the deer, either.

The small otter was deep in thought, when he was grabbed from behind. He jumped straight up, letting out a terrified screech.

"What's the matter with you, you wart?" scolded Branch. "I've been calling and calling, and you haven't heard a word I've said."

"You scared me," breathed Bumble. "I thought it was Olwin."

"It might have been, too. You stay next to me, now."

"I want to walk with Cabbage."

"Then go ahead. But no more wandering out here."

Bramble had heard his mate calling the pup, and he increased his pace until he was even with them.

"What's wrong?"

"This stubborn pup of yours won't listen to anyone. He

was wandering around out here like there was nothing more to worry about than a sticker patch."

"I saw something funny," blurted out Bumble, eager to change the subject. "It was all big, but it wasn't a wolf, and it was too different to be Olwin."

Bramble looked away in the direction the small otter was pointing. A deep frown crossed his brow. It had been near where he saw the shadowy forms. The vague sense of unease he felt returned, and he tried to brush it aside as he reassured his pup.

"More of the killer wolves. They are probably trying to follow us to Thorn. They may think they will find more food there."

"This was bigger than a wolf," insisted Bumble.

"Then it must be Olwin. He may be following, too, rather than confronting us. Then he'd be free to do whatever he wanted, once he had his road through Thorn. We're small potatoes to what he has in mind."

Morley and Basil came to stand beside the otters.

"We've been seeing some strange goings-on," said Basil. "I thought it must be my eyes playing tricks, but Morley's been seeing it, too."

"Very strange. Not trying to attack, or even get close. Just lurking."

"It must be the killer wolves," replied Bramble.

The companions had gone ahead, in order not to lose sight of the gleaming bright shaft of light from the sword Blackpaw carried.

Morley lowered his voice as much as he was able without being silenced by the wind.

"Do you think Blackpaw is leading us into a trap?"

"Erinoult's sword wouldn't have been bright if the badger had meant to trick us. Granny knew that when she let him carry it."

"You mean it would have just been dark?" asked Branch.

"Most likely. But I don't think all these strange doings are any of Blackpaw's work. And I, for one, am going to try to offer him my trust. He's had a bad time of it, and I don't think it's been easy for him."

"I don't like it," mumbled Basil. "He's been rotten all along. Don't see that he's changed all that much. And that sword might glow like that for any badger. It came from a badger set, after all."

"Let's try to give him a fair chance," urged Bramble. "That might be just the thing he needs to bring him back to our side completely."

The muskrat nodded agreement, and Basil gave in reluctantly.

"All right. I'll go on trying to think the best."

"That's a good animal. I'm sure we'll find it the surest way to win him over."

Basil had turned to say something else, but groaned loudly, after bumping his nose painfully on a very solid tree that he had mistaken for another shadow in the dim light from the blown dust.

The animals halted suddenly, and reaching out, found themselves surrounded by the tall trunks of trees.

There was a faint, faraway sound of wind through the upper branches, but where the companions stood, the storm had passed, and they blinked at each other in surprise, being able to see each other plainly for the first time since the wind had begun.

FOLLOWING AFTER GRUFF AND GREYSTONE

The animals hardly dared to breathe, and they waited for the woods to disappear, as they had done before.

Finally, Morley reached out and touched one of the tall, dark gray trees.

"It's real enough," he said, going over to test another one.

"Real enough to bump my nose on," groaned Basil.

"Is this Thorn Wood, Granny?" asked Bramble, turning to the old badger.

She looked carefully about her, and tested the air once or twice, and moved closer to one of the ancient gray trees.

"This is Thorn," she said, after another moment's pause.

"Smell the oldness here."

The companions cautiously began to explore, turning every few moments to see if they were beset by the killer wolves they knew had been following them.

Bramble stood beside Branch, looking into the green darkness beyond the outer eave of the forest. It smelled of silence, and deepness, and secrets of ages long since gone.

There was a smell of danger present in the still air, too, but it did not seem to raise their hackles.

"Look, Granny," chittered Bumble, who had raced about, testing everything out with his paws.

He and Cabbage stood beside the trunk of an ancient, enormous tree, whose top rose completely out of sight above them.

"What is it?" asked Beryl.

"Funny writing, all over it," chirped Bumble.

"It's all squiggly!" piped Cabbage.

"It looks like someone wrote it a long time ago," finished the small otter pup.

"It does look old," agreed Basil, running a paw over the surface of the tree where the writing was.

"Older than we know, or can guess," confirmed Granny, looking at the strange, moss-covered markings. "Give me that chart, Bramble. I think we may have found the way into Thorn."

"Should we get this out now, Granny? What if Olwin is out there?" asked Acorn.

"It won't make any difference. We have to take a chance, to see if we are heading right."

Bramble had handed the wrinkled chart to Granny, who hurriedly unfolded it and scanned it briefly.

"Just as I thought. Look! This writing here on the tree is right on the spot on the chart."

All the friends gathered closer, so they could see over Granny's shoulders.

"It's the sign of the moon!" chittered Bumble. "Just like your Gruff said to follow."

"Oboy!" cried Cabbage. "Now there'll be treasure and dragons, and everything."

"Let's hope not," said Branch, trying to hold her squirming pup.

"Then this is the way in?" asked Blackpaw, looking closely at the chart, then at the ancient runes.

"This is the door to Thorn that Gruff talked of. I don't know what it was like for him to find it, coming through the old woods and all, but I'm sure I'm as glad to see it as he must have been."

"I wonder if he knew what it was, Granny?" asked Bramble.

"He and Greystone only knew it was a road to the Falls. I don't think they ever imagined it to be anything like it was."

"They were lost, too, just like us," reminded Basil.

"Maybe that's the only way you ever find it," said Morley. "It seems like if you're out looking for it, you never get there. Seems like it just gets farther and farther away."

"And the minute you're thoroughly lost and confused, here you are," concluded Stump grimly.

The old badger could not help laughing.

"That seems to be the way of it, Stump."

"Which way are we to go, Granny? We all looked at the chart, but only enough to try to get us to Thorn. Where do we go now?" asked Basil.

"We'll keep on the way it was meant for us to go. We didn't have much to do with finding this, so I guess we'll just go on ahead, and see where it leads us."

"Do you think those louts are still out there?" asked Morley. "I hate to think they'll just wait until we're safely through Thorn, and then attack."

"If they're there, they're certainly quiet about it," replied Bramble. "And I haven't ever heard a really quiet killer wolf."

"Me either," agreed Acorn. "They always seem to be snarling or growling."

"Olwin may be keeping them behind. He knows them

as well as anyone does. He may have thought of that, and just be following us himself."

"If that's true, there's nothing we can do about it, Bramble," said the old badger. "We have to either stay here until we starve, or go on to see what new thing lies ahead. Olwin is not one that we are likely to have to deal with, I don't think. These are the realms of Old Bark now."

Morley's eyes widened.

"I'd forgotten that."

"Do you think he's friendly?" asked Ash.

"I don't think there's a question of that," replied Granny. "And he couldn't be any worse than Olwin."

"I don't think he's anything at all like Olwin," said Bramble firmly.

"Will we get to see him?" asked Bumble.

"I hope he's more fun than that old Olwin," chimed in Cabbage.

"I guess we'll meet him when he's ready for us to," said Granny. "But we won't be doing anything until we get beyond his front doorstep."

Morley kept glancing uneasily about the clearing.

"Let's move, one way or the other. I keep thinking Olwin is watching us."

"Or someone," added Bramble. "I think I've had that feeling too, Morley. Makes my hackles rise. I can't quite put my paw on it, and whenever I turn around to look, there's nothing there."

"Exactly!" snorted Stump. "My hackles have been crawling since that stone talked to us in Granny's cave, but this is something different."

"It would be easier if we just knew where Olwin was," said Basil. "At least we'd know where we stood with him."

Blackpaw spoke up.

"You'll never know where you are with a man like Olwin. You could be standing beside him, and still not know."

"You should know," grumped the mole, although there was no malice in his voice.

"I have more reason to know than any of you. I have made a bad misjudgment, but I've come to my senses, I think. I had no business beyond my own kind. It did sound awfully good, though, for a while. Olwin has a way of attacking your weakness. He knew mine was loneliness, so he offered me great power over all those about me."

"Well, that's all done and gone," said Bramble. "I guess we all go through that, sooner or later. Only it seems you had an especially hard time of it."

"But it has taught me a good lesson in the process," said Blackpaw, looking down at the still glowing sword he held. "And this has finally opened my eyes."

"Erinoult was here with you all the time," said Granny softly. "At the proper moment, he set things right, and as they should be."

"I should have known better," went on Blackpaw. "But it was like I couldn't help myself. Olwin made it all seem so good, and that everything he was doing was for the best, for all kinds, man and animal."

"That's the way of it, when you're dealing with those that have those powers," said Bramble. "Look at all the things he did. Food out of nowhere, and all those beds in the sleeping tent, and the way he treated those poor louts from the north. It's no wonder you fell under his spell. He's a very powerful man, and he's out on his own trail, and too bad for those who oppose him."

"He wouldn't let us play with those swords he gave us," complained Cabbage.

"Or talk, or chase each other," pouted Bumble.

"I'm glad I bit him," went on the beaver pup.

"Me, too," agreed Bumble. "And I'm glad we got his old cloak and Granny's sword back."

"We'll ask Old Bark about that cloak, if we ever meet him," said Bramble. "I've never heard of anything like that, but then I'm not much at anything beyond my own lore."

"It seems like we're all getting lessons in everyone's lore," snapped Morley. "Even when we don't want it."

"I can see your point," mulled Stump. "I'm not much on anything outside my own, and sure enough, I find out I was right all along."

"Hush, you wicked thing," scolded Granny. "You've been telling me for years that you felt like life was passing you by, and that you'd always wanted to go with Gruff and Greystone when they took their little journeys, but you'd always had something come up that wouldn't wait."

"Well, I did!" grumbled the mole.

"Now you're off on one of those adventures, and all I hear is mumbling and snorts about it."

"It's not like I thought it would be."

"Nothing ever is, old fellow," laughed Bramble. "And the worst of it is not being able to sit down in front of the fire to talk it all over. But I'm as guilty as you about that always having something else to do when it came time for an adventure, Stump. I remember sitting looking at the lorebook my great grandsires handed down to me, and all those empty pages in the back, wondering if I'd ever have anything to add to them. And I was always more than a little busy when an opportunity would come along to go anywhere outside my old boundaries."

"We lost the lorebook," said Branch sadly. "It was at Granny's when the killer wolves burned her house."

The otter's eyes grew a deeper brown.

"I'd forgotten that. And all the other things we left, too. My snug den, and all the books, and the boat."

"And my kitchen," added Branch.

"My garden and my boat were nicer than any," put in Morley, wistfully.

Granny Badger's eyes glistened.

"I never cared much about all those things, until now, when they're all gone."

"Well, we'll just have to rebuild," snorted Stump. "And you'll just have to rewrite those stories, Bramble. And I daresay you'll have something to add, after all this is over."

"If we get through it all in one piece."

"We will," said Blackpaw. "We're better off than we were, anyway."

"For now. But we're going to have to travel a far piece before I'm going to get rid of this feeling that we're being watched."

"Let's go on," urged Acorn. "We may be standing here jabbering too long. Those louts might have time to find us."

"Where do we make for, Granny?" asked Bramble, turning to the old she-badger.

She studied the ancient markings on the trees a moment more before she spoke.

"We go east until we reach a forked oak. There will be more markings there."

"The sign of the moon," mused Bramble. "That was what Gruff wrote. And look, there it is, Granny. Why, Gruff came this way, with Greystone."

The old badger clasped her paws together.

"He told me I would make this trip one day. I never believed it, though."

"Let's see if we can find the next markings," said Blackpaw, who began to move ahead, toward the thicker inner woods.

"Be careful! Keep close together now. You pups get between us," ordered Bramble.

"I'll go first," said Blackpaw. "You keep up the rear."

And in a line, single file, the animals set off slowly, in the direction that was marked on the ancient tree, the badger in front, and the otter behind.

As they went on, Bramble's hackles raised again, and the feeling he'd had all through the windstorm grew stronger still, until he could almost feel the danger with his paws. All the other animals grew more restless, and the pups began to whine, although they still pressed forward into the darkening shadows of Thorn Wood.

Bramble turned and looked back in the direction they had come, but there was nothing ever there but the slight movement of the underbrush where the companions had brushed it aside in passing. He thought he heard voices once, although when he stopped to try to listen, they were gone.

As they traveled deeper into the shelter of the ancient trees, the light began to dim, and in the end, Bramble saw that Blackpaw was marking their way again by the light thrown from the blade of Erinoult.

They had gone on but a short way when the humming began, faint at first, but growing louder with every passing second.

THE DEPTHS OF THE INNER WOOD

As the sound increased, the very air about them seemed to jump and move, and the trees wavered in the dim light, blurring and becoming no more than gray forms in the trembling wood. The companions stood frozen, unable to move.

A great shudder of the earth rumbled beneath them, then came a clamor of voices, high and urgent, although none of the companions could understand the tongue. It sounded as if they cried warning, to leave the wood. Those voices were replaced by deep groans and murmurs that came from the earth, or the huge, ancient trees.

They strained to hear what was said, but could not, and at length, those voices, too, passed, and a silence so deep and still settled upon the companions that it seemed as if they would never be able to move or speak again. And then the light went, so suddenly, and so completely, that even the blade of Erinoult was cloaked in total darkness.

At this, Branch, Beryl, and Ash let out low squeaks and moans, and the pups cried aloud. They could neither see nor feel the trees about them, and after reaching out his paw to try to find Branch, Bramble had the distinct sensation that he was alone, although he knew the others were all about him.

The murmur of low drums began throbbing in his ears, and then there came the light and cheering music of a flute, much like the one the otter had fashioned for himself from a river rush. The flute was replaced by a softer reed pipe, and the terror he had felt began to lift.

He called out, finding his voice difficult to use.

"Hello! Branch? Bumble? Are you there?"

He had heard something similar when as a pup he had talked underwater. He could almost imagine the words going out from his mouth in big, silver-dark bubbles.

Very faintly, he heard a reply. Concentrating on listening, he could just make out Branch's voice.

"Here! I'm here, with Bumble."

"What's happened?" came Basil, faintly.

"I don't know. Where are the rest?"

"We're here," answered Blackpaw, speaking for the others.

He sounded as if he had called out from a canyon, and a faint echo rang afterward.

"Where is the sword?" asked Bramble. "We need the light."

"It's gone out," came the faint voice of the badger.

"Granny! You take it! See if you can make it work!" cried Morley, who had begun to think unkindly of Blackpaw again.

"I can't see where I'm going. I can't make it work, anyhow. If it's dark with Blackpaw, it'll be dark with me."

"Do you think Gruff and Greystone ran into this?" asked Acorn.

Ash tried to calm her babies, but they complained loudly, which set Bumble and Cabbage off anew.

"I don't want to be in this old wood," cried Cabbage. "I can't see."

"There may be a dragon in here," echoed Bumble, staring as hard as he could about him, and sure he had seen the dreadful eyes of a horrible beast in the darkness beyond.

"Hush, children!" scolded Granny Badger. "Hush, and listen."

The pups fell silent, and the companions all tried to hear whatever it was that Granny had alerted them to. At first, there was nothing but their quick breathing, but after a moment more, a faint tinkle was heard, of a faraway bell ringing. It could have almost been Granny Badger's own doorbell, which had hung by her hole in the old, burned wood.

"It sounds like someone ringing a doorbell, Granny," blurted Morley.

"But whose door?" grumbled Stump. "I'm not so sure I want to go calling in this upside-down place."

The bell came again, only louder.

"Was this all in Gruff's story?" asked Bramble. "I don't remember reading anything about this in my lorebooks."

"All Gruff ever said was that Thorn Wood was strange, and that odd things happened there."

"This is plenty odd enough for me," said Basil. "I'm all for seeing if we can't back out of here, and see where the next trail leads us."

"Could this be one of those traps, Granny? Thorn Wood is supposed to be able to get you lost, or worse," said Beryl nervously.

"It could be," agreed Granny. "Since we don't know what we're looking for, we wouldn't know whether this was a false trail or not."

"Then maybe we'd better go back, like Basil said."

"I don't think we can, Morley," replied Bramble. "How are we going to know which way to go, in all this pitch black?"

"We just turn around and go the opposite direction," answered the muskrat. "It's as simple as that."

And to prove his point, Morley turned around, and paws held out before him, he began slowly to pace backward, in the direction he thought they had come from. After no more than a step or two, he bumped painfully into a tree. Feeling along both sides, he touched only other trees, which formed an unpassable barrier.

"This must be the wrong way," he called, trying to hide his disappointment. "I'll try back here, now. This has to be it."

"You may as well save your breath," soothed Granny. "I don't think we're going anywhere but on."

"Nonsense!" snorted Morley. "We came in, and there has to be a way out."

He had run into another wall of trees, exactly as before.

"Then this must be it," he cried, the panic welling up in his voice.

"Here, here, you knothead!" snapped Stump. "You've stepped all over my paws, and there's no need in getting all worked up about this. Why, it's merely total darkness, in a strange wood, filled up with we don't know what all. What's there in that to have the wind up about? Why, it's only just begun, old fellow."

Stump tried to give Morley a reassuring pat, but the muskrat had forced his way past, and was clawing at another solid wall of trees.

"Just keep your head on your shoulders," cautioned Basil. "We're not going to do any good losing our wits

and stumbling around out here. Granny says the only way
to go is on, so that's what we're going to do."

"I don't want to go on," whined Morley. "I want to
leave here."

"Stop it!" commanded Bramble. "Stop it right this
minute. You're scaring the pups."

"I don't care. I've had all I can take. I've been mauled
by killer wolves, and manhandled, and I don't want to
have any more to do with this."

Blackpaw's voice rose over the noise of the others, all
speaking to the terror-stricken muskrat at once.

"This is no worse than the tunnels of Granny's old
hole. Come on, lad, you were brave enough then. We're
all edgy, and I'm as frightened as you, but we've got to
keep together now, more than ever before. We need your
help. It's your turn to spell Bramble with the sword, anyhow. We're counting on you."

The young badger's voice was even and collected, and
full of confidence.

Bramble felt himself a little less afraid, and thanked the
badger.

"That's what we need. Get ourselves busy, and we
won't have time to worry. Here, Morley. Here's the
sword. You can take my place. Just keep close to us, and
keep ready to move when we do."

Morley reluctantly allowed the otter to press the sword
into his paw.

"I still don't like all this blackness. It isn't like being in
a tunnel. It's worse, because I know there's trees all
around, and it's not night."

"It's Thorn Wood," said Stump. "And that seems to be
about natural for here. Nothing else follows the Law, so
why should the sun be shining in broad daylight? Maybe
when it gets dark here, like our night, we'll be able to go

on about our business in the light of day. That must make
good sense here."

"Granny, do you know which way is the way ahead?"
asked Bramble.

"The only direction that the trees aren't growing," she
said, cautiously easing forward.

"We'd better hold on to each other," said Bramble.

He didn't have to repeat himself, for as soon as he had
finished speaking, each of the companions had felt a little
more secure in holding the paw of their neighbor.

Morley, bringing up the rear, was the least satisfied
with the situation, for he had no one behind him to hold
to. For the briefest of moments, he had felt, or imagined
he had felt, he couldn't tell which, the faintest pressure of
touching something.

"A tree," he assured himself. "It must be one of those
old trees."

Still, it had given him the distinct impression that it had
moved when he had inadvertently held his paw back, forgetting that he was the last in line. He tried to recall exactly what he had been thinking.

"Probably just this state I've worked myself into," he
said, loud enough to draw an answer from Acorn, who
was next in front of him.

"What state, Morley?"

"It's just this not being able to see. I feel like I'm all
closed in."

"Just pretend it's a nice snug hole," advised the squirrel
lightly.

"Hole? I never get this feeling in a hole. And this is all
the worse, because I know we're in the middle of Thorn
Wood."

"Keeping your spirits up, old fellow. As soon as it gets

dark, it'll be light," snorted Stump, stalking along in front of Ash and the babies.

Everyone had calmed down somewhat once they had begun moving forward again.

"I wish we had light enough to read that chart, Granny," said Bramble wistfully. "I'd sure like to see if Gruff said anything about all this business."

"I don't think any of this would be on a chart," replied Granny. "What could you say? How would you put blackness on a map, or what it feels like to be completely blind?"

"Still, they might have said something. And if they followed the sign of the moon, then how did they find it? Their way was marked all through Thorn with that sign."

Granny thought a moment, and wondered at what Bramble had said. It was true that Gruff had made no indication on the chart about the strange night that had engulfed them completely. Fear gripped her heart, almost choking her, then she felt it pass.

"Then this can't go on much longer," she replied. "If they were able to find their trail with their eyes, then so shall we."

The old badger sounded so sure that Blackpaw took her at her word, and began trying to see ahead into the heavy cloak of darkness that covered them.

It was eerie, traveling along through Thorn Wood, knowing there were tall, ancient trees all around, feeling them as they wandered aside from their path, and hearing the noise they made high above, as their unseen limbs swung to and fro in an invisible wind.

Bramble began to notice the smells, and marveled at the almost ageless musk and heavy perfume of the underbrush that he could not see. The trees smelled green, and

294 DRAGON WINTER

dark gray, and it seemed to the otter that there was the faintest scent of fall, of a coming winter.

It wasn't the sort of winter that would be a cold, frozen wasteland, but the mild, crisp times he remembered as a pup, with the soft, gentle snow clinging to his fur, and turning into a thousand dazzling colors as he nosed down a smooth slope onto the ice-covered weir where his holt was. That was the kind of winter where you went to tea with all your friends, and spent short afternoons hiking through the silent winter wood, when the silver-white snow squeaked beneath your paws, and your breath would hang in icy puffs in front of your muzzle.

That was the winter that was on the wind, and Bramble wondered if they had come far enough that the dreaded dragon winter would not be felt so harshly.

He had planned, before the attacks of the killer wolves, to take Branch and Bumble and go beyond the Upper Rambling, in hopes of finding a milder season.

"Do you think we've come far enough to go beyond the dragon winter, Granny?" he asked aloud.

"I don't know, but I smell what you mean. A golden fall, with plenty to eat, and lots of side trips to enjoy."

"I feel that, too," said Basil. "I can remember winters like that. There was cold, and you knew it was winter, but it wasn't so harsh. It was fun to be out."

"I know what you mean," put in Acorn. "Why, on winters like that, I don't stay in much at all. Up and out, and having lots of fun. And there'll always be something to eat about, whether you've stored up for winter or not."

The companions' spirits had lightened somewhat, talking about the more pleasant things of their memories, and smelling the soft, golden fall only helped to ease their fears.

Bumble had stopped his whining, and was tramping

along, Olwin's cloak swallowing him up and dragging along behind him, causing Cabbage constantly to stumble and complain.

"Stop it, you two!" warned Branch.

"He's wearing that old cloak, and I keep walking on it," pouted Cabbage. "He's making me fall down."

Branch was on the verge of scolding Bumble, when the brilliant flashes of lights exploded all about them, and a final, tremendous clap of thunder deafened them, knocking them senseless to the floor of the forest.

MEETINGS

Stunned and frightened, the companions glanced wildly about, half-blinded by the brilliant light. Woods, tall and green, with the golden mantle of warm sunshine, stretched away in all directions, under a pale blue sky, filled with floating white clouds. Crickets burred away in the berry thickets nearby, and the call of birds echoed back from every quarter.

Bramble, his eyes beginning to adjust, looked back in the direction they had come from, or that he thought he could remember them coming from, and discovered that there was no hint of the darkness there, except for one small space between two huge giants that reached upward toward the arms of the blue sky. Just discernible there was a darker shadow than the rest, and the slit between the two trees seemed to mark some sort of arch, for in the rest of the forest, although filled with majestic elm, and ash, and oak, there were none near as large.

The otter blinked and stared about him, his ears still ringing, and flashes drifting before his eyes.

A soft, bubbling brook ran cheerfully nearby, straight through a small clearing, and bright flowers of blue, red, and yellow grew on both sides. There was even a deep, still weir in the backwater of the stream, which ran to the very eaves of the wood.

"Where are we?" stammered Basil, trying to get his bearings.

"I don't know, but at least it's light," replied Morley. "I never heard tell of anything like all these goings-on. First you can't see your paw in front of you, and then you get so much light you can hardly open your eyes."

Stump snorted.

"What did I tell you? Probably just got dark in Thorn. Only this is what dark looks like."

"There's the door we came through," said Bramble.

"I can see it, too," said Acorn.

"Granny, are you all right?" asked Branch, helping the old badger to stand.

"Goodness, but that was a start! I think I'm all of a piece."

Blackpaw had paced a few steps toward the stream.

"It looks like sweet water. Just in time, too."

"Where's Cabbage?" asked Beryl. "And Bumble?"

"I've got my babies here," answered Ash. "Stump was in front of me, and then I think Bumble and Cabbage."

The companions, regaining their vision and collecting themselves, quickly counted noses, and tried to search out the area, in case the pups had gotten separated from them when they entered the brilliant flashing of the light.

"Branch, did you see Bumble at all before this happened?" asked her mate.

"It was dark, but he was there, I thought. I heard Cabbage complaining about falling over that cloak."

"And then it happened," added Beryl. "I heard those two, going on like they always do, and then the next thing

I knew, we were here, and I couldn't see anything, or hear anything, for a little while."

"They were in front of me," insisted Stump. "Or I think they were. They were fighting about something, as usual."

"Then maybe they're still not through that dark part," suggested Morley. "Maybe we should go back and search."

"That's the only place they could be," agreed Blackpaw.

"Perhaps they're just not through yet," added Ash, echoing the others.

"They are always off somewhere they're not supposed to be," said Branch. "They were playing, and got lost from us when all this light came."

"Then we'd best get back to call them. They're most likely scared by now, if they've found we're gone."

"Come on, Basil. We'll just slip back there into that dark place, and call out. I'm sure they can't be far."

The beaver nodded, and the two friends started out toward the odd-shaped dark shadow that appeared between the two huge trees. As they approached, they could see that the darkness began there, but didn't go on either side of the trees. It was like a long, dark tunnel between two lights.

"Look at that," mused Basil. "This hole only goes between here."

He walked around the side of one of the huge trunks, and looked behind it.

Bramble had gone around the other way, and they met behind, and looked out over the same small clearing, onto the stream and brilliant warm sunshine.

"Can you see us?" called Basil to the others.

All the animals chorused an answer.

"Be careful!" cautioned Branch. "We don't want to get everyone separated."

Bramble had stepped back in front of the two enormous trees. There before him in the place where only the forest behind should have been was a gaping black hole that ran from the ground all the way up as high as the otter could see.

"Maybe we'd better ask Granny about this," he said at last, after thinking to himself a few moments.

"The pups are in there," said Basil stubbornly.

"We don't know that, and I'm not sure what we're dealing with here."

Granny and Blackpaw crossed the clearing and joined them.

"Here's the chart. Let's see what Gruff and Greystone found out about these strange goings-on, or if they found them at all."

The old badger carefully laid out the worn chart, and Blackpaw laid the sword of Erinoult down on one edge to hold it, and they all knelt on the sweet-smelling grass to study the map.

"I can't make anything out of this that would be anything like what we went through," said Granny at last.

"Neither can I," agreed Blackpaw, his brows furrowed into a worried frown.

The others had come to stand beside them, each peering carefully at the old chart.

"Well, it certainly won't tell us where Bumble and Cabbage have gotten to," said Beryl. "And if no one else is going in there to look for them, I will."

She tried hard to keep her fear from overcoming her, but her voice broke, and she was near tears.

"We'll find them, don't you worry," assured Morley. "They can't have gotten away far."

"We're going," said Bramble. "I just wanted to make sure there wasn't something we might be able to find on the map that would tell us where we are, or where this door leads."

"It's dark there," said Blackpaw, staring into the strange gloom.

"I can hardly see how it is," agreed Basil. "It's so bright here, and yet you can't see anything there."

Stump had edged closer to the dark hole's entrance.

"Why, you can see a little," he cried. "I think I can make out trees there."

All the companions rushed forward, and stared into the strange doorway.

"You can see outlines, I think. It's like looking at something under a full moon, only darker."

"Come on," said Bramble. "Let's see if we can get the pups. They must be wondering where we are."

Bramble took a deep breath and stepped forward, followed closely by Basil. They had hardly moved more than a paw's length, but the sun was suddenly gone, and a great roaring filled their ears.

After the thundering noise had diminished, and Bramble's eyes became accustomed to the dark again, he turned to his friend.

"Look! I can see Granny and Blackpaw back there. And Branch, too."

"There's Beryl," said the beaver. "But they look all funny."

"Its like looking at someone through water," went on Bramble. "It looks dark there, from here."

"But it isn't."

"No, we know that. But if you were walking along on this side, you'd hardly notice, because everything looks dark."

"I wonder what all that noise is when you go through?" asked Basil. "I thought my ears were going to pop."

"I don't know. It must have something to do with Thorn or all the other strange things we've found here."

"Well, let's hurry up and find those two wanderers. I don't like it here on this side."

"Neither do I," said Bramble, shivering, and trying to remember how the warm sun had felt on his fur a few moments before.

"Cabbage! Bumble!" cried Basil loudly, raising his voice so that it would carry a great way in the dark wood.

Bramble called out, trying to keep the worry from his voice, so it wouldn't frighten the pups.

"Let's don't lose sight of that place," warned Basil, suddenly turning around. "I don't want to wander too far in here and lose the place we came in."

Bramble stopped.

"Maybe one of us should stay here, and keep calling out, and one of us can look."

Basil was sure he had been staring straight at the strange door that separated the two parts of the wood, but now he could see nothing but the dark shadow of the trees.

"Look!" he cried, grasping the otter's paw.

They ran back toward where they had come from, and the terror only lifted when very dimly, through the outer blackness that hung heavily about them, they saw the door once more.

"I thought it had gone," breathed Basil heavily, relieved.

"I did, too. No wonder the pups could have gotten off without us. That door is easy to miss, unless you're right on it."

"It's not easy to miss going through," replied the beaver. "You sure know it when you're in it."

"Where can they have gotten to?" asked Bramble, lifting his nose to see if he could detect any traces of the two lost pups.

It was difficult, for the smell of Thorn Wood was heavy and oppressive, and his nose kept picking up ancient tree smells and bitter-smelling rot from the underbrush, and it was all hidden beneath a heavy scent of a place that had not seen sunlight for a great many years.

"No wonder all the animals live on the other side," said Bramble aloud. "This is most depressing."

"It gets darker there," said Basil, pointing in front of them, where a deeper gloom began.

"I wonder why we didn't see this place before we walked into it?"

"Probably too sudden a change. All that darkness. You can't see it, unless you're looking for it. Why, we just stepped through it a few paces, and thought we'd lost it."

Bramble shook his head before he went on.

"But I can't figure where the pups would have gotten to. Surely they wouldn't have gone off by themselves."

The beaver turned quickly.

"Is it possible that Olwin or some of those killer wolves could have followed us through the dark?"

Bramble's heart turned to ice inside him.

"I'd put them out of my mind. I don't see how they could have kept up with us. And I don't think they would have kept quiet if they had been with us when the light disappeared."

"Olwin could have," replied the beaver.

"Olwin did!" came a different voice, from behind the startled animals.

They whirled, and were face to face once more with the cloaked figure of the red-bearded man.

He smiled wickedly.

"So we meet again, do we? And such manners. You haven't even greeted the True King."

"You!" chorused the two friends. "Where are the pups?"

"Ah, you notice that I have recovered my lost property. Yes, indeed, those two whelps gave me a hard time of it, and the nasty lads thought they'd finish me by stealing my cloak."

Olwin threw back his head and gave a dark laugh.

"Just like you silly beasts, believing everything that's said. Your precious whelp heard me talk about my cloak of power, and he thought I meant the cloak I wore. But that's neither here nor there, now. What matters is that I have your two brats safe, and I am on the verge of my greatest triumph of all."

"Give us the pups," said Bramble grimly. "We want no more to do with you. You have your doorway. You can settle your own accounts with Old Bark without us. All we ask is to be left alone, to find our own way to a peaceful settlement."

Olwin laughed harshly.

"Is that all you wish, Master Otter? It seems as if you are forgetting one thing of importance here. You haven't knelt to honor the True King. Nor said you were sorry for trying to oppose him."

Bramble's hackles rose, and his tiny paws clamped shut, but he knew he must do what the man asked.

"We'd better do it," whispered Basil. "He has the pups."

"We're sorry, sire," blurted Bramble, feeling the words acrid and bitter in his mouth.

"Now kneel!" ordered Olwin. "And stay there until I tell you to rise again."

The two friends did as they were ordered, and as they knelt, they heard the cries of Bumble and Cabbage. Basil prepared to raise himself, but was called down by the man.

"No further! If you value the worthless lives of these cursed whelps of yours, you'll do exactly as I say."

Basil collapsed back down, as Olwin went on.

"Now, you two, hear me well! Get up and turn around. You lead me to the door you entered, and say nothing when you reach the light. Just say you found the pups, if they ask, and that they're following you."

The companions nodded that they understood.

"Now move!"

They heard the soft whimpers of the two pups behind them, but forced themselves to go on. They marched silently into the darkness, until once more, without realizing it, they had entered the roaring of the thunder, and were standing beyond the shadow of Thorn, blinking in the sunlight, directly into the worried faces of their friends.

And there was another face there, unfamiliar, but kindly, smiling gently at them.

OLWIN TAKES CONTROL

Bramble could not tell if the light were brighter than it had been before, but it seemed that it were so. Basil simply bowed solemnly, and stood staring.

The others were all in a ring about the dignified silver form of the ancient bear.

"Old Bark," whispered Bramble at last, and felt the tears welling up inside him.

Basil started to blurt out that Olwin was following behind them, and that he held the pups prisoner, but before he could speak, Old Bark nodded.

"I know. We are soon to meet Master Olwin. He has long desired such a moment as this."

The bear's voice was deep and mellow, and warm to hear. All the fear began to melt from the animals' hearts.

"But what are we to do?" asked Branch.

"We are to do as he asks," replied Old Bark.

"You mean you'll just do whatever he says?" shot Morley. "What if it's something bad?"

"It is certain to be something disagreeable," nodded the bear. "But it will turn out right, in the end. We have had

307

many disagreements, Olwin and I, and the years have grown long since we have met eye to eye."

"He can make himself a stag," warned Stump. "And a big one, too."

"Not as big as you, though," said Morley. "Nothing is as big as you."

The muskrat stood gazing up at the ancient figure of the bear.

"I think there may be some things as big as I am," said Old Bark softly. "The Great One puts all things in their order, from the least to the most, and sometimes it is the smallest of all that turns out to be the most important. Size is but a fancy, and never says much about the real inside."

"What are we going to do?" moaned Beryl. "He's got the pups, and I know he's an evil man. Now we can't get away from him."

Old Bark shook his great head.

"No, we won't be able to escape him now. His hour is come, as it has often come in the past. There will be a reckoning, as there always must."

"Will you slay him?" asked Ash, holding her tiny babies to her side, although they both were struggling to reach out for the massive silver bulk of the bear.

"Slay Olwin?"

Old Bark raised a great paw, and patted the squirrel, laughing.

"That would make a fine mess of things."

He laughed again, softly to himself, then grew serious.

"No, I don't think we shall slay Olwin. It is not meant to be, and he is carrying out his purpose, dark as it is, beyond Thorn Wood."

"He wants to have your realms, too!" blurted out Stump.

"So indeed he does. Yes, I think he does want these realms, and all that are here."

"And he wants your cloak," added Basil. "The pups said so."

"He will ask for that," agreed Old Bark. "And he shall have it."

"You mean you'll just give up? And let him have everything?" cried Branch.

Granny, who had remained silent, spoke up at last.

"I think I begin to understand you. You fight by not fighting at all."

Old Bark turned.

"It's something like that. You could see it that way, yes."

He smiled again at the old badger.

"I think I have had the pleasure of spending an evening fire or two with your mate, once. A very wise fellow, who went by the name of Gruff, if I'm not mistaken."

Granny's eyes filled.

"He spoke so highly of you, when I could get anything out of him at all. He was always so secretive."

Old Bark laughed again, a deep, clear sound that made the animals feel wonderfully good.

"Secretive, was he? Yes, I imagine it would be difficult to explain about how things are here. Not much you could say about it to someone who has never set foot in Thorn Wood, or beyond."

Bramble remembered Olwin and the pups.

"But what are we to do? He has Bumble and Cabbage. And he's got killer wolves with him, somewhere."

Old Bark's brow furrowed.

"He still has that lot, does he? Poor beasts, caught up in a thing more terrible than their own north."

"You sound as if you're sorry for them," said Basil.

"They've certainly given us a fright or two, and more than one close call."

"No doubt. But they were never meant to be freed from the northland until they had gone through their lessons there. After a few times in that climate, one loses all desire to be savage and cruel. But Olwin has made them fear him, and unleashed them from their boundaries, and set them loose for his own designs."

"What does he want?" asked Blackpaw. "He very nearly drew me into his plans, but aside from vague hints about Thorn, I could never find out what it was exactly that he wanted."

"Oh, I expect he can draw almost anyone in. I wouldn't be too much upset by that, if I were you. Olwin is very clever, and very powerful. He can see what weakness you have, and play up to that, and the next thing you know, you'll be fallen right in with him."

The badger squirmed uneasily.

"That's what happened to me. I guess he knew somehow that I had been exiled from my clan."

All the animals turned to the fidgeting badger.

"You've been exiled?" asked Basil.

"No wonder you were coming to find us," blurted Morley.

"But that's all past. I had vied for the leadership of my clan and lost. They thought in order for the wound to heal more quickly that I should leave them for a turning. I can go back anytime."

"No need now," said Granny softly. "You've found yourself a new clan."

"And I don't think you'll find yourself going back, after all," said Old Bark. "Once the lesson is learned by heart, you go on."

A great rushing noise, like a terrible wind over the tops

of trees, came, and a deep, thundering rumble shook the ground where the animals stood. Great swirls of white mist, exploded by brilliant flashes of light, erupted, and in the next instant, Olwin, clutching the two pups by the scruffs of their necks, appeared.

"Welcome, brother," said Old Bark courteously, as Olwin's eyes adjusted to the brightness.

The man looked paler in the broad sunlight, and not so large as he had seemed before. His red cloak had faded to a dim reddish hue.

"Welcome yourself," snapped the man.

"It's been a few turnings since we've had a chance to chat," went on Old Bark, ignoring Olwin's rudeness.

"Only because you made it so. Blocking up Thorn was a rotten deed."

"You were hasty in your actions, Olwin, and those wolves had no business beyond their proper boundaries."

"They have evened the struggle. And now they wait for all the lands beyond Thorn."

"They shall have a long wait, then. They should be sent back to the north, where they belong. They are causing an imbalance, running loose as they are."

"Oh, that would be fine, would it? Send the wolves back where they belong, and just be nice fellows? And then, I suppose, you'll ask me to give up my plans, and go back to where I should be, at my lessons?"

The bear nodded.

"You know my feelings very well, Olwin."

"Then you shall be disappointed. I have no intention of being tricked by you this time. You have done that often enough in the past. You never told me you could do that bear form. I only found out about that from these miserable beasts."

"You never asked if I could," replied Old Bark.

"There is no need now, for I am going to be rid of you once and for all. Then I shall have Thorn, and all beyond, to myself."

Bumble and Cabbage were whining and wriggling painfully in the man's harsh grasp.

"Give us the pups," said Bramble. "We'll do what you want."

"Oh, no doubt, Master Otter. You can say anything long enough to get your precious whelp back. It's another thing altogether, later. It's then you begin to plot and scheme against the True King."

"The True King is where He should be," said Old Bark evenly. "You will break yourself, trying to fill His shoes, Olwin."

"Liar!" shot the man, advancing a step, holding the pups out before him.

"Do you want these miserable brats back safe?" he asked, a thin dagger of a smile crossing his face.

Old Bark looked straight into Olwin's eyes, but did not answer.

"I know you can't allow anything to die. I know you too well, you soft, meddling fool. You won't refuse me my demand. You have no heart for a fair fight."

"I have no desire to do that," agreed Old Bark. "That is not my place in the scheme of things. It has been at one time, but no longer."

The animals grew restless, and Beryl and Branch wept openly as they saw their struggling pups turn and twist in the cruel hands of the man.

"What is it you wish, Olwin? And remember, our differences have nothing to do with these animals. Give me your word that they will not suffer harm from you if I agree to your terms."

Olwin turned to the companions.

"You see your precious Old Bark?" he sneered. "A lot of good he is doing you now. Look at him! Did you hear? 'Promise me you won't harm them if I agree to your terms.' And to think you went to all this trouble to find this miserable coward to protect you."

Olwin spat in the dirt at Old Bark's feet.

"I would ask you to change to your man form, but I would rather see you like this."

"Don't let him harm the pups," cried Beryl. "Do something!"

"He can't do anything, you waterslime. He has only been able to defeat me in the past by trickery. He's never confronted me and faced me down in an even fight. It's always deceit, and sneaking about, and confusing the issue. But this time, it shall be different."

"You can put them down now," said Old Bark softly. "You have my word I shall do whatever you ask."

Olwin threw back his head and gave a short, vicious snarl of laughter.

"No, no, Master Old Bark, none of that today. I shall hang on to my small captives until I have dealt with you once for all. And then I shall see how I feel about these miserable whelps. Perhaps I shall spare them, perhaps not."

"What can we do?" cried Basil, his paws doubled into fists.

Old Bark shook his head, and said under his breath, "You leave this to me. And don't worry. Things aren't always what they seem."

"Yes, yes, go on and reassure those beasts all you want, you gas bag. Build their hopes so they can see you in your true light once we reach our destination."

"And where might that be?" asked Old Bark.

"Where we are going!" snapped Olwin. "Now get all your belongings, all of you, and lead off. You first, Grand Marshal!"

Olwin laughed such a burst of wicked, hounding laughter that Blackpaw moved for the sword of Erinoult. He was beside himself with shame and rage, and he knew the man had said it to tear him apart from his new friends, and he did not quite realize what he was doing, for the sword seemed to leap into his paw, and before he was aware of it, he had gathered himself and lunged at the man, the blade of Erinoult flashing before him.

Olwin leapt back, and held the two helpless pups before him as a shield.

"You will have to slay them first, good Grand Marshal. And I doubt that your friends of late would love you overmuch for that, if they do indeed love you at all."

Blackpaw, raging, got control of himself with difficulty, and lowered the blazing sword. His paw twitched, and his body jumped from the cold fury that poured through him.

"Leave it alone, good badger," said Old Bark. "This is not your work."

"It's all right, Blackpaw," said Bramble. "You can't fight him while he has the pups. Come away."

"Good lad! Stout lad!" shot Stump. "We're behind you! Pay no attention to him."

"See, Grand Marshal? You have won their affection, just as I told you you would if you did everything I said and followed my plans as I laid them."

Olwin smiled savagely.

"Now be so kind as to hand me my sword!"

Blackpaw stood glowering, then flung the blade carelessly at Olwin.

"What? Surely you have told your new friends all?" said the man, retrieving his lost prize.

"Go on with your gibberish," shot Morley. "You have the upper hand now, but we'll wait."

Olwin's face hardened.

"How about this?" he called, and lifted Bumble out before him, spinning him around.

He placed the other pup on the ground; a cage appeared, and the struggling animal was forced into it.

Then, with his free hand, he held the sword to Bumble's warm throat.

"Now you will tell me you're nothing but a vicious beast, and you are sorry for going against me. Swear me allegiance, and the pup shall live. All of you! Everyone, now! Swear that you shall serve me, and me alone, until you have no breath left!"

The companions muttered and stammered through the man's request.

"Now, once more! All together!" Olwin said. "And let me hear you, Old Bark!"

The huge bear did as he was ordered, and at last the man put Bumble into the cage with Cabbage.

"And now we go to witness your last and most daring performance of all," sneered Olwin.

"Where are you taking us?" demanded Bramble.

"To the Falls," replied Olwin. "We are going to see how well our friend swims."

Olwin's dark, savage laughter filled the animals with dread, and they watched with horror as Olwin prodded the great silver bear with his foot, and turned him in the direction away from Thorn Wood.

They hardly spoke as they plodded along hopelessly, toward a rising bluff, tree-covered, and strewn with huge rocks. Beyond that, they could see a vast green expanse, where the trees and rocks gave way to green lawn.

And then they heard the terrible roar of water, tumbling and falling from a great height, to land with deafening thunder on rocks far below.

THE FALLS

On the seemingly endless journey from the small clearing where they had come into the light, and met Old Bark, to the Falls, which was heard growing louder as they neared it, the animals despaired, and their hearts ached to see the magnificent silver bear cuffed and cursed by Olwin. Nor did it gladden their hearts to hear the pitiful cries of Cabbage and Bumble, carted along roughly in the cage slung over Olwin's back.

Bramble's spirit was cloaked in a nagging dread, and he had to force himself to keep putting one paw in front of the other. His mate followed him, sobbing softly into her paws, and behind her came Beryl, openly tearful, and darting long gazes at the bear and the cage on Olwin's back. Stump was silent, which was unusual, but the mole didn't feel like speaking, for he had begun to lose any hopes that they would ever escape this man or be free again.

Olwin turned to Granny as they trudged along.

"Does this not please you, old one? You are here in your precious forest, and here is that rogue bear of yours, tame as you please, not giving anyone any trouble. Did I

317

not say to you but a day or two past that I would soon
have Old Bark's claws pulled? And that I would make
him pay dearly for all the grief and mischief he has done
me?"

The man reached out a toe of his boot and kicked the
bear.

"Now we shall see the proper end of it. And you shall
all witness the fate of those who stand in the way of the
True King."

"There is always time to change your mind, Olwin,"
said the bear, his voice steady.

Bramble marveled that the huge animal had so much
self-control in the face of such circumstances.

Olwin laughed harshly.

"It's that way, is it? Here you stand, all your defenses
breached, and I am in control, yet you would offer me
terms?"

Olwin's red beard turned a deeper shade, and bobbed
as he bent, laughing.

"There is the Law," reminded Old Bark, a little more
sternly.

"Law? It is only for the weak."

"It is for every living thing, brother. You have broken
it over and again, but there is forgiveness for even that, if
you but ask it."

"Ask forgiveness for winning? Never, you thick-headed
beast! This is the way of the order of things. *I* am the
Law!"

The bear nodded solemnly.

"You are in truth a part of it," he agreed. "But we all
must yield willingly to it, or we become separated, and
lost."

"You are lost from your wit, if you think I am about

to turn you free, after all this time I've spent trying to fashion an attack that would carry me here."

Olwin shook his head rapidly.

"No, no, my friend, you are much mistaken if you think I shall give up so hard won an advantage."

"You need no force to stay here, Olwin. All creatures, no matter where they've come from, or what they've done, are welcome. That is also the Law."

"You speak of it as if you wrote it! But I have no dealings with it, for it is not mine. I make my own code, and follow it."

"We are allowed to do that," nodded the bear. "For it is that way that we find it is, after all, no good. It grows lonely there, all alone."

"What would you know of that?" sneered Olwin. "You have managed to sit here like a crown prince, enjoying the weather, and eating only the most choice of morsels that your subjects have brought you. I am the one who has suffered from this pact. I am the one that roams half-starved among all the rabble of mankind and half the beasts of the world, with no place to turn to, no home to call my own. It is small wonder I have sought so long to oust you from these parts, so that I may enjoy my leisure after so much trial."

"You are welcome to stay, as always, Olwin. It was not I who exiled you from these realms."

"Where are we?" asked Bramble, after having listened for a good while.

"Thorn Wood," replied Old Bark. "On our way to the Falls."

"But you're talking about it as if we were somewhere else," said Morley, shyly. "Somewhere that's special."

"It is someplace like that," nodded the bear.

"Now you can see why I've been so long in storming

these realms," boomed Olwin. "All the best of everything
is here. I'm tired of the scraps and leftovers I've been
given until now."

"You can have all you ask for," said Old Bark. "All
that is necessary is that you ask."

"I don't ask boons of anyone!" ranted Olwin. "I take
what I want. I have no stomach for the likes of you! Take
what you want, that's my thought! There are ways to get
anything, if you have the wit and courage to find it."

"Why do you two want to fight?" asked Basil. "Didn't
you hear Old Bark? He said you're welcome to stay here.
No one is trying to stop you. There's no need to create all
this fuss."

"I've heard all of it before," snapped Olwin. "Oh, I'm
welcome here, all right, as long as I do things *his* way,
and not change anything, or alter any of the rules. But I
have my own ideas about how I want to behave, and I
want no interference from this one, or any of his other
meddling friends."

Olwin prodded Old Bark on with the sword of Erinoult.

"Once he has gone, there will be no one left to stop me
or stand in my way."

"I am not the one who stands in your way, Olwin,"
said Old Bark evenly. "You know that."

"But you'll be the first to go. You have given me
enough trouble in the past."

"It was not I," insisted the bear. "You bring on your
own troubles."

"There would be no trouble if you were out of the
way."

"There is still the Law, Olwin. I have been given
Thorn Wood, and the Falls, and beyond to keep, just as

you have been given those realms on the other side of the Boundaries."

"There's nothing left there," grumbled the mole. "There's no wonder he's so anxious to move in here."

"Hush, Stump!" warned Granny.

Olwin whirled and lashed the small animal viciously across his back, sending him sprawling.

Olwin's face was an ugly mask.

"I am very lenient with you, earth scum! I will have plans for you later. My allies from the northlands haven't had their proper breakfast yet, and I'm saving them a treat they dearly love. You'll do nicely for the first course, as soon as I've dealt with this meddlesome traitor."

Basil and Acorn helped the stunned mole up.

A strange change came across Old Bark's broad muzzle, and his eyes grew a fiery red for a moment, but he remained where he stood, and said nothing. Something in the way the bear had looked for that brief instant gave Bramble new hope.

Olwin kicked Old Bark again, and the companions followed on, Stump between Acorn and Basil, who helped him limp along.

The noise of the Falls had grown louder still, and as the small band of friends crossed the low brow of an oak-covered hill, they came into full view of a vast clearing that was all a deep green lawn, with flowers of all colors laced through it. And beyond the edge of the grass, where it ran down to blue sky abruptly, the full force of the noise from the cascading water was heard.

It sounded to Bramble like the noise they had heard when they had come through the darkness of the wood into the brilliant sunlight on the other side. It was difficult to hear with the constant roar, and a fine, white mist rose in swirling, rainbow motions from the tumult below, and hung near where the cliff rose up from the raging pools.

Olwin was shouting something to Old Bark that Bramble didn't hear, and as he did so, he thrust the wooden cage that held the two pups out in front of him. The man walked briskly toward the ledge, the cage resting dangerously near the drop. Old Bark shook his head, and made a reply, but hesitated a moment to turn to the companions.

Suddenly the horror of what Olwin had planned swept over the friends, and they all wept, and raced to the side of the great silver bear.

He stood silently, his coat covered in tiny droplets of water that reflected back the sun, making him appear to be all light.

"Here, here, this will never do!" he called above the roar.

"We don't want to lose you," cried Branch, tears streaming down her muzzle.

"You can't leave us. What'll we do without you? We're no match for Olwin," said Basil.

"Olwin can't defeat you," replied the bear. "Even with all the power he has, he can't overcome your goodness."

"He has the pups! And he's going to make you jump into that," called Basil, pointing.

Old Bark looked toward the white mist shroud that hung above the thunder of the raging water.

"That's nothing. Olwin doesn't know about the Falls, or he certainly wouldn't be going to make me jump there. And we'll have your pups safe. You must trust me. No matter what you think, or what happens, just remember that it will all turn out right in the end. Keep saying that over to yourselves. Believe me."

Something in the bear's manner calmed the animals,

and although they still hung back in terror as he plodded toward Olwin, they repeated to themselves over and over what Old Bark had said.

As the bear neared Olwin, the man shouted out, his eyes shining.

"I have defeated you at last, traitor! You are in my hands now, and I shall confess to you, your fate is going to be short and painless. It could have been otherwise, but I am a fair man, even to my enemies."

"You have not defeated me, brother. I have not fought you."

Olwin's face reddened.

"You have fought me every step of the way," he shrieked. "I have never been free of you. You were responsible for the defeats my armies suffered when I sent them against you in Thorn Wood, but I have accomplished alone what even they could not do."

"Your armies defeated themselves," said Old Bark. "I have nothing to do with your armies."

"You caused the wood to do all its vile tricks! There is no need to try to whine and plead your innocence, you miserable wretch. You know your guilt as well as I."

"I have no guilt where you are concerned, brother, for I have not lifted my hand to you, now or ever."

"Then who has been responsible? Answer me that, before I send you to your well-earned end."

"The True King."

"*I* am the True King!" shrieked Olwin. "*I* am!"

His face had gone livid, and his eyes started from his head.

Bramble, horror-struck, and unable to hear what was being said, only saw his pup dangled dangerously close to the edge of the drop that ended in the raging torrent below.

"You fiend!" screamed Olwin. "Now you shall feel my wrath!"

The man advanced toward Old Bark, and in the process dropped the cage to the ground.

Olwin brandished the darkened sword of Erinoult, and threatened Old Bark with it, forcing the bear backward, toward the ledge.

"Be gone!" cried Olwin, lunging.

Old Bark, smiling, stepped back over the drop, and disappeared from sight. The animals, frozen where they stood, watched in horror as the bear vanished into the roaring tide.

Olwin had turned, his face that of one possessed.

"Now," he shouted, "I am True King! I am the ruler of Thorn!"

Bramble had gathered himself for a spring, and was on the verge of leaping forward when a ghostly gray shape appeared from nowhere and flew directly at Olwin.

"Bumble!" cried Branch, darting forward.

The pups, frightened senseless, and silent until the moment Old Bark had gone over the cliff, began to cry out.

FEATHERS ON A BREEZE

Suddenly alone on the green lawn above the dreadful roar of the raging water, the companions bolted to the terrible ledge, and freed the hysterical pups.

As Branch fumbled with the latch on the cage, Bramble crept near the sheer drop-off, and poked his nose carefully over, so that he could see the crashing river far below, and the huge whirlpools and torrents that churned ceaselessly and sent up the white spray that wet the grass on the cliffside high above. He trembled inwardly, for there was no way either animal or man could fall into that watery caldron and hope to survive.

He shook his head, as Blackpaw and Stump crept near him to peer over the ledge.

"Is there any way he could have gotten away?" shouted Stump, although he winced when he saw the rushing white flood.

"What happened to Olwin? Did something attack him?" asked Acorn, who had joined them.

"It was the big wolf, in the cave of Erinoult," answered Bramble. "I'd thought more than once that I'd seen him. He was the largest of them all, and I think their leader."

"He sent Olwin over the side," breathed Morley, his voice full of wonder. "I wonder why? He was an ally of the man."

"Perhaps. But it may have been vengeance for the treatment Olwin had given the wolves." Blackpaw fell silent, thinking, before he went on. "I remember that Olwin said the leader of the killer wolves bore him no great good will. He was thought to be dead, according to Olwin."

"Maybe after the battle in the tunnels!" suggested Acorn. "Maybe the wolf didn't ever go back to Olwin after that."

"There was never any wolf that large around Olwin's camp. That could be the answer," said the badger.

"But it doesn't answer what has happened to Old Bark, or what we're going to do now."

Bramble shook his head sadly, tears filling his eyes.

Granny, who had come and stood gazing over the roaring falls below, turned to the others.

"The pups are safe, and we no longer need fear Olwin or his armies. That is a beginning."

"We just found Old Bark. I hate to have lost him so soon," cried Basil.

"I begin to see why Gruff was never able to talk much about here, or Old Bark," went on Granny. "It's difficult to say how you feel."

Bumble, after much effort, had managed to free himself from his mother's hugs.

"Is that old wolf gone?"

"And Olwin?" shot Cabbage, his curiosity overcoming his fear.

Beryl squeezed the young beaver.

"You don't have to be afraid of them anymore," she

said, although her eyes, too, were filled with glistening tears.

She turned away from the ledge where the great silver bear had gone over.

"I don't want to look at it anymore. It's frightening, and it reminds me of him."

"I know," said Bramble. "I was thinking the same thing. I had always dreamed about what it would be like to see the places that were in my lorebooks. The Falls, and all the other places that were mentioned, always seemed like magic, and I would try to think what they would be like." The otter smiled sadly. "I never thought that it would be like this, or that we'd get to meet Old Bark just long enough to lose him."

"Shouldn't we at least try to find a way down, so we can search?" asked Blackpaw, gazing hopelessly at the wild river.

Stump nodded.

"I think we may as well do that. There's no sense hanging about here any longer. And we may find a camp we can use somewhere there, or a place to settle down, until we think of what we're going to do now."

"At least we only have to worry about finding shelter and food," added Acorn. "No more killer wolves or humans."

Basil wrinkled his whiskers and frowned.

"That seems almost too easy, after all we've been through."

"How long has it been?" asked Morley, trying to remember back to the afternoon he had been invited to tea at Granny Badger's house, to have a meeting on the problem of what should be done about the oncoming winter.

Beryl's eyes widened.

"You know, I've forgotten entirely what my own kitchen looked like. I can't tell you if the curtains were yellow or blue, or what color the table was."

Branch tried to concentrate, and her eyes grew gray-brown with the effort.

"I think there was a small table near the window," she mused aloud. "Or was it the other way around? A small window? I think there was a reed mat on the floor, and we had green and yellow teacups."

"Blue!" insisted Bumble. "They were blue, and there was a place by the hearth where I could roast nuts when it got cold."

The old badger laughed softly.

"You know, I can remember what happened when I was just weaned, but I'm getting bad about what happened yesterday."

"Maybe that's best of all, Granny," said Basil. "I don't care to remember much of what happened these past few days, either."

"Is that all it's been?" asked Bramble. "I guess it just seems a long time."

"We only left Granny's, and then it all really started," agreed Morley. "First the wolves, and then the man armies, and then Olwin."

"And then Old Bark," said Blackpaw. "Only we never really got to know him at all."

"At least we got to see him. And I know for certain now that it wasn't him who had anything to do with those strange killings that everyone was always saying he did."

"Never!" shot Branch. "Didn't you see him? Those deer and the poor muskrats must have been attacked by the killer wolves. They must have been there for a long time before they got around to our settlement."

"And Olwin did it. That makes sense, when you think

of it. No one had seen anything of the killer wolves for a long, long time, until he set them free from their boundaries. And I guess he gathered those armies of mankind, too, to try to get into Thorn."

Bramble looked over the great heads of the ancient trees that stretched away below them, beyond the white mist cloud of the river and falls.

"It still seems like a shame, though," said Beryl. "All our old wood gone, and our homes. And all those other creatures, too, that lived there."

"It certainly doesn't take mankind long to stir up a fine brew of mischief," grumbled the mole. "Olwin has done his fair share there."

"And after all that, he ended up at the bottom of this for his trouble," said Morley, gazing fearfully over the edge that dropped away into the thundering water.

"And brought down by the very ones he had used to butcher all the others," said Basil.

Blackpaw paced about on the green lawn, and finally sat down heavily.

"I don't know why I should feel sorry for him, but I do," he said. "And the killer wolf, too."

"Those are strange feelings, indeed," said Bramble, "but I feel the same. I know Olwin was not the best of sorts, and he was going to use Bumble and Cabbage to get his own ends, and he even made Old Bark jump."

Bramble suddenly fell silent.

"But did he?" he went on at last. "I had the feeling that Old Bark wasn't afraid of Olwin, or what he might do."

"Whatever, Old Bark is gone," snapped Stump gloomily. "Nothing could live through that, no matter how good or kind he was, or how good a swimmer. I don't think

even *you* could get through that safely, Bramble, and
you're one of the best swimmers of all."

The otter nodded.

"Yet he seemed to be trying to tell us something. I
have the feeling that maybe he did come through it in a
piece."

Blackpaw shook his head.

"I'd like to believe that, more than anything, but there's
no sense in putting a fancy hope in our heads where there
is no cause. I'm sure we all feel that, but it won't bring
Old Bark back."

"You may be right," agreed Morley, "but I still want to
go on hoping that maybe we'll be able to find him if we
search the river, up and down."

"We'll have to find a way to get there, first," said
Acorn, shading his eyes and looking across the vast, unbroken cliffs.

"It certainly won't do to try to get down here," said
Bramble. "The rocks are wet and slippery, and I'm afraid
we'd all come to the same fate as our friend."

"Maybe if we try farther up," suggested Acorn. "We
haven't seen what lies on beyond this part of the wood.
Those cliffs seem to stretch all the way as far as I can see,
but there is bound to be a back way."

"What do you think, Granny? Do you have any ideas?"

The old badger frowned.

"I have a lot of ideas, but none of them make much
sense. If I had my wits about me, I'd join Old Bark over
the Falls. That would be the easiest way down for my old
bones."

"You'll do no such thing," grumbled Stump. "I won't
stand having to be the oldest one of this little company."

Granny looked long at her friend.

"You old baggage, you're always full of just the right

cheery words to say, aren't you? Well, you don't have to worry about being the oldster of the party. I'm not jumping yet, although my poor paws tell me that would be the kindest."

"There must be some way down," agreed Bramble. "These cliffs have to have a back door. Perhaps we can scout on both sides here, and see which way our path should be."

"Do you think we dare risk the chance of splitting our party?" asked Blackpaw. "Our best safety lies in staying all together. And we do have the babies and ladies to consider."

"You may have a point. I don't really know if we are beyond the reach of more danger or not. I may be overly relieved, knowing that Olwin is gone. There may be more dangerous things yet that we haven't seen."

"Not here," chittered Bumble. "This is Old Bark's realms."

"But Olwin and the killer wolf got in somehow," corrected Basil. "There may be more that got through than those two."

"Do you think there are more killer wolves in Thorn?" asked Ash, holding her babies closer to her.

Bramble looked carefully around him, at the outer eaves of the woods that swayed gently in the warm breeze, and at the deep green darkness within. Aside from his own party, nothing unusual stirred, and a feeling of peace and silence filled his heart.

Yet there was something.

He suddenly came full alert, and stared harder at the dark shadows that the trees cast.

Was there a movement there? He couldn't be sure, but he turned to Stump, and without pointing, or moving too quickly, he spoke.

"Don't look surprised, Stump, but turn around here, and see if you can see anything out there under the largest of that stand of elms. I'm not sure what, if anything, it is, or if there is anything, if it's friendly. I do feel like Bumble, since this is Old Bark's wood, there can't be much to harm us."

The mole casually stretched, got up, and began a leisurely look about him.

"I don't see anything, Bramble, but I have a definite feeling there's something there. Call it my mole nose, if you will. There's something there, and I don't think they mean us any good."

The others looked about themselves, searching for a place of hiding or an avenue of escape. There was nothing but the wide, open lawn, broken by low flowers that grew profusely about the great circle of the clearing. They would have no hopes of gaining the shelter of the trees, and they weren't sure what would be waiting there even if they did break for cover.

Blackpaw sat down heavily, and said grimly, "It seems our backs are to this cliff, then. There's no place for us but here. We'll make a stand as best we may."

"We are poorly armed for that," said Bramble. "But this seems the spot that is chosen for us."

"I wish I had my sword back," chittered Bumble. "That old Olwin never did let me play with it."

"Do you think it's a dragon?" gasped Cabbage, his eyes wide with fear.

"If it is, we'll bite his tail, and see if we can't get his treasure," cried Bumble, darting back and forth at his mother's side.

"I hope he goes away," said Cabbage. "I'm getting hungry."

"Hush, you two. There are no dragons," said Branch,

although she began to doubt herself, looking at the strangely peaceful eave of the wood.

There was a chilly edge of fear that had crept across the companions, and Bramble had made what plans he was able to try to stand as best they could if they were attacked by whatever foe lurked in the concealment of the forest.

He had turned aside to say something further to Stump when a great, chilling cry went up from the part of the wood directly in front of them, turning the animals' blood to ice. Across the open lawn loped a hundred or more gray killer wolves, their great jaws gaping and drooling, revealing their bared, terrible yellow fangs.

"Jump!" cried a voice, very faint, but very distinct, from far below. It was but barely audible over the roar of the falls and the dreadful howling of the advancing killer wolves.

Bramble had barely a glimpse of something silver-white far below.

"Jump! Jump for your lives!" came the voice again.

The otter looked behind him, and saw the wolves were but a single spring away.

"Come on then!" cried Bramble, sweeping up his pup as he leapt.

He caught his breath, and felt himself falling, easily and gently, spinning in midair, and he heard Bumble giggle once. As he spun about, he watched the figures of the others, all floating as gently as a duck's feather on an afternoon breeze.

And then there was a blazing, deafening roar and flash, and a second or two of the sensation of icy water all about him, and then nothing but a soft silence, filled with a steady white glow.

A SNUG STUDY

How long they had been senseless, or how long it had taken them to fall into the icy river, the companions had no way of knowing. It might have been a mere blink of an eye, or yet again, it could have been years passing as they rolled and tumbled, supported by the white mists over the roaring falls.

Bramble was to find later that all the animals had experienced his feeling of well-being and gladness, and a sharp sense of expectancy. And it seemed that all the questions he had been full of disappeared, not so much that they were all answered, but simply because he no longer concerned himself with them. The feeling of gladness was overpowering, and swept aside all fear or dread.

Bumble laughed again, and the others, all around him, echoed that laughter. Even the sudden chill of the water was refreshing, and brought to mind frosty weirs on cheerful winter mornings, where the frozen water caught in the fine sunlight and spun it into spiderwebs of brightness. And then that was what Bramble remembered, those brilliant white flashes of light, like sunshine on fine-powdered snow.

A faraway music was playing, and the otter thought it odd that now that they were falling toward the rushing torrents of the river he could no longer hear the crash and thunder of the water. The music grew louder still, and a low, soft sound of horns being blown was heard, as if some unseen signal were being given upon their arrival.

It was here that Bramble blinked his eyes and looked around him.

He sat on a quiet finger of grass lawn that met a quietly rippling pool. There was no sign of the raging torrents he had seen from above, and the noise of that dreadful fall was gone, replaced by the soft murmur of wind through treetops and the chuckle of the stream that fed the weir. Broad shafts of warm sun beamed through the high tops of the trees, making golden reflections on the clear water, and taking away the last of the chill.

He whirled, getting to his feet, and saw Branch and Bumble come gliding swiftly toward him, through the deep water of the pool. At his side, not far from him, Morley and Stump lay as if napping, their features untroubled, sleeping peacefully in the warm hand of the sun.

The squirrels called Bramble from the broad branch of a stout oak.

"Look, Bramble! No need to store up for winter here!" cried Acorn, holding out a paw and letting a dozen fat acorns fall to the ground.

"And it doesn't smell like winter anymore," added Ash, holding her babies close to her.

Bramble, raising his muzzle to test the air, caught the fresh, new smell of late spring. Nowhere, in any direction, could he pick up any hint of the cold, bleak weariness that had heralded the coming of the dragon winter.

"What's this?" he asked himself, although Granny Badger, who had appeared beside him, answered.

"This is below the Falls, if I'm not too amiss. Even Gruff never came this far, I don't think. If he did, he never mentioned it."

"But what happened? Why aren't we pond bait? I never thought anything could survive the Falls."

"That is what is thought. More of the magic, I suppose. Only those who know dare use the steps of that path."

"I would have sworn we would all have perished," said the otter, shaking his head in disbelief.

"So would anyone think, looking at that horrible place, yet it conceals the fairest places of all."

Bramble knit his brow.

"If Olwin and the killer wolf came over, then they must have been let down as easily as we were. And Old Bark, too!"

Blackpaw, dripping wet, but otherwise in good spirits, came and shook himself off next to the otter.

"Whew!" he cried. "I'm not much of a swimmer, I must admit. Digging and dirt suits my fancy better."

"Well said," snorted a sleepy Stump, arising. "Sensible sort of lad, after all."

"Are we late for tea?" called Morley, his eyes wide open, but still obviously in some pleasant place in a dream.

"Tea! Tea, you laggard fellow, tea you say? How you torture my poor tongue, for want of a taste of it!" lamented Stump. "And a few of Granny's scones wouldn't be too far amiss, if I were to have my druthers."

Bumble had galloped clumsily ashore, and ran wildly about everyone, first one way, then the other. He was soon joined by Cabbage, who seemed to have forgiven him about the tripping he had suffered at stepping on Olwin's cloak.

Branch, breathing hard after a brisk swim, laughed.

"There they are, at it still!"

"Never will be any different," agreed Beryl.

"They must get it from their sires," chuckled Basil. "Bramble and I have been known for a trick or two ourselves."

"Do you suppose this was what Old Bark was talking about, before?" asked Bramble, ignoring the beaver's remark. "He did say not to worry, and that we would have the pups back safely."

"That's right," said Branch.

"And he wasn't worried when he went over the side," chittered Bumble. "I saw him smile. He waved at me."

"Me, too!" echoed Cabbage. "Olwin was being real mean to him, and he tried to stab him with a knife, but Old Bark just smiled, and then he told me not to be afraid."

"And the next thing you know, old Olwin was yelling, and jumping toward Old Bark with Granny's sword. I knew he couldn't hurt him, though. Nothing can hurt Old Bark."

"Not even that old killer wolf that got Olwin."

"What did Old Bark say to you, Bumble?" asked Granny.

"He was standing right there by the cage, and even while Olwin was hollering and jumping around, he bent down and told me not to be afraid, that it was going to be fun."

"Me, too. He told me, too! And he said that he was going to show us a lot of fun things, once we got over the Falls."

"That sounds as if he meant to see us, here, wherever this is," said Basil. "That's all it could mean."

"Is this over the Falls? I guess it must be. But what a ride. I was scared silly when those killer wolves jumped out of the wood, but after we jumped, I wasn't afraid anymore. Not after I saw we weren't falling like I thought we were going to."

"That's how I felt, Branch. It was strange. And I guess we wouldn't have thought of jumping into all that roar if we hadn't been scared into it," said Beryl.

"I hope nothing came along to scare those killer wolves," grumbled the mole. "I'm just beginning to feel good again, without having to worry about ending up in someone's stewpot."

"Speaking of stewpots, I might be ready for a meal," concluded Morley. "I can't remember when I had a decent meal last that didn't come out of a knapsack or off some magician's table."

"Maybe we can find something," said Granny. "There may be berries and nuts here, and if I can find a good spot to build a nice stone oven, I'll be willing to wager I can remember my recipes for blueberry tarts. I think there's enough starter left in my sack to have the makings, and enough to make more, too."

"Why don't we see if we can't find a good place to shelter, and try to rest a bit, and eat, and then we'll set out to find Old Bark," said Bramble. "I know he's here, somewhere."

"We'd best leave a sentry, too," suggested Blackpaw. "Don't forget Olwin and the wolf."

"I'd like nothing better," snapped Stump. "But it seems that we can't be rid of his likes too easily. I was hoping maybe the wolf had done us a favor, but now I see that it just means we have them both to contend with."

"I'd rather deal with the wolf, anytime," said Basil. "At least he was honest."

"I feel bad, sort of, about those poor wolves we had to slay," said Morley. "Especially after we found out that Olwin was making them do all those things. Poor brutes, they weren't responsible for going beyond their boundaries."

"I never thought I'd feel bad about a killer wolf, but I do. Don't want them for my neighbors, but then again, I can't say that I'd go out of my way to do them any harm, if I could help it," snorted Stump.

"Let's just hope we don't have to anymore," said Granny. "Perhaps that's all been left behind us, above the Falls. You can get too used to living like that, and then, before you know it, you're as hardhearted as Olwin."

"I hope there's no need, either," said Blackpaw. "Erinoult's sword is lost. It went over the Falls with Olwin."

"That's a fine way to take care of someone's property!" started Morley, indignantly.

"Hush, Morley! I don't hold Blackpaw to fault. He had to surrender it. But we don't have any weapons left, now. The other sword is gone, too," said Granny.

Bramble turned to the muskrat.

"You were carrying that one, Morley. The same thing must have happened to it."

"Good riddance, if we don't have any more use for them!" blurted out the muskrat. "We were doing nicely without them until those killer wolves came."

"I'm glad they're gone," said Branch. "I hated it when Olwin had made the pups his soldiers. It was awful."

"And I didn't help any," answered Blackpaw. "I thought that would be wonderful, being Grand Marshal. Olwin had a way of beguiling you into what he wanted."

"At least it's over and done," replied Branch. "I don't have to worry so, now."

"It wasn't any fun being a soldier," chirped Bumble. "You never get to have any fun."

"And you can't cry, or talk out loud," added Cabbage. "I'd rather just be me."

"Good lad!" put in his father. "That's what it's best of all to be."

The companions had gathered themselves, and began to prepare to search out a place where they could shelter and lay out their long overdue meal.

A sudden movement in the shadow of the forest behind him caused Stump to turn and squint.

"What's that?" he cried, pointing to where he thought he had seen the movement.

"Where?" chorused the rest of the animals.

"There! Just there! See?"

Nothing stirred but a few floating honeybees that were hovering near a great bed of wildflowers. A bird's song came from somewhere farther into the forest, but other than the snoring of the breeze, nothing else stirred.

"It was there," insisted the mole. "I couldn't be sure of it, but I know something was there."

"I think we've all been overtaxed and tired," soothed Bramble. "To say nothing of hungry. After a nap and a meal, I'm sure we'll all feel better."

"I won't be able to nap, now," shot Stump. "Whatever that was, it means there is someone else besides us here."

He paused a moment, wrinkling his brow.

"I know Old Bark went over the Falls, and I know Olwin and a big lout of a killer wolf did, too. Now I've done the same thing, and here I am, so I feel just as sure that they are all here, too."

"I don't mind running into Old Bark," said Morley.

"I'm even for seeking him out. He'll be able to handle Olwin, now."

"What course, Granny? Are we to wait upon those tea scones a bit longer?" asked Bramble.

The old she-badger smiled good-humoredly.

"We've come this far without them. I don't think it'll do more than whet our appetite to do without them a little longer."

"Good. Let's go on then, and see if we can't discover where Old Bark is, and get free of these sticker burrs, Olwin, and that wolf. They begin to wear my nerves thin," said Blackpaw. "The quicker we find Old Bark, the quicker we'll have our rest as well."

"That could have been Old Bark I saw," said Stump. "I only caught a quick glimpse."

"It could have been the killer wolf, too, or Olwin."

"Let's hope not, Basil," said the otter. "But there's only one way to find out, and that's to follow Stump's nose, and see where it leads us."

"Let's get on with it then," grumbled the mole. "I'm beginning to tire of this journey."

Bramble was on his feet first, and turned once more to look back at where the dreadful torrents should have been. He could see nothing above but pale blue sky, filled with floating, fleecy clouds, and the tops of the trees, reflecting back the golden green light on the leaves.

"Thorn Wood is indeed a strange place," he said, half aloud. "Stranger than my lorebooks ever hinted at."

A brief recollection came to the otter, and he remembered sitting in his snug den, on that faraway day, looking glumly at the unfilled pages of his lorebook, and telling himself that he would never have an adventure worth adding to the tale. And now it was gone, lost in Granny Badger's ruined hole in their old wood, and he was on an

DRAGON WINTER   343

adventure so great he hardly dared think that there would ever be an end of it, although that was the way with great journeys, or great adventures. You were suddenly caught up in the middle of them, and then, for no apparent reason at all, you were just as suddenly out of them.

It was too much for the otter to think about.

And he was on the point of not thinking on it anymore when he, too, caught sight of a silver-gray blur moving off through the forest before them.

Bramble hardly had time to notice the small green door that opened before him, and his surprise was complete when he found himself in a low, snug study, and Old Bark, sitting before a fireless hearth, chuckling softly, and beckoning him to sit down beside him on a curved green bench that was fashioned in the likeness of a flying swan.

AN END OF AN ADVENTURE

"Well met, my friend. Come, sit here, and we'll exchange what news we have, and visit for a while."

Old Bark spoke softly, and for a moment, Bramble tried to think of how he had gotten there, but gave up, and sat where the huge bear had bidden him.

"This isn't unusual for this side of the Falls, although I suppose it must be something of a start to you."

"Oh no," chittered Bramble, feeling suddenly very young again, with a warm glow growing inside him. "We were getting used to that. And we had run into Olwin."

"Olwin," mused the bear. "Yes, my brother Olwin is definitely one to give you a few lessons in quick reversals."

"Is he here, too?" asked the otter.

"Olwin? No, old fellow, he can't stay here. Or he could, if he wished to give up his mad plan to become True King. When he does, he'll be able to stay here."

"And that killer wolf? He went over the Falls, too."

"Poor soul, he's returned to where he belongs, to finish out his lesson, without the interference of Olwin."

"I'm glad," said Bramble. "I fear them, and they aren't

345

the most pleasant sort, but I'm glad that things have been put back in their proper order."

"Well, that could or couldn't be," said the bear. "Things have been altered by Olwin's mischief, but I think, on the whole, that everything has more or less come back to normal."

"Does that mean we're at the end of our journey?" asked Bramble.

Old Bark smiled.

"What does it feel like to you?"

"Well, I feel all calm, now. I wasn't a moment ago, before I came in here. I was walking along in a strange wood, going to look for you."

"You see, when you think a thing here, it already happens," answered the bear. "You were thinking of me, and here we are, having a nice chat."

Bramble's eyes widened.

"You mean I got here just because I was thinking about you?"

"Exactly. Everyone else has already had a nice visit, just before you arrived."

"Branch? And Bumble?"

"Branch, yes. And Bumble and I always have the greatest fun. Cabbage, too."

Bramble shook his head.

"I don't understand."

"I expect you will when you get used to it. It's so simple. Just think about it."

"But what's going to happen now?"

"What do you want to happen now?" asked Old Bark.

"Why, I guess I'd like to settle back in my den chair, and prop my paws before a nice fire, and have some blueberry tea, and one of Granny's tea scones, and be talking about the grand adventure we'd just had."

"And?"

"And then, I'd like to be able to write it all down again, because I lost the lorebooks when the killer wolves burned our old holt."

"Anything more?"

"Well," went on the otter, thoughtfully, I'd like to have Bumble grow up to be healthy and strong, and settle down near us on the river."

He stopped abruptly.

"Any river, just as long as it's sweet and clear, with enough trips to it so we won't get bored."

"What about all the things you've seen? Do they bother you?"

"No, I don't think so," replied Bramble. "I'll put them all in the lorebooks, so maybe someone else can read about it, too."

"And mankind?" asked Old Bark.

Bramble wrinkled up his brow.

"I haven't had dealings with any but Olwin. And I didn't care for him so much."

Bramble heard Old Bark laugh, and looked up. Where the bear had been now sat a large, handsome man, much like Olwin, but with a flowing silver-white beard, and clear gray eyes.

"We can't let you leave knowing only Olwin," laughed the man, although it still sounded like Old Bark's voice.

"Olwin was surprised when he heard us say you were a bear," breathed the otter. "He said you were a man, but I didn't know."

"Well," said Old Bark, twisting about, and reappearing as the more familiar form of the bear. "I prefer this disguise. It suits me more, at times."

"Do you live here? Below the Falls?" asked Bramble.

"Sometimes, my friend. I live many places, yet I live here, too."

Bramble shook his head.

"This is all so confusing. I'm here, but I hardly know it, and all these strange things begin to make sense."

"I think I hear someone calling you, Bramble," said Old Bark, turning his head and listening intently to a sound the otter did not at first catch.

"They're calling for you. You'd best go now. We shall have many meetings to look forward to, you and I. But for now, we must say our farewells."

Old Bark arose and smiled at Bramble, and the otter, very suddenly, began to cry, although he was not unhappy. Before he could blink the tears from his eyes, he looked about himself, and there in a circle, all in the same cozy kitchen as he had remembered in his old holt, or in one very much like it, were all his friends, their eyes shining, applauding.

Branch sat with Bumble at her lap, and next to her were Basil and Beryl. Cabbage leapt about beside their chairs, clapping his paws loudly. The gruff mole, teacup in hand, was snorting and sniffling, and turning to tell Morley to please pass him another scone. Granny sat beside the squirrels and their babies, and next to her was the stalwart young badger Blackpaw, his paw on the back of Granny's chair.

"That was the most wonderful story!" cried Branch, barely able to keep her tears back.

"Bravo!" shouted Morley, upsetting his tea saucer and causing Granny Badger to look at him over the top of her nose.

"Where was the treasure?" chittered Bumble loudly.

"And the old dragon?" shouted Cabbage.

"Where *was* the treasure?" scolded Granny. "Surely

there was something, somewhere. Gruff would have had a
little dragon hoard, just to keep the pups happy."

"I think the best treasure of all is right here," said
Bramble, his eyes clearing. "With my friends around the
fire."

He looked down at his paws, and there was a thick
lorebook, with many pages of maps, and drawings of
killer wolves, and strange men, and armies clashing
beneath huge trees. He frowned, deep in thought.

There too was a drawing that reminded him of something like a waterfall, only more turbulent and wild.

And on the very last page of all was the form of a
bear, sitting in a snug room, on a bench that was fashioned in the shape of a flying swan. At the other end of
the bench was the tiny outline of an otter.

Bramble's thoughts raced.

He looked about him once more, and all seemed the
same, yet changed. His friends were there, yet the sun
was shining, and there was no hint of any winter in the
air. He struggled to remember what it was the meeting
had been called for.

A dragon winter?

Was that what they were to discuss?

He could hardly remember.

Looking out the window at the fresh flowers in the
fragrant earth, it was hard for him to think of how a
dragon winter must be.

"Well, if we're all through here," said Morley, rising
stiffly, as if he'd been sitting for a long time, "I think I'd
best be tending my spring cleaning. Lots to do before I
can launch the boat."

"My turnips need looking after," snorted Stump. "I
wasn't sure they were going to take, but this last batch of
fine weather has done it."

"Do you need any help cleaning up, Granny?" asked Branch.

"I'll help you clean up the cookies," offered Bumble, helpfully.

"Me, too!" shouted Cabbage.

"You two! Off with you now. You've had a dozen apiece while we were listening to Bramble's story."

"They've had enough," agreed Beryl. "I'll never get him to eat supper tonight."

"That was very fine, Bramble," said Blackpaw, coming to stand by the otter, who was still staring distantly into the woods beyond the garden hedge.

Had he seen a silver-gray figure there at the very wood's edge?

He thought so.

A figure very much like the silver bear at the end of the book in his paws.

As Bramble later remembered, adventures always began suddenly, without much warning, and they often ended the same way. Yet he was sure he had seen Old Bark, there where the seven oaks spread their boughs over the little clearing.

He would find the bear, he thought, and see what it all meant, although deep inside, when he turned it over in his mind, he remembered what Old Bark had asked, and what he had answered.

"Well," he said aloud, holding his paw out to his mate, and waving to Granny on the way out into the fine, warm afternoon, "it's going to be a lovely spring."

"It always is, after a dragon winter," came a voice, startlingly clear.

It was Old Bark!

Bramble whirled, his heart pounding, but when he

looked to see where he'd gone, there was only Branch and
Bumble, smiling up at him.

And it turned out, as was said, to be the finest spring of
all, and the animals, each one, lived on beyond winter,
and all danger, until the bear came again, sometime much
later, and led them farther on into the higher meadows
beyond the Falls.

Bramble's story grew in length, and still grows even
now, until it is supposed we will all be included, and sit,
at the end of it all, in that snug kitchen with Granny and
the rest, to listen to it read, and wait for the return of the
great silver bear.

ALL TIME BESTSELLERS
FROM POPULAR LIBRARY

☐ THE BERLIN CONNECTION—Simmel	08607-6	1.95
☐ THE BEST PEOPLE—Van Slyke	08456-1	1.75
☐ A BRIDGE TOO FAR—Ryan	08373-5	2.50
☐ THE CAESAR CODE—Simmel	08413-8	1.95
☐ DO BLACK PATENT LEATHER SHOES REALLY REFLECT UP?—Powers	08490-1	1.75
☐ ELIZABETH—Hamilton	04013-0	1.75
☐ THE FURY—Farris	08620-3	2.25
☐ THE HAB THEORY—Eckerty	08597-5	2.50
☐ HARDACRE—Skelton	04026-2	2.25
☐ THE HEART LISTENS—Van Slyke	08520-7	1.95
☐ TO KILL A MOCKINGBIRD—Lee	08376-X	1.50
☐ THE LAST BATTLE—Ryan	08381-6	2.25
☐ THE LAST CATHOLIC IN AMERICA—Powers	08528-2	1.50
☐ THE LONGEST DAY—Ryan	08380-8	1.95
☐ LOVE'S WILD DESIRE—Blake	08616-5	1.95
☐ THE MIXED BLESSING—Van Slyke	08491-X	1.95
☐ MORWENNA—Goring	08604-1	1.95
☐ THE RICH AND THE RIGHTEOUS —Van Slyke	08585-1	1.95

Buy them at your local bookstores or use this handy coupon for ordering: